THE
VIOLETS
OF
MARCH

SARAH JIO is the #1 international, *New York Times*, and *USA Today* bestselling author of ten novels. She is the host of the Mod About You podcast and also a longtime journalist who has contributed to *Glamour*, *The New York Times*, *Redbook*, *Real Simple*, *O: The Oprah Magazine*, *Bon Appétit*, *Marie Claire*, *Self*, and many other outlets, including NPR's *Morning Edition*. Her books have been published in more than twenty-five countries. She lives in Seattle with her husband, three young boys, and three stepchildren.

sarahjio.com
 sarahjioauthor
 @sarahjio
 @sarahjio

By Sarah Jio

All the Flowers in Paris
Always
The Look of Love
Goodnight June
Morning Glory
The Last Camellia
Blackberry Winter
The Bungalow
The Violets of March

THE
VIOLETS
OF
MARCH

SARAH JIO

ORION

An Orion paperback

First published in Great Britain in 2020 by Orion Fiction,
an imprint of The Orion Publishing Group Ltd
Carmelite House, 50 Victoria Embankment,
London EC4Y 0DZ

An Hachette UK company

1 3 5 7 9 10 8 6 4 2

A CIP catalogue record for this book is
available from the British Library.

ISBN (Mass Market Paperback) 978 1 4091 9079 0
ISBN (eBook) 978 1 4091 9080 6

Printed and bound in Great Britain by Clays Ltd, Elcograf S.p.A.

www.orionbooks.co.uk

To my grandmothers,
Antoinette Mitchell and the late Cecelia Fairchild,
who instilled in me the love of art and writing
and a fascination with the 1940s

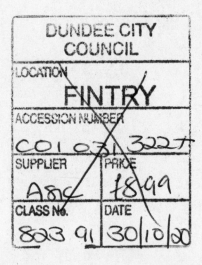

"And the riverbank talks of the waters of March / It's the end of all strain, it's the joy in your heart."

—From "Waters of March" by Antonio Carlos Jobim

The Violets of March

Chapter 1

"I guess this is it," Joel said, leaning into the doorway of our apartment. His eyes darted as if he was trying to memorize every detail of the turn-of-the-century New York two-story, the one we'd bought together five years ago and renovated—in happier times. It was a sight: the entryway with its delicate arch, the old mantel we'd found at an antique store in Connecticut and carted home like treasure, and the richness of the dining room walls. We'd agonized about the paint color but finally settled on Morocco Red, a shade that was both wistful and jarring, a little like our marriage. Once it was on the walls, he thought it was too orange. I thought it was just right.

Our eyes met for a second, but I quickly looked down at the dispenser in my hands and robotically pried off the last piece of packing tape, hastily plastering it on the final box of Joel's belongings that he'd come over that morning to retrieve. "Wait," I said, recalling a fleck of a blue leather-bound hardback I'd seen in the now-sealed box. I looked up at him accusatorily. "Did you take my copy of *Years of Grace*?"

I had read the novel on our honeymoon in Tahiti six years

prior, though it wasn't the memory of our trip I wanted to eulogize with its tattered pages. Looking back, I'll never know how the 1931 Pulitzer Prize winner by the late Margaret Ayer Barnes ended up in a dusty stack of complimentary books in the resort's lobby, but as I pulled it out of the bin and cracked open its brittle spine, I felt my heart contract with a deep familiarity that I could not explain. The moving story told in its pages, of love and loss and acceptance, of secret passions and the weight of private thoughts, forever changed the way I viewed my own writing. It may have even been the reason why I *stopped* writing. Joel had never read the book, and I was glad of it. It was too intimate to share. It read to me like the pages of my unwritten diary.

Joel watched as I peeled the tape back and opened the box, digging around until I found the old novel. When I did I let out a sigh of emotional exhaustion.

"Sorry," he said awkwardly. "I didn't realize you—"

He didn't realize a lot of things about me. I grasped the book tightly, then nodded and re-taped the box. "I guess that's everything," I said, standing up.

He glanced cautiously toward me, and I returned his gaze this time. For another few hours, at least until I signed the divorce papers later that afternoon, he would still be my husband. Yet it was difficult to look into those dark brown eyes knowing that the man I had married was leaving me, for someone else. *How did we get here?*

The scene of our demise played out in my mind like a tragic movie, the way it had a million times since we'd been separated. It opened on a rainy Monday morning in November. I was making scrambled eggs smothered in Tabasco, his favorite, when he told me about Stephanie. The way she made him laugh. The way she understood him. The way they *connected*. I pictured the image of two Lego pieces fusing together, and I shuddered. It's funny; when I think back to that morning, I can actually smell burned eggs and Tabasco. Had I known that this is what the end of my marriage would smell like, I would have made pancakes.

I looked once again into Joel's face. His eyes were sad and unsure. I knew that if I rose to my feet and threw myself into his arms, he might embrace me with the love of an apologetic husband who wouldn't leave, wouldn't end our marriage. But, no, I told myself. The damage had been done. Our fate had been decided. "Good-bye, Joel," I said. My heart may have wanted to linger, but my brain knew better. He needed to go.

Joel looked wounded. "Emily, I—"

Was he looking for forgiveness? A second chance? I didn't know. I extended my hand as if to stop him from going on. "Good-bye," I said, mustering all my strength.

He nodded solemnly, then turned to the door. I closed my eyes and listened as he shut it quietly behind him. He locked it from the outside, a gesture that made my heart seize. *He still cares. . . .* About my safety, at least. I shook my head and reminded myself to get the locks changed, then listened as his footsteps became quieter, until they were completely swallowed up by the street noise.

My phone rang sometime later, and when I stood up to get it, I realized that I'd been sitting on the floor engrossed in *Years of Grace* ever since Joel left. Had a minute passed? An hour?

"Are you coming?" It was Annabelle, my best friend. "You promised me you wouldn't sign your divorce papers alone."

Disoriented, I looked at the clock. "Sorry, Annie," I said, fumbling for my keys and the dreaded manila envelope in my bag. I was supposed to meet her at the restaurant forty-five minutes ago. "I'm on my way."

"Good," she said. "I'll order you a drink."

The Calumet, our favorite lunch spot, was four blocks from my apartment, and when I arrived ten minutes later, Annabelle greeted me with a hug.

"Are you hungry?" she asked after we sat down.

I sighed. "No."

Annabelle frowned. "Carbs," she said, passing me the bread basket. "You need carbs. Now, where are those papers? Let's get this over with."

I pulled the envelope out of my bag and set it on the table, staring at it with the sort of caution one might reserve for dynamite.

"You realize this is all your fault," Annabelle said, half-smiling.

I gave her a dirty look. "What do you mean, my fault?"

"You don't *marry* men named Joel," she continued with that *tsk-tsk* sound in her voice. "Nobody marries Joels. You date Joels, you let them buy you drinks and pretty little things from Tiffany, but you don't marry them."

Annabelle was working on her PhD in social anthropology. In her two years of research, she had analyzed marriage and divorce data in an unconventional way. According to her findings, a marriage's success rate can be accurately predicted by the man's name.

Marry an Eli and you're likely to enjoy wedded bliss for about 12.3 years. Brad? 6.4. Steves peter out after just four. And as far as Annabelle is concerned, don't ever—*ever*—marry a Preston.

"So what does the data say about Joel again?"

"Seven point two years," she said in a matter-of-fact tone.

I nodded. We had been married for six years and two weeks.

"You need to find yourself a Trent," she continued.

I made a displeased face. "I hate the name Trent."

"OK, then an Edward or a Bill, or—no, a Bruce," she said. "These are names with marital longevity."

"Right," I said sarcastically. "Maybe you should take me husband-shopping at a retirement home."

Annabelle is tall and thin and beautiful—Julia Roberts beautiful, with her long, wavy dark hair, porcelain skin, and intense dark eyes. At thirty-three she had never been married. The reason, she'd tell you, was jazz. She couldn't find a man who liked Miles Davis and Herbie Hancock as much as she did.

She waved for the waiter. "We'll take two more, please." He whisked away my martini glass, leaving a water ring on the envelope.

"It's time," she said softly.

My hand trembled a little as I reached into the envelope and pulled out a stack of papers about a half-inch thick. My lawyer's assistant had flagged three pages with hot pink "sign here" sticky notes.

I reached into my bag for a pen and felt a lump in my throat as I signed my name on the first page, and then the next, and then the next. Emily Wilson, with an elongated *y* and a pronounced *n*. It was the exact way I'd signed my name since the fifth grade. Then I scrawled out the date, February 28, 2005, the day our marriage was laid to rest.

"Good girl," Annabelle said, inching a fresh martini closer to me. "So are you going to write about Joel?" Because I am a writer, Annabelle, like everyone else I knew, believed that writing about my relationship with Joel as a thinly veiled novel would be the best revenge.

"You could build a whole story around him, except change his name slightly," she continued. "Maybe call him Joe, and make him look like a total jerk." She took a bite and nearly choked on her food, laughing, before saying, "No, a jerk with *erectile dysfunction*."

The only problem is that even if I had wanted to write a revenge novel about Joel, which I didn't, it would have been a terrible book. Anything I got down on paper, if I could get anything down on paper, would have lacked imagination. I know this because I had woken up every day for the past eight years, sat at my desk, and stared at a blank screen. Sometimes I'd crank out a great line, or a few solid pages, but then I'd get stuck. And once I was frozen, there was no melting the ice.

My therapist, Bonnie, called it clinical (as in terminal) writer's block. My muse had taken ill, and her prognosis didn't look good.

Eight years ago I wrote a best-selling novel. Eight years ago I was on top of the world. I was skinny—not that I'm fat now (well, OK, so the thighs, yes, maybe a little)—and on the *New York Times* best seller list. And if there were such a thing as the *New York Times* best life list, I would have been on that, too.

After my book, *Calling Ali Larson*, was published, my agent encouraged me to write a follow-up. Readers wanted a sequel, she told me. And my publisher had already offered to double my advance for a second book. But as hard as I tried, I had nothing more to write, nothing more to say. And eventually, my agent stopped calling. Publishers stopped wondering. Readers stopped caring. The only evidence that my former life wasn't just a figment was the royalty checks that came in the mail every so often and an occasional letter I received from a somewhat deranged reader by the name of Lester McCain, who believed he was in love with Ali, my book's main character.

I still remember the rush I felt when Joel walked up to me at my book release party at the Madison Park Hotel. He was at some cocktail party in an adjoining room when he saw me standing in the doorway. I was wearing a Betsey Johnson dress, which in 1997 was *the ultimate*: a black strapless number that I'd spent an embarrassing amount of money on. But, oh yes, it was worth *every penny*. It was still in my closet, but I suddenly had the urge to go home and burn it.

"You look stunning," he had said, rather boldly, before even introducing himself. I remember how I felt when I heard him utter those words. It could have been his trademark pick-up line, and let's be real, it probably was. But it made me feel like a million bucks. It was so Joel.

A few months prior to that, *GQ* had done a big spread on the most eligible "regular-guy" bachelors in America—no, not the list that every two years always features George Clooney; the one that listed a surfer in San Diego, a dentist in Pennsylvania, a teacher in Detroit, and, yes, an attorney in New York, Joel. He had made the Top 10. And somehow, *I* had snagged him.

And lost him.

Annabelle was waving her hands in front of me. "Earth to Emily," she said.

"Sorry," I replied, shuddering a little. "No, I won't be writing about Joel." I shook my head and tucked the papers back into the envelope, then put it in my bag. "If I write anything again, it will be different than any story I've ever tried to write."

Annabelle shot me a confused look. "What about the follow-up to your last book? Aren't you going to finish that?"

"Not anymore," I said, folding a paper napkin in half and then in half again.

"Why not?"

I sighed. "I can't do it anymore. I can't force myself to churn out 85,000 mediocre words, even if it means a book deal. Even if it means thousands of readers with my book in their hands on beach vacations. No, if I ever write anything again—if I ever write again—it will be different."

Annabelle looked as if she wanted to stand up and applaud. "Look at you," she said, smiling. "You're having a breakthrough."

"No I'm not," I said stubbornly.

"Sure you are," she countered. "Let's analyze this some more." She clasped her hands together. "You said you want to write something *different*, but what I think you mean is that your heart wasn't in your last book."

"You could say that, yes," I said, shrugging.

Annabelle retrieved an olive from her martini glass and popped it into her mouth. "Why don't you write about something you actually *care* about?" she said a moment later. "Like a place, or a person that inspired you."

I nodded. "Isn't that what every writer tries to do?"

"Yeah," she said, shooing away the waiter with a "we're fine, and no we would not like the bill yet" look, then turning back to me with intense eyes. "But have you actually *tried* it? I mean, your book was fantastic—it really was, Em—but was there anything in it that was, well, *you*?"

She was right. It was a fine story. It was a best seller, for crying out loud. So why couldn't I feel proud of it? Why didn't I feel *connected* to it?

"I've known you a long time," she continued, "and I know that it wasn't a story that grew out of your life, your experiences."

It wasn't. But what in my life could I draw from? I thought about my parents and grandparents, and then shook my head. "That's the problem," I said. "Other writers have plenty to mine from—bad mothers, abuse, adventurous childhoods. My life has been so vanilla.

No deaths. No trauma. Not even a dead pet. Mom's cat, Oscar, is twenty-two years old. There's nothing there that warrants storytelling, believe me; I've thought about it."

"I don't think you're giving yourself enough credit," she said. "There must be something. Some spark."

This time I permitted my mind to wander, and when it did, I immediately thought of my great-aunt Bee, my mother's aunt, and her home on Bainbridge Island, in Washington State. I missed her as much as I missed the island. How had I let so many years pass since my last visit? Bee, who was eighty-five going on twenty-nine, had never had children, so my sister and I, by default, became her surrogate grandchildren. She sent us birthday cards with crisp fifty-dollar bills inside, Christmas gifts that were actually cool, and Valentine's Day candy, and when we'd visit in the summers from our home in Portland, Oregon, she'd sneak chocolate under our pillows before our mother could scream, "No, they just brushed their teeth!"

Bee was unconventional, indeed. But there was also something a little *off* about her. The way she talked too much. Or talked too little. The way she was simultaneously welcoming and petulant, giving and selfish. And then there were her secrets. I loved her for having them.

My mother always said that when people live alone for the better part of their lives they become immune to their own quirks. I wasn't sure if I bought into the theory or not, partly because I was worried about a lifetime of spinsterhood myself. I contented myself with watching for signs.

Bee. I could picture her immediately at her Bainbridge Island kitchen table. For every day I have known her, she has eaten the same breakfast: sourdough toast with butter and whipped honey. She slices the golden brown toasted bread into four small squares and places them on a paper towel she has folded in half. A generous smear of softened butter goes on each piece, as thick as frosting on a cupcake, and each is then topped by a good-size dollop of whipped honey. As a child, I watched her do this hundreds of times, and now, when I'm sick, sourdough toast with butter and honey is like medicine.

Bee isn't a beautiful woman. She towers above most men, with a face that is somehow too wide, shoulders too large, teeth too big. Yet the black-and-white photos of her youth reveal a spark of something, a certain prettiness that all women have in their twenties.

I used to love a particular photo of her at just that age, which hung in a seashell-covered frame high on the wall in the hallway of my childhood home, hardly in a place of honor, as one had to stand on a step stool to see it clearly. The old, scalloped-edge photo depicted a Bee I'd never known. Seated with a group of friends on a beach blanket, she appeared carefree and was smiling seductively. Another woman leaned in close to her, whispering in her ear. *A secret.* Bee clutched a string of pearls dangling from her neck and gazed at the camera in a way I'd never witnessed her look at Uncle Bill. I wondered who stood behind the lens that day so many years ago.

"What did she say?" I asked my mother one day as a child, peering up at the photograph.

Mom didn't look up from the laundry she was wrestling with in the hallway. "What did *who* say?"

I pointed to the woman next to Bee. "The pretty lady whispering in Aunt Bee's ear."

Mom immediately stood up and walked to my side. She reached up and wiped away the dust on the glass frame with the edge of her sweater. "We'll never know," she said, her regret palpable as she regarded the photo.

My mother's late uncle, Bill, was a handsome World War II hero.

Everybody said he had married Bee for her money, but it's a theory that didn't hold weight with me. I had seen the way he kissed her, the way he wrapped his arms around her waist during those summers of my childhood. He had loved her; there was no doubt of that.

Even so, I knew by the way my mother talked that she disapproved of their relationship, that she believed Bill could have done better for himself. Bee, in her mind, was too unconventional, too unladylike, too brash, too *everything*.

Yet we kept coming to visit Bee, summer after summer. Even after Uncle Bill died when I was nine. The place was kind of ethereal, with the seagulls flying overhead, the sprawling gardens, the smell of the Puget Sound, the big kitchen with its windows facing out onto the gray water, the haunting hum of the waves crashing on the shore. My sister and I loved it, and despite my mother's feelings about Bee, I know she loved the place too. It had a tranquilizing effect on all of us.

Annabelle gave me a knowing look. "You *do* have a story in there, don't you?"

I sighed. "Maybe," I said noncommittally.

"Why don't you take a trip?" she suggested. "You need to get away, to clear your head for a while."

I scrunched up my nose at the idea. "Where would I go?"

"Somewhere far away from here."

She was right. The Big Apple is a fair-weather friend. The city loves you when you're flying high and kicks you when you're down.

"Will you come with me?" I imagined the two of us on a tropical beach, with umbrella cocktails.

She shook her head. "No."

"Why not?" I felt like a puppy—a scared, lost puppy who just wanted someone to put her collar on and show her where to go, what to do, how to be.

"I can't go with you because you need to do this on your own."
Her words jarred me. She looked me straight in the eye, as if I needed
to absorb every drop of what she was about to say. "Em, your marriage has ended and, well, it's just that you haven't shed a single tear."

On the walk back to my apartment I thought about what Annabelle
had said, and my thoughts, once again, turned to my aunt Bee. *How
have I let so many years pass without visiting her?*

I heard a shrill, shrieking sound above my head, the unmistakable sound of metal on metal, and looked up. A copper duck
weather vane, weathered to a rich gray-green patina, stood at attention on the roof of a nearby café. It twirled noisily in the wind.

My heart pounded as I took in the familiar sight. Where had I
seen it before? Then it hit me. *The painting. Bee's painting.* Until that
moment, I had forgotten about the five-by-seven canvas she'd given
me when I was a child. She used to paint, and I remember the great
sense of honor I felt when she chose me to be the caretaker of the
artwork. I had called it a masterpiece, and my words made her smile.

I closed my eyes and could see the oil-painted seascape perfectly:
the duck weather vane perched atop that old beach cottage, and the
couple, hand in hand, on the shore.

I felt overcome with guilt. Where was the painting? I'd packed
it away after Joel and I moved into the apartment—he didn't think
it matched our decor. Just like I'd distanced myself from the island
I'd loved as a child, I had packed away the relics of my past in boxes.
Why? For what?

I picked up my pace until it turned into a full-fledged jog. I
thought of *Years of Grace. Did the painting accidentally end up in a box
of Joel's things too? Or worse, did I mistakenly pack it in a box of books*

and clothes for the Goodwill pickup? I reached the door to the apartment and jammed my key into the lock, then sprinted up the stairs to the bedroom and flung open the closet door. There, on the top shelf, were two boxes. I pulled one down and rummaged through its contents: a few stuffed animals from childhood, a box of old Polaroids, and several notebooks' worth of clippings from my two-year stint writing for the college newspaper. Still, no painting.

I reached for the second box, and looked inside to find a Raggedy Ann doll, a box of notes from junior high crushes, and my beloved Strawberry Shortcake diary from elementary school. That was it.

How could I have lost it? How could I have been so careless? I stood up, giving the closet a final once-over. A plastic bag shoved far into the back corner suddenly caught my eye. My heart raced with anticipation as I pulled it out into the light.

Inside the bag, wrapped in a turquoise and pink beach towel, was the painting. Something deep inside me ached as I clutched it in my hands. The weather vane. The beach. The old cottage. They were all as I remembered them. But not the couple. No, something was different. I had always imagined the subjects to be Bee and Uncle Bill. The woman was most certainly Bee, with her long legs and trademark baby blue capri pants. Her "summer pants," she'd called them. But the man wasn't Uncle Bill. No. How could I have missed this? Bill had light hair, sandy blond. But this man had thick, wavy dark hair. *Who was he? And why did Bee paint herself with him?*

I left the mess on the floor and walked, with the painting, downstairs to my address book. I punched the familiar numbers into the phone and took a long, deep breath, listening to the chime of the first ring and then the second.

"Hello?" Her voice was the same—deep and strong, with soft edges.

"Bee, it's me, Emily," I said, my voice cracking a little. "I'm sorry it's been so long. It's just that I—"

"Nonsense, dear," she said. "No apologies necessary. Did you get my postcard?"

"Your postcard?"

"Yes, I sent it last week after I heard your news."

"You heard?" I hadn't told very many people about Joel. Not my parents in Portland—not yet, anyway. Not my sister in Los Angeles, with her perfect children, doting husband, and organic vegetable garden. Not even my therapist. Even so, I wasn't surprised that the news had made its way to Bainbridge Island.

"Yes," she said. "And I wondered if you'd come for a visit." She paused. "This island is a marvelous place to heal."

I ran my finger along the edge of the painting. I wanted to be there just then—on Bainbridge Island, in Bee's big, warm kitchen.

"When are you coming?" Bee never wastes words.

"Is tomorrow too soon?"

"Tomorrow," she said, "is the first of March, the month the sound is at its best, dear. It's absolutely *alive*."

I knew what she meant when she said it. The churning gray water. The kelp and the seaweed and barnacles. I could almost taste the salty air. Bee believed that the Puget Sound was the great healer. And I knew that when I arrived, she would encourage me to take my shoes off and go wading, even if it was one o'clock in the morning— even if it was forty-three degrees, which it probably would be.

"And, Emily?"

"Yes?"

"There's something important that we need to talk about."

"What is it?"

"Not now. Not over the phone. When you get here, dear."

After I hung up, I walked downstairs to the mailbox to find a credit card bill, a Victoria's Secret catalog—addressed to Joel—and a large square envelope. I recognized the return address, and it only took me a moment to remember where I'd seen it: on the divorce papers. There was also the fact that I'd Googled it the week before. It was Joel's new town house on Fifty-seventh—the one he was sharing with Stephanie.

The adrenaline started pumping when I considered the fact that Joel could have been reaching out to me. Maybe he was sending me a letter, a card—no, a romantic beginning to a scavenger hunt: an invitation to meet him somewhere in the city, where there'd be another clue, and then after four more, there he'd be, standing in front of the hotel where we met so many years ago. And he'd be holding a rose— no, a sign, and it would read, I'M SORRY. I LOVE YOU. FORGIVE ME. Exactly like that. It could be the perfect ending to a tragic romance. *Give us a happy ending, Joel*, I found myself whispering as I ran my finger along the envelope. *He still loves me. He still feels something.*

But when I lifted the edge of the envelope and carefully pulled out the gold-tinged card inside, the fantasy came to a crashing halt. All I could do was stare.

The thick card stock. The fancy calligraphy. It was a wedding invitation. *His* wedding invitation. Six p.m. Dinner. Dancing. A celebration of love. Beef or chicken. Accepts with pleasure. Declines with regret. I walked to the kitchen, calmly bypassing the recycle bin, and instead set the little stack of gold stationery right into the kitchen trash, on top of a take-out box of moldy chicken chow mein.

Fumbling with the rest of the mail, I dropped a magazine, and when I reached down to pick it up, I saw the postcard from Bee, which had been hiding in the pages of *The New Yorker*. The front featured a ferry boat, white with green trim, coming into Eagle Harbor. I flipped it over and read:

Emily,

> *The island has a way of calling one back when it's time. Come home. I have missed you, dear.*

All my love,

Bee

I pressed the postcard to my chest and exhaled deeply.

Chapter 2

March 1

Bainbridge Island could never hide its glory, even under the cover of darkness. I watched from the window as the ferry loomed into Eagle Harbor, passing the island's pebble-covered shores and shake-shingled homes that clung courageously to the hillside. Glowing orange interiors beckoned, as if the people inside were making one extra place as they gathered around fireplaces to sip wine or hot cocoa.

Islanders reveled in being an eclectic bunch: Volvo-driving mothers whose executive husbands commuted to Seattle via ferry, reclusive artists and poets, and a handful of celebrities. Rumor has it that before their split, Jennifer Aniston and Brad Pitt purchased nine acres on the west shore, and everybody knows that several former *Gilligan's Island* cast members call Bainbridge home. Clearly, it's a good place to get lost. And that's what I was about to do.

From north to south, the island is just ten miles long, but it feels like a continent in its own right. There are bays and inlets, coves and mudflats, a winery, a berry farm, a llama farm, sixteen restaurants, a café that makes homemade cinnamon rolls and the best coffee I've ever tasted, and a market whose wares include locally produced raspberry wine and organic Swiss chard picked just hours before making its appearance in the produce section.

I took a deep breath and looked at my face in the reflection of the window, and a tired, serious woman stared back—a far cry from the girl making her first trip to the island years before. I cringed, remembering something that Joel had said a few months ago. We were getting ready to leave the apartment to meet friends for dinner. "Em," he said, looking me over with a critical eye. "Did you forget to put on *makeup?*"

Yes, I did have makeup on, thankyouverymuch, but the hall mirror revealed pale and plain skin. The high cheekbones that no one in my family but me had, the ones my mother said I must have gotten from the milkman—the cheekbones that everyone said were such an asset—just looked wrong. *I* looked wrong.

I stepped off the ferry onto the ramp that led to the terminal where Bee would be waiting for me in her green 1963 Volkswagen Beetle. The air smelled of seawater, ferry engine fumes, decaying clams, and fir trees, which was exactly the way it had smelled when I was ten.

"They should bottle it, shouldn't they?" a man behind me said.

He must have been at least eighty, wearing a brown corduroy suit. He resembled a professor, with his thick-rimmed reading glasses dangling from his neck—handsome, in a teddy-bear sort of way.

I wasn't sure if he was talking to me, until he spoke again. "That smell," he said, with a wink. "They should bottle it."

"Yeah," I said, nodding. I knew exactly what he meant, and I agreed. "I haven't been here in ten years. I guess I forgot how much I missed it."

"Oh, you're an out-of-towner?"

"Yes," I said. "I'm here for the month."

"Well, welcome, then," he said. "Who are you here to see, or are you just making an adventure of it?"

"My aunt Bee."

His mouth opened wide. "Bee Larson?"

I grinned a little. As if there was any other Bee Larson on the island. "Yes," I said. "You know her?"

"Of course," he said, as though I was expected to know this fact. "She's my neighbor."

I smiled. We had reached the terminal now, but I didn't see Bee's car anywhere.

"You know," he continued, "I thought you looked familiar when I first saw you, and I—"

We both looked up when we heard the unmistakable popping and crackling sound of a Volkswagen engine. Bee drives too fast for her age—for any age, really. But you'd somehow expect an eighty-five-year-old to fear the accelerator, if not respect it. Not Bee. She skidded to a stop, mere inches from our feet.

"Emily!" Bee said as she barreled out of the car, arms flung wide. She was dressed in dark jeans, which were slightly belled at the bottom, and a pale green tunic. Bee was the only woman in her eighties I knew who dressed like she was still in her twenties—well, a twentysomething from the 1960s, maybe; the print on her shirt was paisley.

I felt a lump in my throat as we embraced. No tears, just a lump.

"I was just talking to your neighbor—" I said, realizing that I hadn't gotten his name.

"Henry," he said, smiling at me, extending his hand.

"Nice to meet you, Henry. I'm Emily." There was something familiar about him, too. "Wait, we've met before, haven't we?"

He nodded. "Yes, but you were a child." He shook his head at Bee with astonishment.

"We should get you home, child," Bee said, hurriedly stepping past Henry. "It must be at least two a.m. New York time."

I was tired, but not so much as to forget that a Beetle's trunk is in the front, and I loaded my luggage. Bee revved the engine, and I turned for a parting glance and a wave at Henry, but he was gone. I wondered why Bee hadn't offered her neighbor a ride.

"It's so good to have you, dear," Bee said as she sped away from the terminal. The seat belts in the car didn't work, but I didn't care. Being here with Bee, on this island, made me feel safe.

I looked out the window up into the starry winter sky as the Beetle jerked along. Hidden Cove Road wound its way down to the waterfront, the route's sharp and winding curves evoking Lombard Street in San Francisco. No cable cars could navigate the tangled clumps of trees that part to reveal Bee's beach home. Even if you saw it every day of your life, it never failed to be breathtaking, the old rambling white colonial with its pillared entryway and ebony shutters flanking the front windows. Uncle Bill had urged her to paint them green. Mom said they should have been blue. But Bee always insisted there was no sense in having a white house without black shutters.

I was unable to see if the lilacs were flowering, or if the rhododendrons were as lush as I remembered, or if the tide was low or high. But even in the dark, the place seemed effervescent and sparkling, untouched by time. "Here we are," Bee said, braking so hard that I had to brace myself. "You know what you should do?"

I'd anticipated her next words exactly.

"You should go put your feet in the sound," she said, pointing to the beach. "It would do you good."

"Tomorrow," I replied, smiling. "Tonight I just want to go inside and sink into a sofa."

"OK, honey," she said, tucking a stray lock of my blond hair behind my ear. "I've missed you."

"Me too," I said, squeezing her hand.

I lifted my luggage from the trunk and followed her along the brick pathway that led to the house. Bee had lived here long before she married Uncle Bill. Her parents died in a car wreck when she was in college, and left her, their only child, a fortune, with which she made a singular significant purchase: Keystone Mansion, the expansive old eight-bedroom colonial that had been boarded up for years. Since the 1940s, a local debate had raged over which was Bee's most eccentric act: buying the enormous house or having it redone, just once, inside and out.

Nearly every room afforded a view of the sound through big casement windows that rattled on windy nights. My mother always said the house was far too large for a woman who didn't have children. But I think she was just jealous; she lived in a three-bedroom rambler.

The big front door creaked as Bee and I entered. "Come," she said. "I'll make a fire and then get us a drink."

I watched as Bee piled logs into the fireplace. It occurred to me that I should have been doing this for her. But I felt too tired to move. My legs ached. Everything ached.

"It's funny," I said, shaking my head. "All those years in New York, and I never once made a trip to visit you. I'm a terrible niece."

"Your mind was elsewhere," she said. "And besides, fate has a way of bringing you back when it's time to come back."

I remembered the words on her postcard. In a way, Bee's definition of fate felt more like my failure, but her intention was kind.

I looked around the living room and sighed. "Joel would have liked it here," I said. "But I never could convince him to leave work long enough to make the trip."

"It's a good thing," she said.

"Why?"

"Because I don't think we would have gotten along."

I smiled. "You're probably right." Bee didn't have much patience for pretense, and Joel was wrapped in layers of it.

She stood up and walked around the corner to the room she called the "lanai," where she kept a full wet bar. The space was enclosed almost entirely by windows, aside from one wall where a large painting hung. I remembered the canvas I'd tucked into my suitcase before leaving New York. I wanted to ask her about it, but not yet. I'd learned long ago that discussing Bee's art, like many subjects in her life, was off limits.

I thought of the night when I was fifteen, when my cousin Rachel and I snuck into the lanai, found our way into that cabinet with its dark British cane doors, and drank four shots of rum each while the adults played cards in the other room. I remember wishing the room would stop spinning. It was the last time I drank rum.

Bee returned with two Gordon Greens, a mixture of lime and cucumber muddled together with gin, simple syrup, and a sprinkle of sea salt. "So, let's hear about you," she said, handing me a glass.

I took a sip, wishing I had a story to tell Bee. Any story. I felt that lump in the back of my throat again, and when I opened my mouth to say something, there were no words, so I looked down at my lap instead.

Bee nodded as if I had just made perfect sense.

"I know," she said. "I know."

We sat there together in silence, staring at the fire's hypnotic flames, until I felt my eyelids get heavy.

March 2

I don't know what woke me the next morning: the waves crashing into the shore, so loud it seemed possible they were reaching out like sea arms to knock on the door, or the smell of breakfast in the kitchen—pancakes, which no one ate anymore, certainly not adults, and certainly not adults in New York. Or maybe it was my phone that jarred my eyes open, the cell phone that was ringing somewhere between the cushions of the couch. I hadn't made it to the guest room the night before; fatigue got the better of me—fatigue or emotional exhaustion. Or both.

I pushed the quilt aside—Bee must have draped it over me after I'd fallen asleep—and started digging around frantically for the phone.

It was Annabelle.

"Hi," I said quietly.

"Hi!" she said, startling me with her cheerfulness. "I just wanted to make sure you made it all right. Everything OK?"

In all honesty, I wished I could be like Annabelle and let it all out. I wanted to cry big fat glorious tears. God knows, I needed to.

She was staying at my place for the month, as her upstairs neighbors had taken up the trumpet. "Have there been any calls?" I asked, knowing that Annabelle would understand exactly whom I was talking about. I knew I sounded pathetic, but we had long since given each other permission to be pathetic around one another.

"Sorry, Em, no calls."

"Right," I said. "Of course. So, how are things there?"

"Well," she said, "I ran into Evan at the café this morning."

Evan is Annabelle's ex, the one she didn't marry on account of his dislike of jazz, and, well, other things, too. Let's see . . . he snored. And he ate hamburgers, which was a problem because Annabelle is a vegetarian. And then there was the business of his name. Evan is not a marriageable name.

"Did you two talk?"

"Sort of," she said. Her voice suddenly sounded distant, as if she might have been doing two things at once. "But it was awkward."

"What did he say?"

"Well, he introduced me to his new girlfriend, *Vivien*."

She said *Vivien* as if it were a name for some kind of dreaded health condition—like a rash, or maybe a staph infection.

"Do I sense some jealousy here, Annie? Remember, *you're* the one who broke it off with *him*."

"I know," she said. "And I don't regret the decision."

I didn't buy it. "Annie, I know Evan," I said, "and I know that if you called him right now and told him how you really felt, he'd be yours. He still loves you."

There was a silence on the other end of the line, as if she was considering my idea.

"Annie?" I said. "Are you there?"

"Yeah," she said. "Sorry, I had to set the phone down. The UPS guy just showed up at your door and I needed to sign for a package. Do you always get this much mail?"

"So you didn't hear a word I just said?"

"Sorry," she said. "Was it important?"

I sighed. "No."

Despite the fact that she believed she was a hopeless romantic, and despite her research, when it came to love, Annabelle had honed the fine art of relationship sabotage.

"Well, call me if you want to talk," she said.

"I will."

"Love you."

"Love you too, and stay away from my Laura Mercier moisturizer," I said half playfully, half seriously.

"I think I can manage that *if*," she said, "you promise me you'll work on things in the tear department."

"Deal."

When I found my way into the kitchen, I was surprised not to find Bee there tending the stove. Instead, there was a plate of pancakes, a few strips of bacon stacked in a neat little pile, and a jar of homemade raspberry jam waiting at the table next to a note:

Emily,

I had to go into town to run some errands, and I didn't want to wake you. I've left you a plate of your favorite buckwheat pancakes and bacon (reheat in the microwave—forty-five seconds on high). I'll be back this afternoon. I put your things in the bedroom down the hall. Make yourself comfortable. And you should take a walk after breakfast. The sound is beautiful today.

Love,

Bee

I set the note down and looked out the window. She was right. The gray-blue water, the patchwork of sandy and rocky shore—it was breathtaking. I had the urge to run out there right at that moment and dig for clams, or lift up rocks and look for crabs, or strip down and swim to the buoy the way I had done in the summers of my childhood. I wanted to immerse myself in that big, beautiful, mysterious body of water. The thought, for a second, made me feel alive again, but it lasted only a second. So I slathered my pancakes in Bee's raspberry jam and ate.

The table was just as I remembered, covered with the yellow oilcloth printed with pineapple, a napkin holder decorated with seashells, and a stack of magazines. Bee reads each issue of *The New Yorker*, cover to cover, and then clips out her favorite stories, plasters them in Post-it notes containing her comments, and mails them to me, no matter how many times I tell her that she really shouldn't bother; I have a subscription to the magazine.

After I'd set my plate in the dishwasher, I walked down the hall, peering into each room until I found the one where Bee had placed my bags. In all the years I'd visited her as a child, I had never set foot in *this* room. In fact, I didn't recall it ever being there. But Bee had a habit of keeping certain rooms locked, for reasons my sister, Danielle, and I would never understand.

Yes, I decided, I would have remembered this room. The walls were painted pink—which was strange, because Bee hated pink. Near the bed there was a dresser, a nightstand, and a large closet. I looked out the paned window that faced the west side of the shore and remembered Bee's suggestion to go on a walk. I decided to unpack later and head for the beach. I was too weak to resist its magnetism any longer.

Chapter 3

I didn't bother changing my clothes or brushing my hair, preparations I would most certainly have made in New York. Instead, I threw on a sweater, jammed my feet into a pair of army green rubber boots that Bee kept in the mudroom, and made my way outside.

There is something oddly therapeutic about trudging through marshy sand, the feeling of squishiness below the feet signaling to the brain that it's OK to just let go for a while. And that's what I did that morning. I didn't scold myself, either, when my mind turned to Joel and a thousand little random memories from the past. I crushed a hollowed-out crab shell with my boot, crunching it into a thousand pieces.

I picked up a rock and threw it into the water as far and as hard as I could. *Dammit. Why did our story have to end like this?* Then I picked up another, and another, throwing them violently into the sound, until I slumped over on a nearby piece of driftwood. *How could he? How could I?* In spite of everything, there was a small part of me that wanted him back, and I hated myself for it.

"You're never going to skip a rock with a throw like that."

I jumped at the sound of a man's voice. It was Henry, walking slowly toward me.

"Oh, hi," I said self-consciously. Had he been watching my tantrum? And for how long? "I was just . . ."

"Skipping rocks," he said, nodding. "But your technique, sweetheart—it's all wrong."

He bent down and picked up a smooth sand-dollar-thin rock and held it up to the light, scrutinizing every angle. "Yes," he finally said. "This one will do." He turned to me. "Now, hold the rock like this, and then let your arm flow through like butter as you release it."

He threw it toward the shore and it flew across the water, where it did a little six-hop dance on the surface. "Rats," he said. "I'm losing my touch. Six is terrible."

"It is?"

"Well, yeah," he said. "My record's fourteen."

"Fourteen? You can't be serious."

"As I live and stand here," he said, crossing his heart with his hand the way you do when you're eleven years old. And a member of a *Boy Scout troop*. "I was once the rock-skipping champion of this island."

I didn't feel like laughing, but I couldn't help myself. "They have competitions for rock skipping?"

"Sure do," he said. "Now you try."

I looked down toward the sand and reached for a flat stone. "Here goes," I said, winding up and then letting go. The rock hit the water and belly flopped. "See? I'm terrible."

"Nah," he said. "You just need practice."

I smiled. His face was worn and wrinkled like an old leather-bound book. But his eyes . . . well, they told me that somewhere inside the smile lines resided a young man.

"May I interest you in a cup of coffee?" he asked, pointing up the shore to a little white house above the bulkhead. His eyes sparkled.

"Yes," I said. "That sounds wonderful."

We walked up the concrete steps that led to a moss-covered pathway. Its six stepping-stones deposited us at Henry's entryway, under the shadow of two large old cedar trees standing sentry.

He opened the screen door. Its screech rivaled that of a few seagulls from the roof who squealed in disapproval as they flew back toward the water.

"I've been meaning to get this door fixed," he said, slipping off his boots on the porch. I followed his lead and did the same.

My cheeks warmed from the fire roaring and crackling in the living room. "You make yourself comfortable," he said. "I'll put the coffee on."

I nodded and walked to the fireplace, with its dark mahogany mantel lined with seashells, small shiny rocks, and black-and-white photos in simple frames. One of the pictures caught my eye. Its subject wore her blond hair curled and styled close to her head, the way women did in the 1940s. She oozed glamour, like a model or an actress, standing there on the beach with the wind blowing her dress against her body, the outline of her breasts and her thin waist visible. There was a house in the background, Henry's house, and those cedar trees, much smaller then, but just as recognizable. I wondered if she had been his wife. Her pose seemed too suggestive for a sister. Whoever this was, Henry adored her. I was sure of it.

He approached with two big coffee mugs in hand.

"She's beautiful," I said, picking up the photo and sitting down on the couch with it for a closer look. "Your wife?"

He looked surprised by my question, then answered, simply, "No." He handed me a mug and then stood up and ran his fingers along his chin, the way men do when they're confused or unsure about something.

"I'm sorry," I said, quickly replacing the frame on the mantel. "I didn't mean to pry."

"No, no," he said, suddenly smiling. "It's silly, I guess. It's been more than sixty years; you'd think I'd be able to talk about her."

"Her?"

"She was my fiancée," he continued. "We were going to be married, but . . . things didn't work out." He paused as if changing his mind about something. "I probably shouldn't be—"

We both looked up when we heard a knock at the door. "Henry?" It was a man's voice. "Are you home?"

"Oh, it's Jack," Henry said, turning to me. He said the name in a familiar way, as though I was expected to know him.

I watched from the living room as he opened the door and welcomed a dark-haired man about my age. He was tall, so tall that he had to duck a little when entering the house. He wore jeans and a gray wool sweater, and even though it was only midmorning, the faint shadow visible on his jawline hinted at the fact that he hadn't yet shaved, or showered, either.

"Hi," he said a little awkwardly, as his eyes met mine. "I'm Jack."

Henry spoke for me. "This is Emily—you know, Bee Larson's niece."

Jack looked at me, and then back at Henry. "Bee's *niece*?"

"Yes," Henry replied. "She's visiting for the month."

"Welcome," Jack said, tugging at the cuff of his sweater. "Sorry, I didn't mean to interrupt; I started cooking and halfway through the recipe realized I was out of eggs. You don't happen to have two, do you?"

"Of course," Henry said as he headed to the kitchen.

While Henry was gone, my eyes met Jack's, but I quickly looked away. He rubbed his forehead; I fiddled with the zipper on my sweater. The silence was as thick and stifling as the murky sand on the beach outside the window.

A splash sounded in the water outside. I startled, catching my foot on the edge of the side table, helplessly watching the little white vase sitting atop a stack of books topple to the ground, where it broke into four jagged pieces.

"Oh no," I said, shaking my head, equally concerned about breaking one of Henry's treasured heirlooms as I was about embarrassing myself in front of Jack.

"Here, I'll help you hide the evidence," he said, smiling. I liked him instantly.

"I'm the world's clumsiest woman," I said, burying my face in my hands.

"Good," he replied, pulling up the sleeve of his sweater to reveal the black-and-blue of a fresh bruise. "I'm the world's clumsiest man." He pulled a plastic bag out of his pocket and carefully picked up what was left of the vase. "We can glue it together later," he continued.

I grinned.

Henry returned with an egg carton and handed it to Jack. "Sorry, I had to run out to the refrigerator in the garage," he said.

"Thanks, Henry," Jack said. "I owe you."

"Won't you stay?"

"I can't," he said, glancing my way, "I really should get back, but thanks." He turned to me with the look of an accomplice. "Nice to meet you, Emily."

"Nice to meet you," I said, wishing he didn't have to go so quickly.

Henry and I watched from the window as Jack made his way back to the beach. "He's an odd one, that Jack," he said. "Here I have the prettiest girl on the island in my living room, and he can't even stay for coffee."

I was certain I was blushing. "You're much too kind," I said. "Look at me. I just rolled out of bed."

He winked. "I meant what I said."

"You're a dear," I said.

We chatted through a second cup, but a glance at my watch told me that I'd been gone for almost two hours. "I should probably head back, Henry," I said. "Bee is going to wonder."

"Of course," he replied.

"I'll see you on the beach," I said.

"Anytime you're passing by, please, stop in."

The tide was out now, exposing a secret layer of life on the shore, and walking back, I found myself picking up shells and big pieces of bubbly emerald green kelp and popping the air bubbles out of the slimy flesh the way I had so many years ago. A rock sparkled in the sun, and I kneeled down to retrieve it, which is when I heard footsteps behind me. Animal footsteps, and then shouting.

"Russ, here boy!"

I turned around, and in an instant, a big and bumbling golden retriever tackled me with the strength of an NFL defensive back. "Whoa!" I yelled, wiping my face, which had just been licked.

"I'm so sorry," Jack said. "He snuck out the back door. I hope he didn't scare you. He's harmless, all one hundred and eight pounds of him."

"I'm fine," I said, smiling, brushing some sand off my pants, before kneeling down to give the pooch a proper greeting.

"And you must be Russ," I said. "Nice to meet you, fellow. I'm Emily."

I looked up at Jack. "I was just on my way back to Bee's."

He snapped the leash on to Russ's collar. "No more stunts like that, boy," he said, before looking at me. "I'll walk with you; we're heading your way."

It was a minute, maybe longer, before either of us spoke. I was content with the sound of our boots on the rocky shore.

"So, do you live here in Washington?" Jack finally said.

"No," I said. "New York."

He nodded. "Never been."

"You're kidding," I said. "You've never been to New York City?"

He shrugged. "I guess I've never had a reason to go. I've lived here all my life. Never really considered leaving."

I nodded, looking at the sprawling expanse of beach. "Well, being on the island again"—I paused and looked around—"I guess it makes me wonder why I ever left. I don't miss New York at all right now."

"So what brings you here this month?"

Didn't I already tell him that I'm visiting my aunt? Wasn't that explanation enough? I wasn't about to explain that I was running from my past, which in a sense I was, or that I was trying to figure out my future, or that, heaven forbid, I'd just been divorced. I took a deep breath and said instead, "I'm doing research for my next book."

"Oh," he said. "You're a writer?"

"Yes," I said, swallowing hard. I hated the self-importance of my tone. *Could any of this really be considered research?* As usual, the moment I started talking about my career I began to feel vulnerable.

"Wow," he said. "So what do you write?"

I told him about *Calling Ali Larson* and he stopped suddenly. "You're kidding," he said. "They made that into a movie, right?"

I nodded. "How about you?" I said, suddenly eager to change the subject. "What do you do?"

"I'm an artist," he answered. "A painter."

My eyes widened. "Oh, wow, I'd love to see your work some-time." But the second I spoke, I felt my cheeks burn with embarrass-ment. *Could I be any more awkward, any rustier? Have I completely forgotten how to talk to a man?*

Instead of acknowledging the statement, he flashed a half grin before kicking his foot in the sand, dislodging a piece of driftwood that had been trapped. "Can you believe the beach this morning?" he said, pointing to the debris scattered along the shoreline. "There must have been quite a storm last night."

I loved the beach after a storm. When I was thirteen, a banker's bag washed up on this same beach with exactly $319 inside—I know because I counted out every bill—along with a waterlogged hand-gun. Bee called the police, who traced the remnants to a bank rob-bery gone wrong seventeen years prior. *Seventeen years.* The Puget Sound is like a time machine, hiding things and then spewing them back onto its shores at the time and place of its choosing.

"So you said you've lived here on the island all your life—then you must know my aunt."

He nodded. "Know her? You could say that."

Bee's house lay a few steps ahead. "Would you like to come in?" I said. "You could say hello to Bee."

He hesitated, as if remembering something or someone. "No," he said, squinting as he looked cautiously up toward the windows. "No, I better not."

I bit the edge of my lip. "OK," I replied. "Well, I'll see you around, then."

That was that, I told myself, making my way to the back door. *Why did he seem so uncomfortable?*

"Wait, Emily," Jack called out from the beach a few moments later.

I turned around.

"Sorry," he said. "I'm a little out of practice." He pushed a piece of his dark hair out of his eyes, and the wind blew it right back where it was. "I was just wondering if you'd like to come to dinner," he said, "at my house. Saturday night at seven?"

I stood there looking at him, waiting to open my mouth. It took a few seconds, but I found my voice, and my head. "I'd love that," I said, nodding.

"See you then, Emily," he said, grinning bigger.

I had noticed Bee watching us from the window, but when I entered the house from the mudroom she had moved to the couch.

"So I see you've met Jack," she said, her eyes fixed on her crossword puzzle.

"Yes," I said. "He was at Henry's today."

"Henry's?" Bee said, looking up. "What were you doing there?"

"I was on a walk this morning, and I ran into him on the beach." I shrugged. "He invited me in for coffee."

Bee looked concerned.

"What is it?" I asked.

She set her pencil down and looked up at me. "Be careful," she said cryptically, "especially with Jack."

"Careful? Why?"

"People aren't always who they appear to be," she said, tucking her reading glasses into the blue velvet case she kept on the side table.

"What do you mean?"

She ignored my question in a way that only Bee could. "Well, is it twelve thirty already?" She sighed. "It's time for my nap."

She poured herself a demitasse of sherry. "My medicine," she said with a wink. "I'll see you later this afternoon, dear."

It was clear that there was some kind of history between Bee and Jack. I could see it on his face, and I could hear it in her voice.

I leaned back on the couch and yawned. Enticed by the allure of a nap, I found my way to the guest bedroom and curled up in the big bed with its pink, ruffled comforter. I picked up the novel I'd bought at the airport, but after battling through two chapters, I tossed the book on the floor.

I freed my wrist from the constraints of my watch—I can't sleep with any hardware on—and opened the drawer of the bedside table. But as I dropped the watch inside, I noticed something in the shadows.

It was a journal, a diary of some sort. I picked it up and ran my hand along the spine. It was old, and its intriguing red velvet cover looked worn and threadbare. I touched it, instantly feeling a pang of guilt. What if this was an old diary of Bee's? I shuddered, setting it carefully back inside the drawer. A few moments passed, and I found myself with the diary in my hands again. It was too irresistible. *Just one look at the first page, that's all.*

The pages, yellowed and brittle, had a pristine feel that can only be cultivated by the passage of time. I scanned the first page for a clue, and found it in the bottom right corner, where the words *Manuscript Exercise Book* were typed in black ink, along with standard publisher's jargon. I recalled a book I'd read long ago in which a character from the early twentieth century used such a notebook to write a novel. *Is this a draft of a novel, or a private diary?* Fascinated, I turned the page, extinguishing my feelings of guilt with ample amounts of curiosity. *Just one more page, then I'll put it back.*

The words on the next page, written in the most beautiful penmanship I'd ever seen, sent my heart racing. "The Story of What Happened in a Small Island Town in 1943."

Bee had never written, at least not that I was aware. Uncle Bill?

No, the lettering was clearly the work of a female. Why would it be here—in this *pink* room? And who would leave off their byline, and why?

I took a deep breath, and turned the page. *What would be the harm in simply reading a few lines?* When I took in the beginning paragraph, I could no longer resist.

I never intended on kissing Elliot. Married women don't behave like that, at least not married women like me. It wasn't proper. But the tide was high, and there was a cold breeze blowing, and Elliot's arms were draped around my body like a warm shawl, caressing me in places where he shouldn't have been, and I could scarcely think of much else. It was like how we used to be. And even though I was married now, even though circumstances had changed, my heart had managed to stay fixed in time—frozen, as if waiting for this very moment—the moment in which Elliot and I found our way back to this place. Bobby never held me like this. Or maybe he did, but if so, his touch didn't provoke this kind of passion, this kind of fire.

And yes, I never intended on kissing Elliot on that cold March night, nor did I plan for the unspeakable things that happened next, the chain of events that would be my undoing, our undoing. But this was the chain of events that began in the month of March of 1943, events that would forever change my life and the lives of those around me. My name is Esther, and this is my story.

I looked up. *Esther? Who is Esther? A pen name, perhaps? A fictional character?* I heard a knock, and instinctively pulled up the comforter to hide the pages I was reading.

"Yes?" I said.

Bee opened the door. "I can't sleep," she said, rubbing her eyes. "How about we make a trip to the market instead?"

"Sure," I said, even though I really wanted to stay and keep reading.

"I'll meet you out front, when you're ready," she said, staring at me for a few seconds longer than was comfortable before breaking her gaze. I was starting to get the feeling that people on the island were all in on some big secret—one that no one had any intention of sharing with me.

Chapter 4

The Town and Country Market was just a half mile from Bee's home. I used to walk there as a girl, with my sister or my cousins, or sometimes all by myself, picking purple clover flowers along the way until I had a big round bunch, which, when pressed up to your nose, smelled exactly of honey. Before the walk, we'd always beg the adults for twenty-five cents and return with pockets full of pink Bazooka bubble gum. If summer had a flavor, it was pink bubble gum.

Bee and I drove in silence along the winding road up into town. The beauty of an old Volkswagen is that if you don't feel like talking, you don't have to. The engine noise infuses uneasy stillness with a nice, comforting hum.

Bee handed me her shopping list. "I have to go talk to Leanne in the bakery. Can you get started on this list, dear?"

"Sure," I said, smiling. I knew I could still find my way around the market, even if I was seventeen the last time I'd stepped foot in the place.

The Otter Pops were probably still on aisle three, and, of course, the cute guy in the produce department would be there, with the sleeves of his T-shirt rolled up high to show off his biceps.

I scanned Bee's list—salmon, arborio rice, leeks, watercress, shallots, white wine, rhubarb, whipping cream—which hinted that dinner would be drool-worthy. I decided to start with wine, since it was closest.

The Town and Country Market's wine department looked more like the cellar of an upscale restaurant than the limited selection typical of a regular grocery store. Nestled below a small flight of stairs was a dimly lit, cavernous room where dusty bottles seemed to cling perilously to the walls.

"Can I help you?"

I looked up, a little startled, and noticed a man about my age walking toward me. I backed up abruptly and almost knocked over a display of white wine. "Oh my gosh, sorry," I said, steadying a bottle that was bobbing like a bowling pin.

"No worries," he said. "Are you looking for a California white, or maybe something local?"

There were few lights in the room, so I couldn't make out his face, not at first. "Well, I really was just . . ." And just then, as he approached me and reached for a bottle on the upper shelf, I saw his face, and my mouth fell open. "God, is that you, *Greg*?"

He looked down at me, shaking his head in disbelief. "Emily?"

It was eerie and exciting and uncomfortable, all at the same time. There, standing in front of me, wearing a grocery store apron, was my teenage crush. And even though it had been almost twenty years since I'd last seen him, his face was as familiar as it had been the day I let him remove the top of my Superwoman bikini and run his hands along my chest. I was sure it meant that he loved me and we'd get married one day. I was so sure of this, in fact, that I scratched "Emily + Greg = Love" with a paper clip on the back of the paper towel dispenser in the women's restroom at the market. But then the summer ended, and I went home. I checked my mailbox every day for five months, but no letters. No calls. And then the next summer, at Bee's, I walked along the beach to his house and knocked on his door. His younger sister, whom I never liked, informed me that he'd left for college and that he had a new girlfriend. Her name, she said, was Lisa.

Greg was still incredibly handsome—but he was older now, more weathered. I wondered if I looked *weathered.* I instinctively glanced at his left hand for a wedding ring. There was none.

"What are you doing here?" I said. It still hadn't hit me that this was his place of employment. I'd always imagined Greg as an airline pilot or a forest ranger—something bolder, something bigger, something, well, more Greg. But a grocery store clerk? It didn't fit.

"I work here," he said, grinning proudly. He pointed to his name badge and then ran his hand through his bleached-blond hair. "Wow—it's so good to see you," he continued. "It's been, like, what, fifteen years?"

"Yeah," I said. "Wait, maybe even *longer.* That's crazy."

"You look great," he said, which made me feel self-conscious.

"Thanks," I replied, tugging at my collar. I looked down at my feet. Oh God. The rubber boots. Everyone fantasizes about running into old flames while wearing slimming cocktail dresses, and here I was in a balled-up wool sweater from the back of Bee's closet. Oops.

Even so, Greg, with the same boyish good looks and gray-blue eyes exactly the color of the sound on a stormy day, was making me feel as good as he looked.

"So what brings you back to the island?" he said, smiling, propping his elbow against the wall. "I thought you were some fancy writer in New York."

I grinned. "I'm visiting Bee for the month."

"Oh really," he said. "I see her here shopping every once in a while. I've always wanted to ask her how you were." He paused. "But I guess I always chickened out."

"Chickened out?"

He rubbed his hand along his forehead. "I don't know," he said. "I guess at our core, we're all still sixteen, right? And didn't you break up with me?"

I smiled. "No, you left for college." He had a certain warmth, a certain energy that I liked.

"So why here, why now, after all these years?" he said.

I sighed. "*Well*, it's a little complicated."

"I can do complicated."

I rubbed the finger where my wedding ring had once been. "I'm here because . . ." I paused and searched his face for approval, or disapproval, which was crazy because what did I care what my boyfriend from a million years ago would think of my marital status, and then I finally blurted it out: "I'm here because I just got divorced, and I needed to get the hell out of New York City."

He put his hand on my shoulder. "I'm sorry." He said it as if he meant it, which made me decide that I liked Grown-up Greg a lot more than Teenage Greg.

"I'm OK," I said, praying that he wasn't a mind reader.

He shook his head in disbelief. "You haven't changed at all."

I didn't know what to say, so I said, "Thanks." Greg was only saying what every person says to someone they were once romantically involved with, but it woke up my lethargic self-esteem like a dose of epinephrine. I nervously smoothed my hair, then remembered that I needed a haircut—three months ago.

"I could say the same about you," I said. "You look great." I paused. "How has life treated you? Any better luck in the marriage department than I've had?"

I don't know why, but I had somehow pictured Greg blissfully married, living the good life on Bainbridge Island. A great house. A pretty wife. A half dozen kids buckled safely into car seats in a navy blue Suburban.

"Luck?" He shrugged. "No, none here. But I'm happy. I'm healthy. That counts for something, right?"

I nodded. "Of course it does." I have to admit, it felt good to know that I wasn't the only one with a life that hadn't exactly worked out according to plan.

"So really, you're doing all right? Because if you need to talk to anyone, I . . ." He grabbed a towel that hung from his apron and began dusting off a few bottles of red wine on a lower shelf.

Maybe it was the dim lights, or the presence of so much wine, but I felt oddly at ease there with Greg. "Yeah," I said, "I'd be lying if I said this isn't hard. But I'm taking things day by day. Today? Today I feel good." I gulped. "Yesterday? Not so much."

He nodded, then smiled again, looking at me affectionately, his face ablaze with memories. "Hey, do you remember the time I took you to Seattle to that concert?"

I nodded. It felt like one hundred years since I'd thought about that night. My mother had forbidden it, but Bee, ever the miracle worker, convinced her that letting Greg take me to the "symphony" was a grand idea.

"We almost didn't make it home that night," he said, his eyes like portals into the forgotten memories of my youth.

"Well, as I recall you wanted me to stay the night with you at your brother's frat house at the university," I said, rolling my eyes the way I might have when I was a teenager. "My mother would have killed me!"

He shrugged. "Well, can you blame a guy for trying?" He still had it, the spark that had attracted me from the beginning.

Greg quashed the awkward silence that followed by redirecting our attention to wine. "So you were looking for a bottle of wine?"

"Oh, yes," I said. "Bee sent me down for something white. Which one of the pinots would that be?" When it comes to wine, I am one hundred percent idiot.

He smiled and ran his finger along the rack until it stopped mid-shelf, and he pulled out a bottle with the precision of a surgeon. "Try this," he said. "It's one of my favorites—a local pinot grigio made from grapes grown right here on the island. One sip, and you'll be in love."

Another customer was suddenly hovering behind Greg, but before he turned to assist he quickly asked, "Will you let me take you out to dinner? Just once. Just once before you go?"

"Of course," I said instinctively, not stopping to think the invitation through, because if I had, I would have probably—no, definitely—said no.

"Great," he said. His smile illuminated two rows of glistening white teeth, which made me run my tongue along mine. "I'll call you at your aunt's."

"Good," I said, a little dazed. Did that just happen? I made my way up to the produce department to tackle the watercress, when I spotted Bee.

"Oh, there you are," she said, waving at me. "Come here, dear, I want to introduce you to someone."

Standing next to her was a woman, about Bee's age, with dark hair—clearly dyed—and dark eyes to match. I'd never seen eyes that dark. They were nearly black, and quite a contradiction to her creamy, pale skin. There was nothing geriatric about this woman, except for the fact that she was, well, in her eighties.

"This is Evelyn," Bee said proudly. "One of my dearest friends."

"It's so nice to meet you," I said.

"Evelyn and I go way back," Bee explained. "We've been friends since grade school. You actually met her as a child, Emily, but you may not remember."

"I'm sorry," I said. "I don't. I'm afraid I had a one-track mind during those summers: swimming, boys, repeat."

"It's so nice to see you again, dear," she said, smiling as if she already knew me. And there was definitely something familiar about her, too, but what?

Unlike Bee, in her jeans and sweatshirt, Evelyn looked like she could be a senior citizen model. There were no high-waisted pants or thick, rubber-soled shoes. She wore a stylish wrap dress and ballet flats, and yet she seemed genuine and down-to-earth, just like Bee. It made sense that they were best friends. I liked her instantly.

"Wait, I do remember you!" I said suddenly. The glint of her eyes and the light of her smile instantly transported me back to 1985, the summer when Danielle and I stayed with Bee on our own. We had been told that our parents were going on a trip, but I later learned that they had separated that summer. Dad had left Mom in July, and by September they'd patched things up. Mom had lost fifteen pounds and Dad had grown a beard. They seemed strange and awkward around each other. Danielle told me that Dad had a girlfriend, but I didn't believe it, and even if I had, I could never blame Dad for that, or for anything, after the way he had endured my mother's badgering and yelling all those years. Still, Dad had the patience of Gandhi.

But it wasn't their separation that was consuming my mind just then; it was Evelyn's garden. Bee had taken us there when we were children, and it was all rushing back: a magical world of hydrangeas, roses, and dahlias, and lemon shortbread cookies on Evelyn's patio. It seemed like only yesterday that my sister and I sat on the little bench under the trellis while Bee hovered over her easel, capturing on her canvas whatever flower was in bloom in the lush beds. "Your garden," I said. "I remember your garden."

"Yes," Evelyn said, smiling.

I nodded, a little astonished that this memory, buried so deep in my mind, had risen to the surface just then like a lost file from my sub-conscious. It was as if the island had unlocked it somehow. Standing there in the produce section, I recalled the daylilies and the shortbread, which tasted like heaven—and then the fog lifted. I was sitting on a weathered gray teak bench on her patio, wearing that old pair of white canvas Keds—except that they weren't really Keds; they were the generic brand with the fake blue square on the heel. It would have cost exactly eleven dollars more for a pair of *real* Keds, and boy did I want them. I'd clean the bathroom every Saturday for a month, I promised my mom. I'd vacuum. I'd dust. I'd iron Dad's shirts. But she just shook her head and returned home with a pair of knockoffs from Payless Shoe Source. Every other girl I knew had a pair of real Keds, with that trademark blue rubber tag. And so there I sat on Evelyn's patio, fussing with the blue tag that was peeling off the back of my right shoe.

Bee was giving a very disinterested Danielle a tour of the garden when Evelyn sat down next to me. "What's troubling you, dear?"

I shrugged. "Nothing."

"It's OK," she said, squeezing my hand. "You can tell me."

I sighed. "Well, it's really kind of embarrassing, but you wouldn't happen to have any superglue, would you?"

"Superglue?"

I pointed to my shoe. "Mom won't buy me Keds, and the tag on the back of my shoe is falling off and I . . ." I burst into tears.

"There, there now," Evelyn said, handing me a handkerchief from her pocket. "When I was about your age, a girl I knew came to school wearing a pair of the most beautiful red shoes. They sparkled like rubies. Her dad was quite wealthy, and she told everyone that he'd brought them home for her from Paris. I wanted a pair more than anything in the world."

"Did you get some?" I'd asked.

She shook her head. "No, and you know what? I'd still like a pair. So, you asked for superglue, dear, but wouldn't you rather have a pair of—what did you call them?"

"Keds," I said meekly.

"Ah, yes, Keds."

I nodded.

"Well then. What are you doing tomorrow?"

My eyes widened. "Nothing."

"Then it's settled. We'll take the ferry into Seattle and get you some Keds."

"Really?" I stammered.

"Really."

I didn't know what to say, so I just smiled and pulled the rest of the blue rubber tag off the back of my shoe. It didn't matter. Tomorrow I'd be wearing the real thing.

"Evelyn," Bee said, looking at the shopping cart, "I'm making dinner tonight, why don't you join us?"

"Oh, no," she said, "I couldn't. You're just getting settled with Emily."

I smiled. "We'd love to have you."

"Well, then, OK."

"Great," said Bee. "Come by at six o'clock."

"See you then," she said, turning toward the potatoes.

"Bee," I whispered. "You're not going to believe who I just ran into."

"Who?"

"Greg," I said quietly. "Greg Attwood."

"Your old boyfriend?"

I nodded. "I think he just asked me out."

Bee smiled as if this was all part of the plan. She reached for a red onion, examined it, and then shook her head, throwing it back on the pile. She did this a few more times before finding one that pleased her. She said something quietly, under her breath, and when I asked her to repeat herself, she was already across the aisle, filling a bag with leeks. I glanced at the stairs to the wine department and smiled to myself.

Just before six, Bee pulled three wineglasses out of the cabinet and uncorked the bottle of white that Greg had selected for us.

"Light the candles, dear, will you, please?"

I reached for the matches and thought about the dinners at Bee's house during my childhood. Bee never served a meal without candles. "A proper supper requires candlelight," she'd told my sister and me years ago. I thought it was elegant and exciting, and when I asked my mom if we could start the same tradition at home, she said no. "Candles are for birthday parties," she said, "and those only come once a year."

"Beautiful," Bee said, surveying the table before taking a close look at the white wine Greg had recommended. "Pinot grigio," she said approvingly, eyeing the label.

"Bee," I said, sitting at the table as she sliced a leek with a large butcher knife. "I've been thinking about what you said about Jack the other day. What's the story between you two?"

She looked up, a bit startled, then dropped the knife suddenly, clutching her hand. "Ouch," she said. "I cut myself."

"Oh no," I said, running to her. "I'm sorry."

"No," she said. "It's not your fault. These old hands don't work the way they used to."

"Here, let me do the chopping," I said, shooing Bee to the table.

She bandaged her finger, and I finished dicing the leeks, then stirred the risotto, feeling the savory steam rise from the pot to my face with every turn around the pan.

"Bee, it just doesn't make sense that—"

I was cut off by the sound of Evelyn's footsteps at the front door. "Hello, girls!" she said, walking toward the kitchen. In her hands were a bottle of wine and a bouquet of purple lilacs wrapped in brown paper and tied loosely with a strand of twine.

"They're lovely," Bee said, smiling. "Now, where on earth did you find these this early in the season?"

"In my garden," she said as though Bee had just asked her what color the sky was. "My lilac tree always blooms before yours." She said it with an air of amicable competitiveness that only a sixty-plus-year friendship could bear.

Bee mixed her a drink—something with bourbon—and then sent us to the living room while she put the finishing touches on dinner.

"Your aunt is quite something, isn't she?" Evelyn said to me once Bee was out of earshot.

"She's a legend," I said, smiling.

"She is," Evelyn said. The ice in her drink was clinking against the glass, but I couldn't tell if she was doing it on purpose or if her hands were trembling.

"I was going to tell her my news tonight," she said, turning back to me. She said it casually, as if she might have been talking about a new car purchase or a vacation she had booked. But then I noticed tears in her eyes. "I decided, on the way over, that I'd tell her tonight, but then I saw her just now. I saw how good things are, and I thought, Why ruin a perfectly good evening?"

I was confused. "Tell her what?"

She nodded. "I have cancer. Terminal cancer." She said it the way one might say, "I have a cold," simply and straightforward, devoid of the drama it deserved. "I have a month, maybe less, to live," she said quietly. "I've known for a while now, since Christmas. But I haven't found a way to tell Bee. I guess I keep thinking that it might be easier if she just finds out when I'm gone."

"Evelyn, I'm so sorry," I said, reaching for her hand. "But how can you think that Bee wouldn't want to know? She loves you."

Evelyn sighed. "I know she'd want to know. But I don't want our friendship to be about death and dying, when we have so little time left. I'd rather drink bourbon and play bridge and razz her like I always do."

I nodded. I didn't agree with Evelyn's decision, but I understood it.

"Sorry," she said. "It's your first day on the island; I shouldn't be worrying you with my problems. Shame on me."

"I don't mind," I said. "And honestly, it's nice, for once, not to be the one talking about *my* problems."

She took a long sip of her drink and then exhaled deeply. "What would you do if you were in my shoes? Would you tell your best friend and ruin your final days together, or go on happily as you always have until it all just ends?"

"Well, I'd have to come clean, but mostly for selfish reasons," I said. "I'd need my friend's support. But you, you're so strong." I felt myself choking up a little. "I admire your strength."

Evelyn leaned in closer. "Strength? Nonsense. I have the pain tolerance of a four-year-old." She let out a laugh, then whispered, "Now, let's gossip. What can I tell you about your aunt that you don't know?"

My mind flicked through a million unanswered questions, then settled on a weightier topic: the mysterious book I'd found in the bedside table today. "Well," I said, pausing until I could determine whether Bee was still in the kitchen. A clanging pan at the stove let us know that she was. "There is *one* thing."

"What is it, sweetie?" she said.

"Well," I whispered, "today I found a red velvet journal, a diary, in the bedside table in the room where I'm staying. It's really old—dated 1943, I think. I couldn't resist reading the first page, and I was fascinated."

For a second I thought I could see a flicker of recognition in Evelyn's eyes, or maybe remembrance, but the light was quickly extinguished.

"I can't stop wondering if Bee wrote this," I whispered. "But I had no idea that she was ever a writer, and you'd think she would have shared that with me, given my career and everything."

Evelyn set her drink down. "Is there anything more you can tell me about this, this diary? What have you read so far?"

"Well, I've really only read the first page, but I know that it begins with a character named Esther," I said, pausing for a minute, "and Elliot, and—"

Evelyn quickly put her hand to my lips. "You mustn't speak of this story to Bee," she said. "Not yet, anyway."

It occurred to me that maybe this was just an early start at a novel that had never taken shape. God knows I'd had enough of those before my book was published. But why the anonymity? It didn't make any sense. "Evelyn, who wrote it?" The dark shadows under her eyes looked more pronounced now than they had earlier at the market. She took a deep breath and stood up, retrieving a delicately preserved starfish from Bee's mantel. "Sea stars are enigmatic creatures, aren't they? Not a single bone in their body, all cartilage, and fragile, yet they're spirited and tenacious. Brightly colored. Adaptable. Long livers. Did you know that when a sea star's arm is wounded, it can grow another?"

Evelyn returned the starfish to its home on the mantel. "Your grandmother adored sea stars," she said. "Just as she adored the sea." She paused, smiling to herself. "She spent so much time on the shore, collecting bits of beach glass and dreaming up stories about the lives of the crab colonies under the rocks."

"That's so surprising," I said. "I had the impression that my grandmother never liked the sound. Isn't it why she and my grandfather moved to Richland? Something about the sea air and her sinuses?"

"Yes, but—I'm sorry," Evelyn said. "I got lost in a memory." She sat down again and turned to face me. "Now, this diary. Yes, it has found its way into your hands," she said. "You must keep reading it, Emily. The story is important, and you will come to see why."

I let out a deep sigh. "I wish this all made more sense."

"I've already said too much, dear," she said. "It's not my place to talk about. But you deserve to know this story. Keep reading and the answers will come."

She looked lost for a moment, as if her mind had traveled back to the very year when the story of Esther and Elliot began.

"And what about Bee? How can I keep this from her?"

"We protect the ones we love from certain things," she said.

I shook my head, confused. "I don't understand how reading this book would hurt her."

Evelyn closed her eyes for a moment, and then opened them again. "It's been a very long time since I have thought about all of this, and believe me, it was once heavy on all of our minds—heavy and inescapable. But time heals all wounds, and those pages, well, I assumed they were gone, or maybe even destroyed. Yet I always hoped they would surface when they needed to." She paused for a moment. "What room did you say you were staying in, dear?"

I pointed down the hallway. "The pink room."

She nodded. "Yes. Keep reading the book, dear. And you will know when it's time to speak to Bee, but be gentle with her when you do."

Just then, Bee peered around the corner with a steaming platter in her hand. "Dinner's ready, girls," she said, "and I have a bottle of Bainbridge Island white here. Let's fill those glasses."

It was nearly midnight before I made it to bed. Bee and Evelyn had captivated me with their stories of debauchery and drama. There was the time they snuck out of French class to share a bottle of gin with two boys from the football team, and the day they stole the pants from a particularly handsome math teacher while he was swimming at the pool. Their friendship, so seasoned and honest, made me think of Annabelle. I missed her already—our daily and sometimes twice-daily talks, even her not-so-gentle prodding.

I propped up my pillow and climbed into bed, but a few seconds later, I found myself hovering over my suitcase, searching for the little painting I'd brought with me from New York. I found it tucked under a sweater and studied it again. The couple looked natural together, made for each other, even. There was a harmonious quality to the composition—the hands clasped together, the waves cascading onto the shore and the weather vane twirling above. *What will Bee say when she sees the canvas again?* It was a window into a distant corner of Bee's world I knew little of. I wrapped the sweater back around the painting and tucked it away.

The diary beckoned from the drawer, and I obediently pulled it out. I thought about what Evelyn had told me, but mostly I thought about Bee and this mysterious story from so long ago—one that had some kind of connection to her.

Bobby was a fine man. Honest and hardworking. And when he handed me a ring and asked me to marry him on that unseasonably mild January day on the ferry coming back from Seattle, I looked into his eyes and said yes, plain and simple. There was no other answer to give. I would have been a stupid woman to decline his proposal.

There was a war going on, but Bobby was exempt for medical reasons: He was nearly legally blind, and even with his glasses, the ones with such thick lenses you expected them to weigh ten pounds, the Army still wouldn't let him in, even though he wanted so desperately to go. I hate myself for thinking, now, that if he'd gone to war, perhaps none of us would be in this mess.

But Bobby stayed home and pursued a career. And while so many people were out of work on the island, he had a job—a good job in Seattle. He could take care of me, and I suppose that was all any young woman could ask for in those times.

I remember the way he looked when I accepted his proposal, all smiles and grins, with his hands in the pockets of his brown corduroy pants, which always seemed to hang the wrong way. The wind was blowing his thin, straight brown hair to the side, and he almost looked handsome as he reached for my hand. Almost handsome enough.

As fate, or bad luck, would have it, Elliot was on the boat that day too—with another woman. Elliot always had women around. They swarmed like flies. I remember this one because she wore a white silk scarf wrapped around her neck and a red dress that clung to her body like a tight glove.

Before the boat docked, Bobby and I walked past their seats—not that she was using hers; the woman was practically hanging off of Elliot.

"Hello, Bobby, Esther," Elliot said, waving to us. "This is Lila."

Bobby said something polite. I just nodded.

"Well, should I tell them or should you?" Bobby said, turning to me.

I knew exactly what he meant, but I instinctively hid my ring finger, burying it in the side of my dress until I could feel the ring's prongs burrowing into my skin. It was a fine ring, of course—a simple gold band and half-carat gemstone most worthy of admiration. No, it was my history with Elliot that gave me pause.

"We're engaged!" Bobby blurted out, before I could interject. His exclamation was so loud that many of the other passengers seated nearby turned to look at us.

When my eyes met Elliot's, I could see a storm brewing; waves of betrayal, or maybe sadness, churned in those dark brown eyes I knew so well. Then he looked away, stood up, and patted Bobby on the back. "Well, how about that," he said. "Bobby goes and gets himself the prettiest girl on the island. Congratulations, my friend."

Bobby beamed as Elliot turned back to me and just stared. There were no words.

Lila cleared her throat and frowned. "Excuse me, Elliot? Prettiest girl on the island?"

"Next to my Lila, of course," Elliot added, wrapping his arm around her waist so suggestively I had to avert my eyes.

He didn't love her. We both knew that, just like we both knew that Elliot belonged to me, and that I belonged to Elliot.

I could feel his heart aching and cracking at that moment, just as mine was. But I had said yes to Bobby. I had made my decision. In two months, I would be Mrs. Bobby Littleton, even though I loved Elliot Hartley.

It was almost two a.m. and three chapters later before I set the book down. Esther indeed married Bobby. They had a child together, a baby girl. As for Elliot, he was drafted to the South Pacific thirteen days after their wedding, where he watched them exchange vows from the shadows of the back pews. When Bobby slipped the ring on her finger, she thought of Elliot, and when she said her vows, she glanced toward the back of the church and her eyes met Elliot's.

No one had heard from him since he had deployed, and every day, Esther walked to town hall, pushing her baby in the stroller to check the updated casualty list for his name.

As I closed my eyes, I thought about Bee. You'd have to know love, and heartache, to write like this.

Chapter 5

March 3

"Emily," Bee called out from the hallway. I could hear her voice getting nearer, and then the door opened, creaking a little until I opened my eyes and saw Bee's face poke through.

"Oh, sorry, dear, I didn't realize you were still sleeping. It's nearly ten a.m. And *Greg* is on the phone." Her smile was half encouraging, half teasing.

"OK," I said groggily. "I'll be there in just a sec."

I stood up and stretched, put on my sage green fleece robe, and walked out to the living room, where Bee was waiting, phone in hand.

"Here," she said, whispering. "He sounds excited to talk to you."

"Shhh," I hissed at her. I didn't want Greg to get the idea that I was sitting around waiting for his call, because I wasn't. Plus, I hadn't had my coffee yet, and my patience level was at a negative two.

"Hello?"

"Emily, hi."

"Hi," I said, instantly warming when I heard his voice. It had the effect of a double espresso.

"You know," he said, "I still can't get over the fact that you're back on the island. Do you remember the time we found that old rope swing down by Mr. Adler's beach?"

"Yeah," I said, smiling, suddenly recalling the color of his swim trunks: green, with blue trim.

"And you were afraid to try it," he said, "but I promised you I'd be waiting in the water to catch you."

"Yes, but you failed to mention the belly flop that would come with the deal."

We both laughed, and I realized that nothing, and everything, had changed.

"Hey, what are you doing tonight?" he asked, a little more self-consciously than the Greg Attwood I had known in the summer of 1988. He had either lost some confidence or gained some humility. I wasn't sure which.

"Well, nothing," I said.

"I was just thinking, maybe, if you wanted to, we could have dinner at the Robin's Nest. A friend of mine opened the restaurant last year, and, I mean, it's nothing compared to New York standards, but we islanders think it's pretty great. It has a terrific wine list."

"That sounds wonderful," I said, grinning. I could sense Bee's eyes on me.

"Good," he said. "Would seven be OK? I can pick you up."

"Yes," I said. "I'll be here."

"Great."

"Bye, Greg."

I hung up the phone and turned to Bee, who had been listening to our entire exchange from the kitchen table.

"Well?" she said.

"'Well,' what?" I replied.

Bee gave me a look.

"We're going out. Tonight."

"Good girl."

"I don't know," I said, grimacing a little. "It feels, well, *weird*."

"Don't be silly," Bee said, folding her newspaper in half. "What else would you be doing tonight?"

"Point taken," I replied, sinking my hand into a jar on the coffee table that held a massive collection of miniature seashells. "It's just that, well, first Greg, then Jack—I'm so rusty at all of this."

When I uttered Jack's name, Bee looked out the window to the shore the way she does when something is too cumbersome to talk about. She would get this way when anyone brought up her late husband, Bill, or when someone asked her about her art.

"Well," I finally said, breaking the silence, "if you don't want to talk about it, that's fine. But if you disapprove of Jack, will you at least tell me why?"

She shook her head and ran her fingers through her gray hair. I loved that she had a bob haircut and didn't succumb to the short, coifed dos of every other woman I knew over the age of seventy. Everything about my aunt provoked a reaction, even her name. I asked her once, as a girl, why she was named Bee, and she told me it was because she was like a honeybee: sweet, but with a terrible sting.

She sighed. "I'm sorry, honey," she said in a distant voice. "It's not that I disapprove. I just want you to be careful with your heart. I was once hurt, deeply, and after all you've been through, I'd hate to see you endure any more pain."

Bee's cautions resonated. I'd come to Bainbridge Island to escape the heartache that seemed so thick and ever present in New York City, not to take the kind of risks that could put me in vulnerable places. Yet, part of my journey, as Annabelle had urged me, was to take life as it came—not to question or to edit myself, the way I did every time I sat down at my computer and typed out a mediocre sentence. This March, my life was a free write.

"Just promise me you'll be careful," Bee said softly.

"I will," I said, hoping I could hold up my end of the bargain.

Greg was twenty minutes late picking me up. I thought of those summers so long ago, when he didn't show up at the rope swing or the movie theater or the beach when he said he would. For a moment I even hoped he *wouldn't* show up. It was more than a bit ridiculous that I was actually going through with this—having dinner with a high school boyfriend. *Who does this?* I panicked. *What am I doing?* Then I saw headlights coming down the road. He was driving fast, as if trying to make up for every lost second.

I clutched the doorknob and took a deep breath.

"Have a good time," Bee said, waving me off.

I walked outside to the patio and watched as he pulled his car into the driveway—the same old light blue 1980s four-door Mercedes he'd driven in high school. The years hadn't been as kind to it as they had been to Greg.

"I'm so sorry I'm late," he said, jumping out of the car. He put his hands in his pockets, then took them out again, nervously. "Things got really busy in the wine department just before my shift ended. I had to help a customer find a bottle of Châteauneuf-du-Pape. She stood there debating between the eighty-two and eighty-six *forever.*"

"Which did she pick?"

"The eighty-six," he said.

"A very good year," I said mockingly. I once dated a man who had the whole wine bit down to a science. He swirled and sniffed and followed up his first sip with things like "a first-rate vintage," or "such a brilliant meritage of flavors." These were the reasons I stopped returning his calls.

"It *was* a good year," he said, smiling boyishly. "It was the year we met."

I couldn't believe he remembered. *I* hardly remembered. But when I did, I remembered *everything*.

I was a flat-chested fourteen-year-old with stringy blond hair. Greg was a tanned hotshot sophomore with hormones pumping through his blood—and I mean *pumping*. He lived a few houses down the beach from Bee's. It wasn't exactly love at first sight, at least for Greg. But by the end of the summer, I was wearing makeup and push-up bras, courtesy of my cousin Rachel, and Greg seemed to notice me for the first time.

"Nice arm," he said, as he watched me tossing a Frisbee to Rachel on the beach one day.

I was so startled that I didn't say anything back. A *boy* had just talked to me. A *cute* boy. Rachel dropped the Frisbee and ran to my side, jabbing her bony elbow into my arm.

"Thanks," I finally blurted out.

"I'm Greg," he said, extending his hand. He didn't say anything to Rachel, which, at the time, I couldn't make any sense of. Boys always noticed her first, and for some odd reason, Greg was looking at me. *Just me.*

"I'm Emily," I said in almost a squeak.

"Want to come down to my place tonight?" he asked, leaning toward me. He smelled of Banana Boat suntan lotion. My heart was beating so loudly, I almost didn't hear the next part. "Some friends of mine are coming over. We're having a bonfire."

I didn't know what a bonfire was. I thought it sounded illegal, most logically something one did while smoking marijuana. But I said yes anyway. I would follow this boy anywhere, even to a possibly illegal, drug-fueled *bonfire*.

"Good," he said. "I'll save a spot for you." And then he winked. "Right next to me."

He was cocky and sure of himself, which made me like him even more. And when he turned to walk back down the beach to his alluringly ramshackle house, Rachel and I watched, mouths gaping wide open, as the muscles in his back flexed with each step.

"Well," she said, sounding very offended. "*He* seems like a real jerk."

I just stared, too stunned to speak. *A handsome guy just asked me out.* But if I'd been able to open my mouth then, I would have said, "He seems absolutely perfect."

Greg ran around to the other side of the car and opened the door for me. "I hope you're hungry," he said, grinning. "Because you're going to love this restaurant."

I nodded and climbed inside the car, which looked like it had seen better days. I brushed what seemed to be a petrified french fry from the seat before sitting down. Inside, the car smelled just like the Greg I remembered: the heady scent of unwashed hair, engine oil, and a hint of cologne.

When he put the gearshift into Drive, his hand grazed mine. "Oh, sorry," he said.

I didn't say anything, but hoped he didn't see the goose bumps that had erupted on my arm.

The restaurant, less than a mile away, must have been a favorite on the island, as the parking lot was jammed with cars. Outside, he led the steep climb toward what looked like an elaborate tree house perched on a hill overlooking the sound. I reached into my purse and discreetly popped two aspirin into my mouth.

"Pretty cool, isn't it?" Greg said, looking around as the hostess went to check on our table.

"Yeah," I said, wondering if this was such a good idea, me going out with Greg.

He said something to the hostess, who pulled out two menus and led us to a table on the west side of the restaurant.

"I thought we could catch the sunset," Greg said, smiling.

I couldn't remember the last time I'd caught a sunset. It occurred to me that this is something people do on Bainbridge Island, something New Yorkers had forgotten about. I smiled at Greg and looked out the window to see clearing ahead, and two orange sunbeams poking through the clouds.

Our waitress brought a bottle of red wine that Greg had selected, and we watched as she filled our glasses. There was a certain quiet crispness to the air. Anxious air, as Annabelle would call it. The wine trickling into each glass sounded unusually loud.

"Can I get you anything else?" she asked.

"No," I said, on top of Greg's "Yes."

I laughed. He apologized. It was awkward.

"I meant, 'Yes, we're fine,'" he said, tugging at his collar.

We both reached for our wineglasses.

"So, is it good to be back, Emmy?"

I relaxed a little in my chair. He hadn't called me Emmy since, well, 1988. It felt good to hear him say it.

"It is," I said unapologetically, spreading a thick layer of butter on a dinner roll.

"It's funny, I never thought I'd see you again."

"I know," I said, looking at his face a little longer, now that the wine had entered my bloodstream.

"So, how did it go with Lisa?" I asked, after another long sip.

"Lisa?"

"Yeah, Lisa, the girl you dated in college. Your sister mentioned her when I came to see you on the beach that next summer."

"Oh, *Lisa*. That lasted about as long as . . . English 101."

"Well," I said, giving him a half grin, "you still could have called."

"Didn't I call?"

"Nope."

"I'm sure I called."

I shook my head, feigning anger. "You didn't."

He tried to manage a smile. "And to think, if I had called you, we could be sitting here, married. An old Bainbridge Island married couple."

He meant it as a joke, but neither of us laughed.

After a tense pause, Greg poured a little more wine into both of our glasses. "I'm sorry," he said. "I can't believe I said that after all you've been through—with marriage and all."

I shook my head. "No apology necessary. Really."

"Good," Greg said, looking relieved. "But I have to say, just sitting here with you now—I'm kind of wishing I could rewind history and go back and do things right. And end up with you."

I couldn't help but smile. "It's just the wine talking."

"There's something I was hoping to show you tonight," Greg said, looking at his watch after the waitress brought the check. "It's not too late for a quick drive, is it?"

"No, of course not," I said.

He set his credit card down before I could even begin to protest. I felt guilty. Even though I hadn't written a book in years, I knew I probably earned him under the table. But it didn't matter. Not on Bainbridge Island. Here, I was just Emmy, Bee's niece, and I kind of preferred her to divorcée-washed-up-author-with-issues anyway. I slipped my purse back under the table and Greg proudly signed the check.

We drove about a mile to what looked like a park. Greg stopped the car and turned to me. "Did you bring a coat?"

I shook my head. "Just this sweater."

"Here." He handed me a navy blue fleece jacket. "You're going to need this."

I might have felt awkward in a fleece and heels, but it didn't faze me, really. Not here, anyway. Not with him. I followed him down a rocky trail that was so steep I reached for his hand to steady me, and when I did, he wrapped his other arm around my waist for added support.

The trail was dark, until we made our way closer to the shore, where I could see the glimmer of the moon on the water and hear the waves rolling softly, gently, as if they were being careful not to wake up a single sleepy soul on the island.

When we reached the beach, my heels sank into the sand.

"Why don't you take them off?" Greg suggested, looking down.

I discarded my pumps and dusted them off, then Greg carefully tucked one into each pocket of his jacket.

"Over here," he said, pointing to a distant object shrouded in darkness.

We walked a few more feet, and with each step, I dug my toes a little deeper into the sand. Even in forty-five-degree weather, I loved the feeling of grit between my toes.

"Here," he said.

It was a rock—well, a boulder—the size of a small house, just sitting there in the middle of the beach. But its most striking feature wasn't its size, but its shape. The boulder perfectly resembled a heart.

"So, this must be where you take all your dates," I said sarcastically.

Greg shook his head. "No," he said in a serious voice. He took a step closer to me, and I took a step back. "The last time I was here I was seventeen," he said, pointing. "I wrote *this*." He crouched down next to the side of the rock, flipped open a mini-flashlight, and illuminated an inscription.

I love Emmy forever, Greg.

We stood in silence; two modern-day observers eavesdropping on our former selves.

"Wow," I finally said. "You wrote that?"

He nodded. "It's kind of strange to see it now, isn't it?"

"Can I see your flashlight?" I asked.

He handed it to me, and I ran the light along the inscription. "How did you do this?"

"With a bottle opener," he said. "After a few too many beers."

I broadened the arc of the light and noticed hundreds of other inscriptions—all declarations of love. I listened for the whispers of lovers across generations of islanders.

Greg turned to face me, and I didn't resist when he leaned in to kiss me, firmly, with intention. I clasped my hands around his neck and let myself weaken in his embrace, trying to ignore the voice inside that told me to stop, to pull back. After the kiss, we stood there for a moment, locked in an awkward embrace, like Tinkerbell and Hulk Hogan trying to do the waltz.

"I'm sorry, I . . ." Greg stammered, taking a step back. "I didn't mean to rush things."

I shook my head. "No, don't apologize." I touched my finger to his soft, full lips. He kissed it lightly, then wrapped his hands around both of mine.

"You must be freezing," he said. "Let's head back."

The wind had found its way into my sweater, and my feet, I decided, weren't cold; they were numb. We walked to the trailhead, and I slipped my heels back on, ignoring the sand that was still caked between my toes. The uphill climb wasn't as bad as I had expected, even in heels. Three minutes later, we were back at the parking lot and in Greg's car.

"Thank you for tonight," Greg said once he'd pulled his car into Bee's driveway. He nestled his head into the crook of my neck, kissing my collarbone in a way that made me feel absolutely woozy. I was happy to be there then, sitting in that old musty-smelling Mercedes in front of Bee's house. The wind was blowing through the cracks of the car's windows, whistling in a faint, lonely sort of way. Something was missing. I felt it in my heart, but I wasn't willing to face it. Not yet.

I squeezed his hand. "Thank you," I said. "I'm glad we got to do this." And it was the truth.

It was late; Bee had already gone to bed. I hung up my sweater and looked down at my empty hands. *My purse. Where's my purse?* I retraced my steps. Greg's car, the rock, the restaurant. Yes, the restaurant—it had to be under the table, where I'd left it.

I looked out the window. Greg's car was long gone, so I grabbed Bee's keys hanging on the hook in the kitchen. I hated being away from my cell phone. She wouldn't mind if I borrowed the car, I reasoned. If I drove fast, I could make it there before the restaurant closed.

The Volkswagen handled as it had when I'd driven it in high school, sputtering and choking between gears, but I made it to the restaurant unscathed. As I opened the doors and walked inside, I noticed an elderly couple making their way out. *How cute*, I thought. The man's right arm was draped around the woman's frail waist, gently steadying her with each step. Her eyes shone with love, as did his. My heart knew it when I saw it—it was the kind of love I yearned for.

As I passed, the man tipped his hat to me and the woman smiled. "Good night," I said as they made their way outside.

The hostess recognized me instantly. "Your purse," she said, holding up my white Coach bag. "Right where you left it."

"Thanks," I said, less grateful to be reunited with my bag than to have witnessed such an endearing display of love.

Back at Bee's, I undressed and crawled under the covers, eager to read more of the love story unfolding in the red velvet diary.

Plenty of people got letters from GIs. Amy Wilson received at least three a week from her fiancé. Betty at the salon bragged about the long, flowery letters from a soldier named Allan stationed in France. I didn't get a single one—not that I really expected to—yet I made sure I was home at precisely two fifteen each day, which was exactly when the postman made his way to our door. Maybe, I thought. Maybe he'd write.

But nobody had heard from Elliot. Not his mother. Or Lila. Or any of the other women he'd dated—and there were many—after me. So I was shocked the day the letter came. It was a dark, early March afternoon, colder and grayer than usual, even though the crocuses and the tulips were pushing their way through the frozen ground, eager to usher in spring. Yet Old Man Winter refused to relinquish his grasp.

The postman came to my door and delivered a certified letter, addressed to me. I stood there in my light blue housedress on the front porch lined with flowerpots—pansies, Bobby's favorite—and gulped, hard. The envelope was wrinkled and battered, as though it had endured a harrowing journey to reach my doorstep. When I saw "First Lieutenant Elliot Hartley" on the return address, I prayed the postman wouldn't notice my trembling hands as I signed for it.

"Are you all right, Mrs. Littleton?" he asked.

"Yes," I said. "I'm just a little jittery today. Too much coffee. I was up with the baby last night." I would have said anything to get him to go away.

He grinned in a way that told me he saw through my story. Everyone in town knew about Elliot and me, even the postman. "Good day," he said.

I closed the door behind me, and I ran to the table. The baby was fussing in the nursery, but I didn't go to her. I was capable of doing only one thing at that moment, and that was tearing the letter open.

Dear Esther,

It's dusk here in the South Pacific. The sun is setting, and as I sit here under a palm tree I have a confession to make: I can't stop thinking about you.

I've thought a lot about whether to write you, and my conclusion is this: Life is too short to worry about the consequences when you love someone as I love you. So I write you this letter as a soldier would, without fear, without question, and without knowing if it might be my last.

It's been close to a year, hasn't it? Do you remember? That day on the ferry coming back from Seattle, I knew I could see hesitation in your eyes when Bobby announced your engagement. Tell me that was what it was, because I have racked my brain for months about why we didn't end up together—why it wasn't you and me, instead of you and Bobby. Esther, since the day we chiseled our names into Heart Rock when we were seventeen, I knew we belonged together—forever.

I sat up in bed and set the pages down. Heart Rock? Wasn't that the same rock Greg had taken me to just tonight? I felt an eerie sense of connectedness to the pages as I picked them up and continued.

I should have told you all of this long ago. Before everything happened. Before you doubted me. Before Bobby. Before that awful day in Seattle. And I will forever be haunted by that.

I don't know if I'll ever see you again. That is the reality of war, and I suppose the reality of love, too. No matter the outcome, I want you to know that my love endures. My heart is, and forever will be, yours.

Elliot

I don't know how long I sat there at the table, just staring at the letter, reading it over and over again, studying it for clues, anything. Then I noticed the postmark: September 4, 1942. It had been sent almost six months ago. Either the military mail system moved at a snail's pace, or—dear Lord—Elliot could be . . . I swallowed hard, and didn't let my mind go a step further.

I don't know how long I let the baby cry—it could have been minutes or hours—but when the phone rang, I sat up, straightened my dress, and answered it.

"Hello?" I said, wiping away tears.

"Dear?" It was Bobby. "Are you all right? You sound upset."

"I'm not," I lied.

"I just wanted to tell you that I'm working late again tonight. I'll be on the eight o'clock ferry."

"OK," I said, without emotion.

"Kiss our sweet angel for me."

I hung up the phone and turned on the radio. Music would help. Music could ease my pain. I sat there at the table, staring at the wall, when "Body and Soul" came on. It was the song Bobby and I had danced to at our wedding. I had thought of Elliot with each step, because it had been our song, and now, as I stood in my living room, I danced alone, and let the music soothe me, since Elliot couldn't:

My heart is sad and lonely
For you I pine, for you dear only . . .

By the second verse, the song felt haunting, cruel, even. So I switched off the radio, tucked the letter into the pocket of my dress, and went to get the baby. I rocked her until she fell asleep again, and while I did, I couldn't stop thinking about what a tragedy it is to be married to the wrong man.

I wanted to read more. I wanted to know what had happened, early on, between Esther and Elliot that had led to this. And I wanted to know, as Esther did, if the love of her life was still alive. I worried about Bobby, too, good and decent Bobby, and the baby. Would Esther leave them if Elliot came home from war? *Would* Elliot come home from war? But it had been a long day and my eyes were closing.

Chapter 6

March 4

"**Y**our mother called last night," Bee said at the breakfast table, her head buried behind the *Seattle Times*. Her face was expressionless, as it always was when she spoke of my mother.

"Mom called . . . *here?*" I asked, applying a generous slather of butter to my toast. "That's strange. How did she know where I was?"

My mom and I weren't close, not in the traditional sense. Sure, we talked on the phone, and I'd visit her and my dad in Portland often enough, but there was always a part of her that seemed distant and closed off. Our relationship was tinged with an unspoken disapproval, one I could never understand. She'd been nearly heartbroken when I chose creative writing as an emphasis in college. "Writing is such an unhappy path," she said. "Do you really want to do that to yourself?" At the time, I shrugged it off. What did my mother know about the literary life? Yet, the words followed me through the years, and haunted me quietly until I began to wonder if she was right.

And as I wrestled with my mother's censure, her natural relationship with Danielle, who was two years younger than me, did not go unnoticed. When I got engaged to Joel, I asked her if I could wear Grandma Jane's veil for my wedding, the one I'd clipped to my hair during dress-up sessions a hundred times as a girl. Instead of giving me her blessing, however, Mom shook her head. "No, I don't think that veil is right for your face," she said in protest. "Besides, it has a tear." I was hurt, but even more so three years later when Danielle walked down the aisle wearing the lace veil, perfectly pressed and mended.

"She called your apartment, and your friend Annabelle told her you were here," Bee said. I could hear that tone in her voice, the one that said she took pleasure in the fact that my mother was out of the loop on my life.

"Did she say whether it was important?"

"No," she said, turning a page of the newspaper. "She just wants you to call her back when you can."

"OK," I said, taking a sip of coffee. I paused and then looked up again. "Bee, what is it with you and my mom?"

Her eyes widened. I knew I'd caught her off guard. After all, I'd never before asked her about family matters. This was new territory for both of us, but there was something about where I was and what I'd gone through that made me feel bolder.

She set the paper down. "What do you mean?"

"Well, I've sensed some tension over the years," I said. "I've always wondered why the two of you don't like each other."

"I love your mother dearly, always have."

I scrunched my nose. "It just doesn't add up," I said. "Then why do you barely speak?"

She sighed. "It's a long story."

"I'll take the short version, then," I said, leaning in closer, clasping my hands around my knees.

She nodded. "Your mother used to come stay with me as a girl," she told me. "And I loved having her. So did your Uncle Bill. But one year things changed."

"What do you mean?"

"Well," she said, carefully choosing her words, "your mother started asking questions about her family."

"What about her family?"

"She wanted to know about her mother."

"Grandma Jane?"

Bee looked out the window at the water. Grandma Jane had passed away about ten years ago. Grandpa was devastated, and so was my mom, though she'd had a complicated relationship with her mother. I'd felt a little indifferent about Grandma's passing, as awful as that sounds. It wasn't that she was unkind to me. Every year on my birthday, even after I graduated from college, she sent a birthday card, with well wishes written in the most beautiful cursive handwriting—so elegant that I needed my dad's help to decipher it. She displayed photos of my sister and me on her mantel. Still, there was something missing about Grandma Jane. Something I could never quite put my finger on.

She and my grandfather left the island when my mom was young and moved to Richland, a city in Eastern Washington that's about as exciting as boiled broccoli. I once overheard Bee talking to Uncle Bill about how they'd been "hiding" there for too many years, that Grandma Jane wouldn't let Grandpa move back to his home, the island.

Every year we'd visit Richland for Christmas, but I never wanted to go. I loved my grandpa, but with my grandma, well, there was just something forced about it that even a child could detect—the sideways glances she'd send my way at the dinner table or the way she'd stare at me when I spoke. Once, when I was eleven, my parents left my sister and me in Richland for the weekend while they went on a trip. Grandma offered us a box of her old clothes from the 1940s, and of course, Danielle and I relished the opportunity to play dress-up. But when I put on a red gown with lace around the bodice, Grandma looked at me, horrified. I can still picture her standing in the doorway of the living room, shaking her head. "Red is not your color, dear," she said. I felt embarrassed and awkward. I pulled the white gloves off my hands and unclasped the costume jewelry from my neck, trying my best to choke back the tears.

Then Grandma walked toward me and put her arm around my shoulder. "You know what you need?" she said.

"What?" I sniffed.

"A new hairdo."

Danielle squealed. "A perm! Give her a perm!"

Grandma smiled. "No, not a perm. Emily needs a new color." She held my chin in her hand and then nodded. "Yes, I've always pictured you as a brunette."

I numbly followed Grandma into the bathroom, where she pulled out a box of hair color and directed me to sit on a little silk dressing chair near the bathtub. "Hold still," she said, combing my hair into sections and methodically applying a black paste that smelled of ammonia. Two hours later, my blond locks were so dark, I cried when I looked in the mirror.

I shuddered at the memory of it. "You grew up with Grandma Jane, didn't you, Bee?"

"Yes," she said. "And your grandfather, too. Right here on the island."

"So what was it that you said about Grandma that drove my mom away?"

Bee looked lost in thought. "Your mother took on a very ambitious project when she was young," she said. "When her efforts failed, she decided that she didn't want to be a part of the family anymore, at least not in the same way she had been. She stopped coming to the island. Eight years passed before I saw her again. That was when you were born. I drove down to Portland to see you in the hospital, but your mother had changed by then."

Bee drifted off again, retreating into her memories, but I was quick to pull her back. "What do you mean, *changed*?" I said.

She shrugged. "I don't know how to describe it other than to say that it was as if the very life had been sucked out of her," she said. "I could see it in her eyes. She had changed."

I shook my head, confused. At that moment, I wished I could talk to my grandfather. He had been in a nursing home in Spokane for years now, and I felt a pang of regret in my heart when I realized that it had been at least two years since I'd visited him. The last time my mother had made the trip, she said he hadn't recognized her—his own daughter. She said he kept calling her by a different name, and that he'd said something to make her cry. Even so, I was overcome with a sudden urge to see him.

"Bee," I said cautiously, "what project did my mother take on?"

She shook her head. "After the blowup with your mother, Bill made me promise not to speak of it again, for her sake, and for all of us."

I frowned. "So you're not going to tell me?"

She clasped her hands together in determination. "I'm sorry, dear. It's water under the bridge now."

"I'm just trying to understand," I said, feeling my frustration rise up into a flush on my cheeks. "All those years, all those summers we visited—this is why my mom hardly spoke to you?"

"I don't really know anymore," she said. "Nobody stays the same. But she still brought you girls here. I will always give her credit for that. She knew how much you enjoyed your summers on the island, as she once did. And no matter what resentment she has for me, I think she managed to put it aside for the sake of you and Danielle."

I sighed and looked out the window. The sound looked angry, its waves churning and swirling and then lashing down on the cement bulkhead with such ferocity that salt water ricocheted off the windows. It didn't seem fair that Bee could keep these secrets from me. Whether it was painful or not, didn't I deserve to know this family story she spoke of?

"I'm sorry, dear," she said, patting my arm.

I sighed and looked away. Bee had always been a stubborn woman, and I'd learned long ago to pay attention to her cues, and to leave some subjects well enough alone.

Bee nodded to herself, as though she was remembering something—perhaps something disturbing. I studied her face, hoping to get a glimpse of whatever she was harboring inside. The light from the window amplified the deep wrinkles that crisscrossed her forehead. I was reminded of something I often forget: Bee was getting old. Very old. And it was apparent to me, for the first time, that my aunt was carrying something heavy on her shoulders—something troubling, definitely, and, I worried, something dark.

I had told Bee that I was heading to the beach for some quiet time. What I hadn't told her, however, was that I was bringing the diary with me. I walked along the shore until I found a log to lean against—not exactly a comfortable sofa, but there was enough beach grass growing around it to cushion my back a bit. Feeling the cool breeze hit my skin, I closed the top button on my sweater and picked up the page where I had left off, eager to dive in again, but then my phone rang. I looked at the screen and saw that it was Annabelle.

"OK," she said, "so I figured that you have either been off having a hot island fling or that you died."

"Alive and well," I said. "Sorry for not calling. I guess I'm getting kind of wrapped up in things here."

"And by 'things,' do you mean a member of the male species?"

I giggled. "Well, sort of."

"Good lord, Emily, tell me everything!"

I told her about Greg and Jack.

"I love that you haven't mentioned Joel once," she said.

My heart sank, the way it did whenever anyone mentioned his name.

"Why did you have to say that?" I said.

"Say what?"

"Why did you have to bring *him* up?"

"Sorry, Em," she said. "OK, change of subject: How are things going over there?"

I sighed. "Wonderfully. There's just something about this place." The seagulls were flapping and squawking overhead, and I wondered if she could hear them.

"I knew it would be better than Cancún," she said.

"You were right. This is exactly what I needed."

I told her about last night's beach kiss with Greg, and she squealed. "And why did you not call me at three in the morning to tell me this news?"

"Because you would have screamed at me for waking you up."

"Yes, I would have," she said. "But I would have still wanted to know."

"Fine," I said. "After my next kiss, if there is a next kiss, I will ring you. Satisfied?"

"Yes," she replied. "And I'm going to want details."

"I can do details."

"You have about three more weeks there, right?"

It seemed too short. And instantly I felt like the child who panics when she starts seeing back-to-school ads on TV in July: *Don't they know that school doesn't start for two whole months?* "I have a lot to figure out before I come home," I said.

"You'll piece it together, Em," she said. "I know you will."

"I don't know, I guess I get the feeling that there's something bigger going on here—something about my aunt and my family. A family secret. And, oh, there's this diary I found in the guest room."

"A diary?" She sounded intrigued.

"It's an old diary that someone kept, from 1943, or maybe the start of a novel. I'm not really sure. Honestly, I feel a little strange reading it. But I have this haunting feeling that I'm supposed to be reading it—that I found it for a reason. Is that weird?"

"No," Annabelle answered quickly. "Not weird at all. I once found my mother's diary from high school and read the whole thing cover to cover. I learned more about my mom in those hours reading under the covers with a flashlight than I have in the thirty-three years I've known her." She paused. "Who did you say wrote it? Bee?"

"That's just it," I said, "I don't know. But I haven't been this engaged in a book in years."

"Maybe you *are* meant to read it, then," Annabelle said. "Wait, didn't you say you had a date with what's-his-name tomorrow night?"

"Yes—well, I'm having dinner with Jack, at his house," I replied. "So, yeah, I guess you could call it a date."

"Emily, if a man cooks for a woman, that, my dear, is a date."

"OK, I guess when you put it that way. And what about you? Any progress with Evan?"

"Nothing," she said. "I think it's sunk. I will just wait patiently for my Edward."

We both knew that according to Annabelle's research, Edward is the name of the most reliable and longest-lasting husband.

"Oh, by the way, Annabelle," I said, "just curious—what does your research say about the name Elliot?"

"Why? Is this mystery bachelor number three?"

I laughed. "No, no, I, um, know someone with the name here, and I was just wondering."

I could hear her fumbling around at her desk. "Ah, here it is," she said. "Elliot, yes—wow, it's a *very* good name. Average length of marriage for Elliots is forty-two years. It still doesn't beat Edward at forty-four, but Elliot is about as good as you can get."

"Thanks," I said, smiling. When I hung up the phone, I realized that I had forgotten to ask her about the names Jack and Greg. But for some reason, that didn't matter to me as much as Elliot's name did. I wanted to know, on Esther's behalf. And I was certain that she'd be pleased with the answer.

Bobby came home at ten to nine, just as he said he would. Bobby was always on time. He took off his blue suit jacket and hung it up in the closet, then walked to the kitchen and greeted me with a kiss.

"I missed you," he said.

This was what he always said.

Then I rewarmed his dinner and sat down with him at the table, watching him spoon the food into his mouth and listening to him recount the details of his day.

This was how our evenings always went.

And then we went to bed, and because it was Wednesday, Bobby rolled over and tugged at the bodice of my nightgown. Bobby always wanted to make love on Wednesdays. But tonight I didn't tense up. I didn't count to sixty and pray for it to be over. Instead, I closed my eyes and imagined that I was with Elliot.

Three years before I married Bobby, I was engaged to Elliot, and for a while, all was right with the world. I remember the chill in the air the day of the clambake. I didn't know it then, but it signaled the beginning of the end.

Frances, one of my best friends, suggested I wear gloves. But my other best friend, Rose, came to my defense: "And hide that ring?" she said. "Nonsense. You can't cover up a ring like that. It would be sacrilegious."

We laughed and primped and powdered our noses. An hour later, we made our way, arm in arm, to the event of the season, the one that drew every man, woman, baby, and child to the beach in Eagle Harbor. Picnic tables and campfires dotted the shore, where freshly harvested butter clams and Dungeness crab roasted near pots of fresh chowder.

On the beach, little strands of white globe lights crisscrossed overhead, and as was the tradition of the island clambake, there was music and dancing. The three of us cheered when "Moonlight Serenade," our favorite recording by Glenn Miller, sounded over the loudspeakers. I started to sway to the music, and as I did I felt Elliot's strong arms behind me. He kissed me on the neck. "Hi, my love," he whispered, leading me to the dance floor. Our bodies moved in unison as the moon shone down on us.

When the song ended, we walked to the bench where Frances was sitting alone. "Where's Rose?" I asked.

Frances shrugged. "Probably off looking for Will."

I detected hurt in her voice, so I let go of Elliot's hand and reached for hers.

"Let's go have some fun, shall we, girls?" Elliot said. He offered us each an arm, and we obliged. Frances perked up immediately.

Will and Rose joined us on a blanket that Elliot had spread out on the beach. We drank beer and ate clams out of tin bowls and reveled in the beauty of the crisp, star-filled night.

Elliot reached into his dark green knapsack and pulled out his camera, fiddling with the flash for a second before gesturing at me to look up. "I don't want to ever forget the way you look tonight," he said, making one, then two, then three snaps with his finger. Elliot was never more than a few feet away from his camera. He could capture a scene in black and white with such poignancy that it almost made you weak.

Looking back, I wish I had prevented Elliot from leaving that night. I wish I could have made time stand still. But shortly before ten p.m., he turned to me and said, "I have to go to Seattle tonight. There's some business I have to attend to. Can I see you tomorrow night?"

I didn't want him to go, but I nodded and kissed him. "I love you," I said, lingering in the moment a few seconds longer before he stood up, brushed the sand off his legs, and began walking to the ferry dock, whistling, as he always did.

The next morning, Frances, Rose, and I caught an early ferry to Seattle to do some shopping. Rose wanted to go to Frederick & Nelson to get a dress she'd seen in the latest issue of "Vogue." Frances needed new shoes. I was just happy to get off the island. I liked being in the city. I must have told Elliot a hundred times how I dreamed of a big apartment downtown with windows overlooking the sound. I'd paint the walls mauve, and the drapes would be cream with little sashes holding them back from the windows, just like in the magazines.

And then, walking out onto the sidewalk on Marion Street in front of the Landon Park Hotel—a big brick building with two enormous columns in front—was Elliot. He was with someone, but it wasn't until the traffic cleared a few seconds later that I could see whom. She was blond and tall, nearly as tall as Elliot. I watched as he wrapped his arms around her in an embrace that lasted an eternity. I was close enough to hear their conversation—well, just bits and pieces of it, but that's all I needed to hear.

"Here's the key to the apartment," the woman said, handing him something, which he immediately put in his pocket.

He winked at her, which sent a chill through my body. I knew that wink. "Will I see you tonight?" he asked.

The noise of a passing truck muffled her response. Then he helped her into a cab and waved as it drove away.

"Will I see you tonight?" My mind suddenly turned to a novel I'd read years prior. Never before had a heroine in a book spoken to me in the way Jane had in "Years of Grace."

My eyes widened. *Years of Grace*! I shook my head in wonderment before turning back to the page.

The fact that Jane, married to Stephen, had pined for another man, going so far as to let herself feel the passions of love, a certain betrayal of her marriage vows, prompted my mother to call the book "rubbish." I told her it had won the Pulitzer Prize and that my high school English literature teacher had recommended it to me, but it was no use. Novels like these, she said, were filled with fanciful, dangerous ideas for a young woman, so I was forced to keep it hidden under my mattress.

As I stood there on the sidewalk that day, it all came rushing back: Jane's story, now so painfully intertwined with mine. There was tenderness in Elliot's voice when he spoke to this woman. I thought of the ties that bind us together, the vows we make, and break. If Jane could give her hand to Stephen and still love another, Elliot could give his word to me and still pine for someone else. It was possible. It seemed poetic in the story—Jane's love for Andre, and for Jimmy, a midlife love—but now, seeing it played out before my eyes, as an outsider, it only felt wrong. Could one not love one person for eternity? Could one not keep his or her promise? Elliot could have any woman he wanted, and until that moment, I'd believed he wanted only me. I'd never been so wrong.

The letter. I remembered the perplexing letter Jane had received from Andre years after their declaration of love. It was all in the story, all tragically detailed. He had broken her heart with his decision to go to Italy instead of returning to Chicago for her. It is why she agreed to marry Stephen, an action that forever changed the trajectory of their lives. It is why she wrote him that cold, blunt letter shortly before the war broke out, snuffing out any further possibility of their love, even if that love still smoldered in her heart for years to come. "When you killed things," Jane had said, responding with decisiveness to Andre's actions, "you killed them quickly." And I knew, at that moment, what needed to be done.

Rose and Frances stood by me in silence, each holding one of my arms, to steady me or to prevent me from darting across the street, or both. But I broke free from their grasp and ran, without caring if I'd be hit, across the street to where Elliot was standing in front of a newspaper vending machine.

I pried the ring, the one Elliot had given me last month, with its enormous pear-shaped diamond nestled between two red rubies, off of my left hand. It was way too extravagant, and I had told him so, but he wanted me to have the best, he had said, even if it meant going into debt for the rest of his life, which I think is what he did. None of that mattered now, though, not after seeing him here with another woman and hearing him say those incriminating words.

"Hello, Elliot," I said coldly, once I'd made my way to the other side of Marion Street.

He looked at once startled and at ease, as though he had everything and nothing to hide. My face felt hot. "How could you?"

A confused expression clouded his face, and then he shook his head. "No, no, you have the wrong impression," he said. "She's just a friend."

"A friend?" I said. "So why did you lie and say you had business to attend to? This is clearly not business."

Elliot looked at his feet. "She's just an old friend, Esther," he said. "I swear."

I clutched my necklace tightly. It was just a little gold starfish that dangled from a simple chain. I'd won it at the street fair years ago, and it had become my good luck charm. I needed all the luck I could get then, because I knew he was lying. I had seen the way she looked at him, the flirtation in her mannerisms, the way they embraced. His hands had been low on her waist. She was more than a friend. Any fool could see that.

I regretted what I was about to do before I did it, but I proceeded just the same. I squeezed the ring in my hand into a tight fist and threw it as far as I could down the sidewalk. We both watched as it skipped along the pavement, until it sputtered and rolled—right into a storm drain.

"It's over," I said. "Please don't ever speak to me again. I don't think I could bear it."

I saw Rose and Frances staring in horror from the other side of the street. It felt like a Herculean effort to walk back to them and away from Elliot. Because, you see, I knew I was walking away, forever, from our life together.

"Wait, Esther!" I could hear him shouting from across the street, through traffic. "Wait, let me explain! Don't leave like this!"

But I told myself to keep walking. I had to. I just had to.

Chapter 7

I read for another hour, unable to look away from the pages, even for ferry horns or beachcombers with barking dogs. True to her promise, Esther didn't forgive Elliot. He wrote to her for months, but she tossed his letters, all of them, into the trash, never opening a single one. Rose married Will and moved to Seattle. Frances stayed on the island, where, to the dismay of Esther, she struck up an unlikely friendship with Elliot.

I looked at my watch, realizing that I'd been away longer than I'd anticipated. I tucked the diary into my bag and walked quickly back to Bee's.

As I opened the door to the mudroom, I heard Bee's footsteps approaching. "Oh good, you're back," she said, peering around the doorway as I stepped out of my sand-covered boots. "I don't know how I managed to forget about tonight," she continued. "It's been on my calendar since last year."

"What, Bee?"

"The clambake," she said, without further explanation. She paused, looking suddenly thoughtful. "Can it be that you've never attended an island clambake?"

Aside from an occasional holiday visit, I'd only been to the island in the summer months. The nostalgia I felt wasn't from personal memories but instead from Esther's account of that magical night.

"No, but I've heard stories," I said.

Bee looked giddy. "Now, let's see," she said, putting her hands on her hips. "You'll need a warm coat. And we'll pack blankets, and wine; must have wine. Evelyn's meeting us there at six."

The beach scene was exactly as Esther had described it. The campfires. The twinkle lights. The blankets spread out on the sand. The dance floor and the canopy of starry sky above.

Evelyn waved at us from the beach. Her sweater looked too light to protect her fragile skin from the cool wind, so I retrieved a blanket from Bee's basket and wrapped it around her thin frame. "Thanks," she said, a little dazed. "I was lost in memories."

Bee gave me a wise look. "Her husband proposed to her here on this beach years ago, the night of the clambake," she said.

I set the basket down. "You two sit down and be comfortable. I'll take your meal orders."

"Clams, with extra butter," Bee said. "And corn bread."

"Asparagus, and just lemon with my clams, dear," Evelyn added.

I left them there together with their memories, and wandered toward the chow line, passing the dance floor, where a few shy teenage girls huddled in a corner, staring at the teenage boys congregating on the opposite side. A staring match ensued. And then, silencing the evening waves curling up on the shore, music began seeping through the speakers, Nat King Cole's "When I Fall in Love."

I rocked to the sound of the melody, allowing myself to be swept away by its reverie, until I heard a voice behind me.

"Hello."

I turned around to find Jack standing behind me. "Hi," I said.

"Your first clambake?"

"Yes," I said. "I—"

We were interrupted by the DJ on the dock. "And look who we have here," he said from his spot on the dock above. His assistant had shone a spotlight on us. I shielded my eyes from the brightness. "A young couple to kick off tonight's dancing!"

I looked at Jack. He looked at me. We heard applause coming from every direction.

"I guess we only have one choice," he said, reaching for my hand.

"I guess so," I replied, smiling nervously as he pulled my body toward his.

"Can you believe this?" I asked, wide-eyed.

Jack spun me around the floor like a pro. "No," he said. "But we might as well give them a show."

I nodded. There was something natural about the way he held me. He whirled me around the floor, and I saw flashes of faces gazing at us. An elderly couple. Children. Teenagers. And Henry. Henry was there, smiling at us from the sidelines. I extended my hand to wave at him when Jack spun me around again, but in a flash he was gone.

When the music ended and another round of applause broke out, I wished we could go on dancing. But Jack pointed to the beach, and I could see that his attention was elsewhere.

"Some friends of mine are waiting," he said. "You could join us."

I felt silly for romanticizing the moment. "Oh, no," I said. "I can't. I'm here with Bee and our friend Evelyn. I promised I'd bring back food, so I guess I better be going too. But I'll see you tomorrow at your house?"

His features clouded for a moment as if he'd forgotten his invitation on the beach. "Right, yes, dinner," he said. "I'll see you then." And then he was gone.

Ten minutes later, balancing a tray full of food, I returned to Bee and Evelyn, huddled under a blanket. We drank wine and ate every last morsel, until our limbs succumbed to the cold. I thought about Jack on the drive home, and the moment we'd shared that evening, coming to no conclusions as I did. It felt good to let my mind drift.

"So?" Bee asked before I turned in that night.

"I loved it," I said.

"It was a beautiful dance," she said.

I hadn't thought she could see the dance floor from her spot on the beach. I smiled. "It was, wasn't it?"

"Good night," she said, stroking the side of my face.

"Night, Bee."

March 5

Dinner with Jack. It was all I could think about the next day. As I washed the dishes after breakfast, I sank my hands into the sudsy water and wondered whether he had thought much about our dance the night before. *Did he feel the spark that I did?* A large soap bubble popped as I rinsed a dish and set it on the drying rack. *Was I reading into things too deeply?* I'd only recently said good-bye to Joel, so it occurred to me, as I was polishing the silverware with a dishcloth, that perhaps my marital status had marred my perception of Jack.

Later that evening, I fumbled through my suitcase, looking for something suitable to wear. Dinner with Greg had been casual, meeting an old friend in a public place. While the fleeting moments I'd had with Jack on the beach were certainly pleasant, there was enough mystery surrounding this man to elevate my nervousness.

Plus, he had invited me not to a restaurant, but to his home, so I chose what I always do in times of wardrobe panic: a wrap sweater, a pair of chandelier earrings, and my favorite pair of jeans. I inched my camisole down a teeny bit, then I shook my head and pulled it up again.

I ran a brush through my hair, which was in desperate need of a trip to the salon, and finished the ensemble with a bit of mascara and a touch of blush. I gave myself a disapproving look in the mirror before turning out the lights. It would have to do.

"You look beautiful," Bee said, peering into my room. I didn't realize she was standing there, and I hoped I had remembered to put the diary away. I glanced over at the bed and was relieved to see that I had.

"Thank you," I said, grabbing my bag and slipping into a pair of flats suitable for walking along the beach to Jack's house.

She looked like she wanted to confide in me, but it was a warning she spoke. "You better not stay out too late, dear. The tide will be high tonight. You might have trouble walking home. Be careful."

But we both knew that her words had two meanings.

I realized after I'd already walked a good distance along the shore that I should have brought a jacket, or maybe even a winter coat. The March breeze was feeling more like an arctic wind, and I hoped that Jack's house wasn't too much farther. My cell phone rang in my purse as I made my way along the beach. I picked it up, the screen displaying a New York number I didn't recognize.

"Hello?" I said. I could hear rustling in the background and car noises—horns and traffic, as if someone was walking on the sidewalk near a busy street.

I gulped. "Hello?" I said again. There was no response, so I put the phone back in my bag, shrugging.

The crescent moon was bright overhead. I looked back along the stretch of beach behind me. *I could turn around. I could go back.* But then the wind picked up again, startling me like a cold glass of water splashed in my face. And I felt compelled to keep walking. Was I responding to a voice whispering in the wind? A feeling? I wasn't sure, but I walked, one foot in front of the other, until I came to Jack's beach cottage. It was exactly as he'd described it, with its gray shake shingles and a big wraparound porch in front.

Like all houses on this stretch of the beach, the home was old, and probably storied. I thought about the couples who had watched the sun set from that porch in the century and a half leading up to this moment, and my heart fluttered a little. But it wasn't until I noticed the duck weather vane twirling in the wind from its perch on the roof that my heart really started to pound inside my chest. *Could this be the home in Bee's painting?*

The warm light in the window beckoned me up the trail that led to the house. I could see a fishing pole draped along the front steps, next to a pair of wading boots. I approached the front door, which was open.

"Hello?" I said cautiously, stepping inside. I could hear music—jazz—and something sizzling on the stove.

"Hi, please come in," Jack called out from another room, most likely the kitchen. "I'm just finishing up in here."

I could smell garlic, butter, and wine—the world's most delicious flavor combination. It made me feel warm, like the first few sips of wine always do. I had brought a bottle of pinot noir snatched from Bee's wine cabinet. I set it down on the entryway table, next to a ring of keys and a large white clamshell filled with spare change.

I looked around from my vantage point in the entryway. The dining room caught my eye with its deep merlot walls and big oak table. I wondered if Jack did a lot of entertaining, with a table like that. Just a few steps to the left was the living room, with a pair of slipcovered sofas and a coffee table constructed of soft gray driftwood. The furnishings were sturdy and masculine, yet everything looked polished, like the pages of a Pottery Barn catalog. Even the magazines on the side table appeared to be deliberately placed askew. I walked over to the fireplace and glanced at the photos he had displayed. One caught my eye: a photo of a woman in sunglasses, a red bikini top, and a delicate linen sarong wrapped around her slim waist. She was on a beach, staring at the cameraman—*Jack?*—adoringly. All of a sudden I felt like an awkward intruder, which was ridiculous, because this woman could have been his sister.

"Hi," Jack said, walking into the living room. "I'm sorry to keep you waiting, but the world stops for béchamel."

Jack was holding two full wineglasses and offered me one. "Hope you like chardonnay."

"Love it."

"Good," he said. He seemed calm and steady, like an old ferryboat, which only seemed to accentuate my nervousness. I hoped he didn't notice. "Let's sit down." He gestured at the sofa that faced the fireplace.

"I'm glad you could come tonight," he said. He was more handsome than I remembered—dangerously handsome, with that dark, wavy hair and dizzying gaze.

"Did you have fun last night?" he asked.

"Yes," I replied. "It was a beautiful night." I prayed I wasn't blushing, even though I knew I was.

"I'm sorry I had to go so quickly," he said, looking concerned.

"Oh, it was fine," I said, looking around the room, eager to change the subject. A series of framed vintage black-and-white photographs on the wall caught my eye—in particular, one of a ferry from long ago. "Your home is lovely." *How could I say something so ordinary?*

"So, how is your story coming?"

"My story?" I immediately thought of Esther's story and wondered how Jack could know about it.

"Your book," he said. "The one you're researching?"

"Oh, yes. It's, um, it's coming along. Slowly but surely."

"Bainbridge is the perfect place for a writer, an artist of any kind," he said. "All you have to do is grab your pen or your brush, and stories, pictures, they come to you."

I nodded. "It does have that effect," I said, thinking more about the story unfolding in the pages of the diary and less about any fiction of my own.

Jack grinned and took a long, slow sip of wine. "Are you hungry?"

"Very."

I followed him into the dining room and sat down at the table, while he brought out an arugula, fennel, and shaved Parmesan salad, a platter of halibut, asparagus drizzled with béchamel, and dinner rolls fresh from the oven.

"Dig in," he said, refilling my wineglass.

"A man who cooks—like this—I'm seriously impressed," I said, reaching for my napkin.

Jack grinned mischievously. "That was kind of the point."

We talked nonstop as the candles flickered on the table. He told me about the time he sleepwalked at summer camp and woke up, embarrassed to discover that he had attempted to crawl into bed with his camp counselor. I reminisced about the time I'd chewed on the end of an ink pen in middle school and didn't realize it had leaked all over my face, permanently staining my upper lip for the next two days.

I told him about Joel, too, but not in a sappy, self-pitying sort of way.

"I just don't understand," he said, shaking his head after I'd shared the story of our marriage's undoing—details I wouldn't have recounted had I not been drinking. White wine gives me loose lips. "I don't understand why he would have let you get away."

I felt my cheeks get hot again. "So what about you? Ever been married?"

Jack looked uncomfortable for a moment. "No," he said. "It's just me and Russ."

I remembered the golden retriever from the beach.

"Russ!" he called up the stairs, and within seconds I heard a thump and then the sound of four paws trudging slowly downstairs, making a beeline for me. First he sniffed my legs and then my hands, before plopping his butt down right on my foot.

"He likes you," Jack said.

"He does? How can you tell?"

"He's sitting on your foot, isn't he?"

"Um, yes." I wasn't sure if this was normal or if it was just a Russ thing.

"He only does that when he likes someone."

"Well, I'm glad I have his approval," I said, grinning as the pooch burrowed his head in my lap, leaving a thousand dog hairs on my sweater. I didn't care.

Jack cleared the table, declining my offer to help, and then motioned me to the back door. "There's something I'd love you to see," he said.

We walked through the backyard, just a small square of tidy lawn dotted with a few stepping-stones, to a tiny outbuilding that resembled a garden shed.

"My art studio," Jack said. "The other day on the beach, you mentioned that you wanted to see some of my work."

I nodded eagerly. I sensed a sacred quality to the place. Jack was letting me inside his secret world. It would be like me inviting him to read one of my sloppy first drafts. And I never let anyone read my first drafts, not even a single sentence.

Inside, there were canvases everywhere—propped up on easels and resting against walls. They were mostly beautiful seascapes, but one portrait, the only one, caught my eye: one of a striking young woman with shoulder-length blond hair staring out at the sound. There was something unsettled about her face, something sad. It was different from any work in the studio. I looked closer at her seductive yet lonely eyes, noting a vague resemblance to the woman in the photo on Henry's mantelpiece, though there was nothing old-fashioned about this woman. *Who is she?* I wanted to know her story, and how she came to be painted by Jack, but it didn't seem right to inquire. The subject of this painting felt untouchable.

Instead I focused on his other works and marveled. "The brushwork, the light . . . these are breathtaking," I finally said, trying not to let my gaze turn back to the mystery woman on the easel. "All of them. You are insanely talented."

"Thank you," Jack said.

It was dark now, but the moonlight filtered in through the studio windows. Jack grabbed a sketchbook and walked toward me, his lips pursed.

"Do me a favor, and sit right there," he said, pointing to a stool in the corner.

I eagerly followed his instructions.

Jack pulled up another stool, sat down, then stood up, circling me with rapt attention. I tugged at my hair and my sweater self-consciously as he set down the sketchbook and approached me slowly, until he was standing directly in front of me. He was so close, I could smell his skin.

Then he reached out and took my chin gently in his hand, tilting my profile into the moonlight. He ran his hands down my neck until they reached the edge of my sweater, sending a tingly feeling down my arms. He opened the neckline until my collarbones were exposed, as well as a hint of my camisole. I felt the cold air brush my skin, but I didn't shiver. Jack may have put this move on all the women he brought to his house—the dinner, the dog, the portrait—but I let my inner cynic slip away.

"Perfect," he said. "Now, sit there for just a second."

I felt quivery and limp, but I managed to hold the pose while Jack sat across from me, sketching furiously. Then he stood up and showed me his drawing.

"Wow," I said. "I mean, it's really good—it's so . . . realistic." As a child, I had my portrait sketched by a street artist in Portland. My nose had looked contorted and my mouth too big. But Jack—he drew *me*.

He carefully detached the sketch from the book and set it on an easel.

We walked back to the house, where deep burnt umber flames flickered in the fireplace. Jack started up his CD player.

"Since I had to run off so quickly last night, I thought we could continue our dance tonight," he said, reaching for my hand.

I was instantly charmed by the old-fashioned gesture. The last time I'd been asked to dance—outside of the prom, of course—I was seventeen, dating a guy two years older who was the lead guitarist in a garage punk rock band. We slow-danced to the Ramones for an incredibly romantic five minutes, until his dad came home from work.

Jack pushed the coffee table aside, leading me to the center of the living room. As he did, a soft big-band orchestra began to play the most beautiful melody.

"It's an old recording of one of my favorite jazz songs," he said, pulling me close to him. "Do you know it?"

I hesitated.

"'Body and Soul,'" he said. "It's one of the most beautiful love songs ever written."

The hair on my arms stood on end.

"Do you know it?" he asked, sensing my reaction.

I nodded. *"Body and Soul"? As in Esther and Elliot's song?* I couldn't be certain if I'd ever heard it before that moment, and yet the melody, the lyrics—I knew it instantly. Of course it was their song. It was haunting and hopeful at the same time. It was made for them.

Jack held me close, so close I could feel his breath on my neck and the firmness of the muscles in his back. He let his lips brush the side of my forehead, as our bodies swayed to the music.

"Girls like you don't wash up on this beach every day," he whispered as the song ended.

We both looked toward the beach, where the waves were crashing into the shore, and Jack suddenly seemed concerned. "The tide's getting high," he said. "I better walk you home."

I nodded, hiding my disappointment. I didn't want to go. Not yet.

When we arrived at Bee's doorstep, he smiled and said, "I have

to go to Seattle, but I'll be back in a few days. I'll call you then."
I tried not to parse his words for deeper meaning.

"Good night," I said. And that was that.

I sulked as I crawled into bed, and I told myself I had no reason. It had been a wonderful night. He had called me special. *Special.* What had I expected? A profession of love? Ridiculous, I told myself. I pulled the diary out of the nightstand, but could feel exhaustion in every bone of my body, so I put it back. And as I drifted off, I couldn't help but feel that I was abandoning Esther, leaving her there alone on those pages to figure out her own problems, to fend for herself. Yet I, too, was fending, in the midst of my own new story.

Chapter 8

"Want to go into Seattle today?" Bee asked over breakfast. That's how people on Bainbridge Island talked about Seattle, as a total immersion experience.

"Why don't you ask Evelyn to come with us?" I suggested. Time was short, though Bee didn't know it.

Bee placed the call. "Why don't you join us today in Seattle? We're catching the ten a.m. ferry to do some shopping. We'd love for you to come."

Two seconds later it was a done deal. Evelyn met us at the ferry terminal, which was reminiscent of a train station, with panoramic views of the water and an espresso stand to satisfy a craving for, say, a tall split-shot mocha, as I had. Bainbridge Islanders frequently walked onto the ferry, leaving their cars tucked cozily away in the terminal parking lot. Since the boat discharged passengers in the heart of the city, there was no need to drive a car, even if getting around meant climbing a few hills. Even in their eighties, these women wouldn't dream of forgoing a city walk for a cab.

Evelyn wore khaki capris, a black boat-neck sweater, and simple ballet flats. "Thanks for saving me from another dull day with the cats," she said.

I smiled. It occurred to me that she didn't look like a person with a terminal illness. She still had her hair—*a wig?* I wondered. Her cheeks shone with color, which could have been courtesy of makeup. But it was mostly that she didn't *act* sick. While the cancer may have ravaged her body, Evelyn would not let it take her spirit.

"So, what's the plan for the day?" I asked as we made our way onto the ferry. Among the first to board, we secured a coveted booth closest to the front of the boat, where views of Seattle's skyline were the best.

"Well," said Bee, making herself comfortable on the vinyl bench seat, "we'll hit Westlake Center, of course, and then there's this delightful little bistro on Marion Street where I thought we could have lunch."

Marion Street. *Isn't that the street in the book where Esther ended her relationship with Elliot for good?* I thought about the gorgeous ring she'd chucked into a storm drain and shook my head. It seemed like such a waste, such an impulsive thing to do. But then again, she'd had her reasons.

I remembered by name the Landon Park Hotel, the place where the tragic scene had transpired. Perhaps Bee, or whoever was the true author, had used historical reference points. I was eager to see if the old hotel still existed, or had ever existed.

"Anyone feel like clam chowder?" Bee said, standing up. She always ordered clam chowder on the ferry, no matter what time it was, no matter that the passage lasted a mere half hour.

"Not for me," Evelyn said.

"I'll have some, if you're heading to the cafeteria," I said. Bee nodded approvingly and walked away.

As soon as Bee was out of earshot, I turned to Evelyn. "How are you feeling?"

"I've had better days."

"I'm sorry," I said, suddenly feeling guilty that Evelyn's accepting my invitation was depriving her of rest.

"Hah," she said. "Not for me, thanks. I'd rather feel sick in Seattle with the two of you than feel sick in bed at home."

I nodded. "When are you planning on telling her?"

Evelyn looked concerned. "Soon."

"I'm getting worried," I said, "about how she's going to take the news."

Evelyn looked down at her hands, so tightly clasped together that I could see the little blue veins poking out. "I'm worried too, dear."

I looked out the window and then back at Evelyn. "It's just that as far as I know, you're the only real friend Bee has."

She nodded. "Are you still reading that diary?"

"Yes," I said. "I can hardly set it down."

She peered down the walkway to see if Bee was returning. "We don't have much time," she said. "I won't be here much longer. But I need you to know something: This story you're reading, it holds many secrets—ones that could change life today. For you. For your aunt. For others."

"I wish you could just tell me what this is all about," I said, hoping I didn't sound too impatient.

"I'm sorry, dear," she said. "This is your journey."

As we moved into open water, I felt time stand still. "Evelyn," I said, looking up from the window. "Did you know my grandma?"

She studied my face for a while before answering. "Yes, dear, I did."

"Maybe you know, then," I said, "what Bee told my mother about Grandma Jane that caused such a rift in the family."

Evelyn nodded. "She told your mother the startling truth about your grandmother," she said.

"Startling?"

"Yes," she replied. "But, Emily, it doesn't have to end this way for your family."

"Evelyn, what does that mean?"

"You can fix things, Emily," she said. "You can bring the story the closure it needs."

I ran my fingers through my hair and sighed. "It's like I'm trying to put together a jigsaw puzzle, and everyone is hiding the pieces from me."

"Be patient," Evelyn said quietly. "You'll find your answers in time. It's the island's way."

I could see Bee making her way back to our booth. "Here we are," she said, returning to her seat. "One clam chowder for you."

"Thanks," I said, opening up a package of saltine crackers and dunking one into the creamy hot soup.

"Evelyn," Bee said, "where's your appetite? You always have chowder on the ferry."

I shot Evelyn a look as if to say, "Now is the right time. Tell her." But she kept her poker face. "I had a huge breakfast this morning; I guess this old stomach of mine just isn't what it used to be."

"Well," she replied, "we're having lunch in a few hours, so it's not like you'll starve."

"So," Bee said cautiously, turning to me. "How was last night at Jack's?"

Evelyn's face lit up. "Jack Evanston?"

"Yes, Jack Evanston," I said.

Evelyn and Bee exchanged a significant look.

"We're two old women who haven't had a date in several decades, Emily," said Evelyn. "Give us a little nugget."

"Well, he cooked dinner," I continued. "Can you believe that? A man who can cook. And he showed me his paintings."

Bee grimaced and looked out the window at the water, but Evelyn ignored her. "The evening sounds like a dream. Did you enjoy yourself?"

"I did," I said. "But I was wondering, with all the visits I made to the island as a child, why didn't I ever meet Jack? I never saw him on the beach."

Evelyn opened her mouth to explain, but Bee cut her off. "Whatever happened to Greg?" she asked.

"Good heavens," Evelyn said, "you have two men chasing after you?"

"She does," Bee said.

Evelyn glowed with nostalgia. "Oh, to be young again."

Just then the ferry's horn sounded, announcing our arrival into Seattle. Energized by the other riders' eagerness to disembark, we walked quickly along the gangway and down the stairs that led to the sidewalk lined with cabs, panhandlers, and pigeons pecking around for crumbs.

Once we reached the crosswalk, Evelyn took a deep breath. "Ah," she said. "I've missed that scent."

It was the same ferryboat-engine-seawater-city smell I'd come to love, but on the Seattle side it was accented by fried fish from the restaurants along the piers.

"Do you ever regret moving back, Evelyn?" Bee said suddenly.

Evelyn looked at me instead of at Bee, as if to fill me in. "Emily, when my husband died ten years ago, I moved back to Bainbridge.

But I had spent my entire married life here in the city—up a ways, on Capitol Hill."

"I'm sorry about your husband," I said. "You must have so many memories here of him."

"Yes," she said. "I do. But the island has always been my home."

We walked in silence up three hills until we came to Marion Street. I held Evelyn's elbow to support her, something Bee would have done had she known about her friend's illness.

"Ah," Bee said. "We're here." She pointed to a restaurant across the street called Talulah's. "Let's sit down. I could use a rest after that walk."

I nodded, and Evelyn quickly agreed.

Inside, the restaurant was cheerful and bright, with its sunshine-colored walls and daffodils in little etched-glass vases on each table. With the exception of a man having coffee and a sandwich at a far table, we were the only people in the place.

It was eleven a.m.—a bit early for lunch, but just the right time for mimosas. Evelyn ordered a round. And by the time we finished our second, we all felt happy, not to mention hungry. Despite the clam chowder on the boat, I guiltlessly ordered a burger.

"So," Bee said after the waitress had cleared our plates. "Where to next?"

I looked out the window and onto Marion Street. "Do you think we can walk along Marion for a bit before heading over to Westlake Center?"

"Sure," Bee said.

She paid the bill and the three of us walked out onto the side-walk. As we passed each building, I looked up for the hotel, the one where Esther had seen Elliot with the other woman. There must have been forty-five Starbucks, but no Landon Park Hotel. And then something caught my eye: a brick building just as Esther had described—with two bold-looking columns in front. And there was a newspaper dispenser nearby too. Coincidence? Then the kicker: About fifty feet away was a storm drain. I froze for a moment. It had to be *the place*. I needed to see for myself, fiction or not.

"Emily?" Bee said, turning around to see what I was doing standing there, motionless, on the sidewalk. "Why are you stopping here? Do you see a shop you want to go into, dear?"

Without looking at Bee, I shook my head. "I just want to check the newspaper headlines," I lied, running across the street in haste, nearly missing a gray sedan. The displeased driver sounded a honk.

And there, on the other side of the road, was the building. It had to be the hotel. "Excuse me," I said to the elderly doorman. "Is this the Landon Park Hotel?"

He looked at me with wide eyes. "Landon Park?" He shook his head. "Why, no, this is the Washington Athletic Club."

"Right," I said. "Of course."

I turned to walk back, this time using the sidewalk.

"Wait, miss," he called out.

"This *used* to be the Landon Park Hotel, but not since the nineteen fifties, when the place nearly burned down."

"Really?" I said, grinning.

He nodded. "It was completely gutted."

I thanked him and glanced across the street to where Bee and Evelyn were standing. They both looked confused, especially Bee.

"I'll be right there," I shouted, pretending to be looking at the newspaper machine, but I was really soaking in the spot where Elliot and Esther's troubles had begun. Standing there made the story feel that much more real, even if they were only figments of someone's daydreams a lifetime ago.

* * *

We skipped the shopping trip and caught the two o'clock ferry. I faked a headache for Evelyn's sake; I could see that she wasn't doing well. She looked pale and fatigued. I knew she needed to rest, but I also knew she wouldn't admit it.

Bee headed to her bedroom for a nap, and I did too. But I didn't plan on sleeping.

I could hear the phone ringing in the kitchen. Busy in the bathroom, where I was bathing the baby, I decided that the caller could wait. But the phone kept ringing persistently, until I'd rung out the washcloth and wrapped her in a little blue terrycloth towel that Bobby's mother had given us. She'd been hoping for a boy.

"Hello?" I finally answered. I didn't mask the annoyance in my voice.

It was Frances. "Esther, you're not going to believe it." Her voice sounded choked up, excited, panicky—all at once.

"Slow down and tell me," I said, adjusting the baby so I could hold the phone more comfortably.

"It's Elliot," she said. When she said his name, I nearly fell to my knees.

"No, no, Frances," I said. "Don't tell me. I can't bear to hear it."

"No," she said quickly. "He's alive. He's fine. And he's home! He's home from the war."

Tears began to well in my eyes. "How do you know this?"

She paused for a minute, as if considering whether to tell me the full truth or the partial version. "Well," she said finally, "because he was here."

"Where?"

"At my house," she said. "He just left."

"What on earth was he doing there?"

I could sense Frances stiffening, and tension swelled within me. I was apprehensive about their friendship, and I couldn't hide it. "Frances," I continued. "What was he doing there?"

"Esther, I don't know what you're implying," she said defensively. "He knows I love photography so he gave me an album with some photos he took in the South Pacific. They're beautiful. You should come see them—coconut trees, beaches, the people he encountered."

I formed my right hand into a tight fist. "Why would he give you a gift?"

"What kind of question is that?" Frances said, sounding hurt. "Let's not forget that we're old friends too, Esther. It was simply a kind gesture."

"And what about me?" I said. "Am I not a friend?"

"Esther, you're married with a child," she said a little more bluntly than I had expected. "He doesn't exactly feel welcome on your doorstep."

The anger was building now, stirring up years of emotions that I'd tried to ignore. "You've always put him above our friendship," I said bitterly. "You've always wanted him for yourself."

Frances was silent.

"I'm sorry," I said. "I didn't mean that."

"Yes you did," Frances said.

"No, no, I didn't. It came out wrong. Can you forgive me?"

"I have to go, Esther." There was a click, and then I heard nothing but the lonely dial tone.

I stared into my closet the next morning, and finally pulled out the fitted blue dress I'd bought in Seattle last year. It had a black belt and a V neckline with a white peony on the lapel, just like the ones in the fashion magazines.

I called Rose. "Hi," I said. "Have you heard the news?"

"About Elliot?" she said. "Yes."

I sighed. "I'm a wreck."

"Why should you be? He's alive."

"Yes, I know, but this island is too small for the both of us."

Rose knew that as well as I did. "Want me to come over? I can catch the next ferry."

"Yes," I said. "Can you meet me for lunch? I can be at Ray's at noon, just after I do my shopping. I'll have the baby, but if I'm lucky, she'll sleep in her carriage."

"Perfect," she said.

Ever since Rose had moved to Seattle, the island felt lonely. I had Frances, of course, but the two of us had grown distant in the past year, for reasons I understood but couldn't bring myself to speak of. Until now.

"Rose," I said, "is Frances in love with Elliot?" It sounded absurd that one of my best friends could love the man I loved, but I had to ask. I had to know. And I knew Rose would have the answer.

"You need to ask her yourself," she said simply. But I didn't have to. Somewhere in my heart, I already knew.

At the market, I could hardly turn down one aisle before I was peering down another to see if Elliot might be there. But instead of him, I ran into Janice Stevens, my next-door neighbor, who was staked out near the canned goods. She was a widow, which is why I tried not to feel irritated by the way she looked at me or the things she said. She was always baking cookies, cakes, and pies, and pointing out the fact that I didn't. Frances told me once that Janice had eyes for Bobby, and perhaps she did. She'd bring over her confections and say things like "You poor man! Esther never bakes for you, so it's my duty as a neighbor to make sure you're looked after." She always wore a fresh application of red lipstick and had a habit of lingering in our doorway longer than I liked.

Even in high school, I'd gotten the feeling that she wanted me to fail, that she was waiting in the wings, ready to swoop in like a vulture as soon as I showed any sign of weakness.

It's partly why I braced myself that morning when I saw her. She looked at me with a saccharine smile and said, "I heard that Elliot is home. Have you seen him?"

Janice knew the mention of Elliot's name was bound to get a rise out of me.

"I saw him this morning," she said.

I feigned interest in a can of tomatoes. "Oh?"

"He's quite tan from the South Pacific," she continued. "He looked so handsome."

"Where did you see him?" I finally asked, caving, even though I knew I shouldn't.

"He was having breakfast with Frances—at Ray's," she said. "Didn't she tell you?"

I dropped the can of tomatoes.

Janice bent down to pick it up and gave me a sly smile. "Frances and Elliot would make a darling couple, wouldn't they?"

"Simply darling," I said, snatching the can out of her hands before pushing my cart past her.

"Oh, Esther, stop," Rose said as we sat at a table at Ray's. "Don't read into things."

"Read into things?" I said. "How can I not? Since Elliot's been home, they've been inseparable."

I knew by the look on Rose's face that she was disappointed in Frances, as I was, but she wouldn't take sides. Rose never took sides.

"Why don't you two talk about it?" she suggested.

I nodded. But I was really wondering what THEY had talked about this morning. Why had Elliot come back from war and taken such an interest in my best friend? Wasn't there some unwritten rule that former lovers are not supposed to carry on with your friends?

Just then, the waiter approached our table, but not to take our orders. He looked right at me. "Are you Esther?"

"Yes," I said, confused.

"Good," he said. "I should have known by the way the gentleman described you. He said you'd be the prettiest woman in the restaurant." The waiter cast an apologetic glance at Rose. "Sorry. You are quite beautiful too, miss." But Rose smiled as if she didn't care, and I knew she didn't.

From behind his back, he pulled out a single tulip, my favorite flower—pure white, with the very tip of each petal tinged red. I had never seen a tulip like that, and it nearly took my breath away.

"For you," he said, handing me the flower, along with a white envelope. My name was written in Elliot's handwriting. I had memorized his e's along with the special embellishment he added to each s.

"Go read it in private," Rose said. "I'll stay with the baby."

"Thanks," I said. She knew I needed to savor every word.

I ran out to the sidewalk and sat down on a bench before tearing open the envelope.

My Dearest Esther,

It's wrong of me to be reaching out to you like this, I know. You're married, and I hear you have a child. But I need you to know something, to set the record straight. Can you meet me, tonight, on the beach in front of my house? I'll be there waiting for you, in hopes that you'll come. And if you do, I'll know we are meant to be together. And if you don't, I will know that it is the end for us, that I must make plans to move on, to leave the island, and let my heart say good-bye. Please say you'll come. Please tell me that despite everything, you'll come. It's a lot to ask, but I pray that the fire that still burns in me also burns in you. I'll be waiting.

Yours,

Elliot

I held the letter to my chest, and a single tear trickled down my face. As I brushed it away, I could see movement from the corner of my eye. But when I turned to look, whatever or whoever it was had vanished.

Chapter 9

March 7

I spent much of the next morning writing, or at least trying to write. The story had inspired me to put words together again, not that the words I typed were amounting to much. After exactly one hour and twelve minutes, I'd hammered out a two-paragraph opener to a new novel that, frankly, stank.

So when Bee knocked on the door, I was eager for a break.

"Feel like a walk?" she asked, leaning into the doorway. "Oh, sorry, I see that you're writing. I didn't mean to disturb you, dear."

I looked outside and could see that the sun had pushed through the clouds; the beach looked sparkling. "No, I'd love to," I said, setting my mug down.

I grabbed my sweater and then slipped on a pair of boots, and we made our way down to the shore. For as long as I can remember, Bee always went left instead of right. And now I knew why. She wanted to avoid Jack's house and whatever history they shared.

"Are you glad you came?" she asked.

"Yes," I said, reaching for her hand and giving it a squeeze.

"I am too," she said. Then she paused and hunched over to examine a little orange starfish caught in a game of tug-of-war between the shore and the waves. Bee gently picked it up, then carefully sent it on its way a few feet out into the sound.

"There, little friend," she said. "Go home."

We walked together for a little while, until she stopped and turned to me. "It's been lonely here," she said.

I had never heard her say anything like that before. Uncle Bill had been gone for at least twenty years, maybe longer. I had always thought she liked her solitude.

"Why don't you come visit me in New York?" I suggested. "You could spend April with me."

Bee shook her head. "I belong here," she said.

I felt a little hurt. *If she's so lonely, why wouldn't she want my company?*

"I'm sorry, honey," she said. "I'm getting older, and . . . you'll see, when you're my age. Leaving your home starts to feel like an epic journey, one I'm afraid I no longer have the energy for."

I nodded as if I understood, but I didn't. I hoped I wouldn't feel tied to my home in my elder years, but maybe it was unavoidable.

"Emily," she said. "There's something I need to ask you. I've been thinking about where you are in life, and where I am, and, well, I wondered if you'd ever consider moving here, living here, with me on Bainbridge Island."

My mouth fell open. For much of my life the island had been my secret place, my personal retreat, but my home?

"Wow," I said. "I'm honored that you'd want to have me. . . ."

"Emily," she said, cutting me off before I could decline her invitation. "I'm leaving the house to you—in my will. The house, the property, everything."

I shook my head in disbelief. "Bee," I said, suddenly concerned. "Is everything all right?"

"I'm only planning ahead," she said. "I guess I wanted you to know that the house was yours, in case you wanted to think about a life here someday. Maybe someday soon."

It was a lot to consider. "Wow, Bee," I said. "I . . ."

"You don't have to say anything. Just know that the choice is yours. You were the only one who loved this place. Your mother, she'd board it up. And your sister would sell it just as fast as that husband of hers could find a buyer. Of course it's yours to sell too, but I know I'm leaving this place in good hands." She paused to watch an eagle fly overhead. "Yes, the home is yours. Just consider me the old lady who occupies one of the bedrooms. You come stay as often as you like, for as long as you like. And don't forget my invitation to move in."

I nodded. "I'll give it some thought," I said, squeezing her hand again.

I heard my phone ringing in my sweater pocket, and when I looked at the screen, I could see that it was a local number.

"Hello?" I answered.

"Emily? Hi, it's Greg."

I had no idea how he got my cell number, but then I realized that after we'd drunk all that wine at the restaurant the other night, I'd scribbled it on a napkin and he'd tucked it into his pocket. Classy.

"Hi," I said, remembering Heart Rock, the kiss, our unfinished business.

"Hey, I was just wondering if you might be free one of these nights. I'd love to have you out to my place for drinks. I'm a terrible cook, so we could order in, or do takeout. Whatever you'd like."

"Um," I said, feeling caught off guard by the invitation. "Sure."

"Great," he said. I could picture his smile. "How about tomorrow night, at seven?"

"Yeah," I said. "That would be . . . great."

"Good," he said. "We can pick up Chinese along the way. See you then."

Bee and I both looked up when we saw Henry waving from his front porch. The smoke billowing out of his chimney mingled with the soft mist rising off the morning tide, creating a thick fog one could disappear into.

"Good morning, you two," he called out.

Bee nodded. "We were just on our way home," she said without pause.

"But surely you can stop for a cup of coffee," he countered.

I'd asked Bee, on the night I arrived, about Henry. Her answer was direct, yet hardly informative. "He's just a very old friend," she had said, her words snuffing out the flame of my intrigue.

Bee nodded at Henry, and I followed her up to the house. It occurred to me that they would have made a very odd couple. They looked awkward standing there together, and it erased any suspicions that they had ever been romantically involved, not that a short man and a tall woman couldn't have an explosive love affair.

I smiled and said, "Coffee sounds wonderful."

Once inside, I sat where I had when Jack came in the door that morning last week. I suddenly remembered the vase.

"Henry," I said. "I have a confession. Your white vase, I . . ."

He winked at me. "I know," he said, pointing to the now intact vase, which was presently resting on the mantel with a single daffodil inside. "As good as new," he continued. "Jack brought it by this morning."

I grinned before hesitating. "This morning?"

Henry looked puzzled. "Yes." He paused for a second. "Is there something wrong?"

"No, no," I said. "It's nothing. I just thought he was in Seattle. He said he was spending a few days there."

Didn't Jack say he'd be away for a few days? Did he change his plans? The discrepancy in the details gnawed at me.

Henry went to pour the coffee, and while I sat down, Bee cased the room like a detective, examining every object slowly and cautiously.

"He's not much of housekeeper, is he?" she said.

"I guess it's the curse of being a bachelor," I replied. But then I remembered Jack's home, perfectly organized and clean—surprisingly clean.

She nodded and sat down in a chair by the window.

"Did he ever marry?" I asked in a whisper, remembering the woman in the photo on the mantel.

Bee shook her head as though the very idea of Henry marrying anyone was, well, crazy. "No," she said.

I looked around the little living room with its wainscot paneling and old plank floors until my eyes stopped at the mantel. I searched the display of beach rocks and frames. The photo was gone.

"Wait," I said, confused. "Last week there was a photo of a woman, an old girlfriend, maybe," I said, conspiratorially. "Do you know the photo I'm talking about?"

"No," she said in a distant voice. "I haven't been here in a very long time."

"You'd know her if you saw her," I said. "She was blond and

beautiful, standing right in front of Henry's house, where the photo was taken."

Bee looked out the window at the sound, pausing the way she does when she's lost in thought. "It's been so long," she said. "I don't recall."

Henry was back with coffee a few minutes later, but Bee seemed uncomfortable and agitated as she sipped hers. I wondered what was bothering her.

I made conversation for the both of us, coaxing Henry into a monologue about his garden. Bee never made eye contact with him, not once. Then, just after she took the last sip of her coffee, she abruptly set the cup down on the saucer and stood up. "Emily, I'm afraid I have a headache," she said. "I think it's time for me to head home."

Henry held up his hand in protest. "Not yet," he said. "Not until the two of you see the garden. There's something I want to show you."

Bee agreed reluctantly, and the three of us walked through the kitchen to the back door that led to the yard behind the house. We'd hardly stepped three feet outside when Bee gasped, pointing to the garden to our right.

"Henry!" she exclaimed, surveying hundreds of delicate light green leaves that had pushed up from the soil in grand formation, showcasing a carpet of tiny lavender-colored flowers, with dark purple centers.

Bee looked astonished. "How did they . . . where did they come from?"

Henry shook his head. "I noticed them two weeks ago. They just *appeared*."

Bee turned to me, and upon seeing my confused face, she offered an explanation. "They're wood violets," she said. "I haven't seen them on the island since . . ."

"They're very rare," Henry said, filling the void that Bee had left when her voice trailed off. "You can't plant them, for they won't grow. They have to *choose* you."

Bee's eyes met Henry's, and she smiled, a gentle, forgiving smile. It warmed me to see it. "Evelyn has a theory about these flowers," she said, pausing as if to pull a dusty memory off a shelf in her mind, handling it with great care. "Yes," she said, the memory in plain view. "She used to say they grow where they are needed, that they signal healing, and hope."

"It's ridiculous, isn't it, Henry, to think that violets can *know*," Bee continued.

Henry nodded. "Harebrained," he said in agreement.

Bee shook her head in disbelief. "And to see them in bloom, in March of all months . . ."

Henry nodded. "I know."

Neither took their eyes off the petals before them, so fragile, yet in great numbers stalwart and determined. I stepped back, watching the two of them standing side by side, sharing a moment of reflection that I could not understand. I knew it then: I was in the presence of something much bigger than just flowers.

Bee and I walked in silence back to the house, she with her secrets and I with mine. And as she napped, I opened my laptop and told myself I couldn't look away until I had another two paragraphs written, but all I could do was stare at the clock at the top of my screen. After eight minutes had passed with no inspiration, I called Annabelle.

"Hi," she said a little limply.

"What's wrong?"

"Nothing," she replied.

I knew her too well to believe that. "Tell me," I said. "I know your voice. Something's wrong."

She sighed. "I told myself I wasn't going to tell you this."

"Tell me what?"

There was silence.

"Annie?"

"All right," she said. "I saw Joel."

My heart started beating faster. "Where?"

"At a café on Fifth."

"And?"

"He asked about you."

I was practically breathless. "What did he say?"

"I told you I shouldn't have said anything."

"Well, you did, and now you have to finish the story."

"He asked me how you were."

"Did you tell him I was here?"

"Of course I didn't. But I did tell him you were dating someone."

"Annie, you did not!"

"I did. Hey, if he can play house with another woman, he deserves to know that you're moving on."

"What was his reaction?"

"Well, if you want me to tell you that he started bawling right there, he didn't. But he didn't look thrilled, either. His face said it all."

"What did his face say, Annie?"

"That it hurt to hear of you with someone else, dummy."

My heart throbbed deep inside. I sat down—I *had* to sit down. I felt weak, and a little sick.

"Em, are you there?"

"Yeah."

"See? I shouldn't have told you. Look what it's going to do to your healing process. Remember, Joel left you. In such a betraying way, I might add."

It was as certain as the freckles on my nose, but somehow hearing Annabelle say it again—well, it stung.

"I know," I said. "You're right." I sat up straighter. "I'm going to be fine. Just fine."

"How many times can we say 'fine'?"

I grinned. "Fine. Do you have any other bombs to drop?"

"Nope," she said. "But there is a tragedy happening in this apartment."

"What?"

"You're out of ice cream."

I remembered my late-night affair with Ben & Jerry's Cherry Garcia before I left for the island. "A tragedy, indeed."

"Bye, sweetie," she said.

As I set my cell phone on the table, Bee's phone began ringing. After four rings, I picked it up.

"Hello?"

"Emily, is that you?"

"Mom?"

"Hi, honey," she said. "So, did you hear the wonderful news?"

"What news?"

"Danielle," she said in a high-pitched voice, "is pregnant!"

I should have said, "That's so exciting!" or "Oh, the miracle of life!" but I just shrugged and said, "Again?" This was Danielle's third child. But as far as I was concerned, it might as well have been her thirteenth.

"Yes, she's due in November!" Mom cried. "Isn't it wonderful?"

That's what she said, but what I heard was: "Why can't you be more like your sister?" I sensed a Danielle lovefest beginning and quickly changed the subject. "So," I said, "Bee said you called. Was this what you wanted to tell me?"

"Well, yes, but dear, I heard about Joel. I'm worried about you. How are you doing?"

I ignored her question. "How did you *hear* about it?"

"Oh, honey," she said, "that's not important."

"It's important, Mom."

"Well," she said, pausing for a moment. "Your sister told me, dear."

"How did Danielle know? I haven't talked to her in months."

"Well, I think she read that you weren't married anymore on the World Wide Web," she said. My mother was the only person, I think on earth, who referred to the Internet that way, yet it was endearing somehow. She also called Google "Goggle."

I remembered my Facebook page. Yes, I had adjusted my relationship status in my profile shortly after Joel had done the same—but there was something wrong, on so many levels, about your own mother hearing about your divorce via Facebook. "I didn't know that Danielle even used Facebook," I said, still a little stunned.

"Hmm," she said. "Well maybe she *Goggled* it."

I sighed. "The point is, Danielle knows. You know. Everybody knows. I was going to tell you, Mom, eventually. But I guess I just wasn't ready to face my family yet. I didn't want to worry you and Dad."

"Oh, honey," she said, "I'm so sorry that you're going through this. Are you holding up OK?"

"I'm doing all right."

"Good," she said. "Honey, was there another woman involved?" This is what everyone wanted to know when they learned of my marriage's demise, so I didn't fault my mother for her curiosity.

"No," I said. "I mean yes, but no, I don't want to talk about it."

I looked down at the phone cord, which I'd somehow wrapped so tightly around my finger that it was cutting off the circulation. I didn't know if I was angry about my mother's obvious prying or angry at Joel for precipitating the reason for the prying. But mostly my finger hurt, so I focused on that, as Mom chattered on. I could see her there, standing in the kitchen in front of that horrible old electric stove—avocado green with the oven mitts hanging from the handle, knitted in rainbow-colored yarn.

"I worry about you all alone, dear. You don't want to end up like your aunt."

"Mom," I said a little more sternly than I had anticipated. "I don't want to talk about this now."

"OK, honey," she said, sounding a bit wounded. "I'm just trying to help." And I suppose in her own way she was.

"I know," I replied. "So, how did you know I was here?"

"I called your apartment. Annabelle said you were staying with your aunt."

Mom never called Bee by her first name. She always referred to her as "your aunt."

"Yeah," I said. "She invited me to stay for the month. I'll be here through the end of March."

"A *whole month*?" She sounded annoyed, or vaguely jealous. I knew she wanted to be here too, but she was too prideful to admit it. She hadn't been to the island since Danielle and I left for college, which is when our summer visits ceased.

"Oh, Mom?" I said. "I wanted to ask you about something."

"What?"

"Well, it's something Bee and I were talking about," I said, pausing.

"What is it, honey?"

I took a deep breath, unsure of the emotional land mines that might lie ahead. "She told me that there was a time, many years ago, when you were working on some sort of project—one that changed your relationship with her."

There was silence on the other end of the line, so I continued. "She said she told you the truth about Grandma. I wish I knew what she meant by that."

I could no longer hear her fiddling around with her spatula and kitchen pans in the background. There was only silence.

"Mom? Are you still there?"

"Emily," she finally said, "what has your aunt told you?"

"Nothing," I replied. "She wouldn't tell me anything, just that you decided not to be a part of the family anymore. She said it changed things between the two of you." I looked over my shoulder to be sure Bee wasn't hovering. She wasn't. "She said you stopped coming to visit. Why, Mom? What happened?"

"Well," she said, "I'm afraid I can't recall the details. And if Bee tries to tell you anything, I wouldn't believe it. She's getting up there in age and her memory is fleeting."

"Mom, it's just that—"

"Emily, I'm sorry, I don't want to discuss this."

"Mom, I deserve to know the story."

"You don't," she said simply.

I frowned.

"Honey, don't be angry," she said, detecting my mood as only mothers can do.

"I'm not angry."

"It's in the past, dear," she continued. "Some things are better left that way."

I could tell by the tone of her voice that the door was closed. Bee, Evelyn, and now my mother had made it very clear that these secrets were not for the taking. If I wanted to know their stories, I would have to work for them.

Later, after Bee's nap, she mixed a gin and tonic for herself, and offered me one. "Sure," I said, leaning back on the couch and enjoying the punch of the first sip, which always tastes like pine needles.

"Did you ever call your mother back?" Bee asked.

"She called here again about an hour ago," I said. "She wanted to tell me that Danielle is having another baby."

"Another one?"

I loved that Bee's response was similar to mine. Perhaps it was just that we were childless, but I think we both agreed that anyone who willingly has more than two children is clinically insane.

I took another sip of my drink and buried my head deeper into the blue velvet couch cushion. "Bee, do you think Joel left me because I never cooked for him?"

"Nonsense, dear," she said, setting her crossword puzzle down.

I tucked my knees into my body and clasped my arms around them tightly. "My mother is so—"

"She's had a more difficult life than you know, Emily," she interrupted.

The statement took me by surprise. "What do you mean?"

Bee stood up. "Here, let me show you something."

She began walking down the hallway, so I followed her. Two doors past the guest room where I was staying, she stopped in front of another door. She reached for the knob and then her pocket, from which she pulled out a key ring and selected a small gold key that she then inserted into the door.

The door creaked open and we stepped inside. I batted away a cobweb from my face. "Sorry," she said. "I haven't been in this room in a very long time."

Next to the small white dresser there was a child's table, set with two pink teacups on saucers, and a Victorian dollhouse. I bent down to pick up a porcelain doll from the floor. Her face was smudged and her brown hair matted. She looked as if some little girl had left her there, just like that.

"What is this room?" I asked, confused.

"It was your mother's room," she said. "She lived here with me for a time when she was very young."

"Why? What about Grandpa and Grandma?"

"Something happened," she said simply. "Your grandparents . . . they were going through a rough patch, so I offered to have your mother come stay with me for a while." Bee sighed, smiling to herself. "She was such a dear little girl. We had the most fun together, your mother and I."

As Bee opened the closet door, I thought of my grandparents and wondered what could have precipitated them leaving their child with her. She reached to the top shelf and retrieved a shoe box. She blew a layer of dust off the lid before handing it to me. "Here," she said. "Maybe this will give some insight into your mother."

Bee pulled the keys from her pocket and they jingled in her hands, which was my cue to walk back to the hallway.

"Thank you," I said, looking at the box in anticipation.

Bee turned toward her room and said, "I'll see you at dinner."

In my room, I set the box down on the bed. *What could be inside? Would my mother approve of me riffling through her things?*

I lifted the lid and peered inside. On top were three dried roses tied together with a shiny red ribbon. When I picked up the little bunch, three delicate petals fell to the floor. Next I pulled out a child's picture book; a long gray feather, which looked like a seagull's; a barrette; a pair of tiny white gloves; and a small, leather-bound volume. It wasn't until I moved it into the light that I could see what it was: a scrapbook. I opened it and waves of emotion flooded my body. On the first page the word *Mother* was handwritten, surrounded by tiny flowers. I blinked hard, and turned the page to find a collage of sorts. There were clippings from magazines, of women with perfectly coiffed hair and pressed dresses. There were dried flowers and black-and-white photos—one of a baby, and one of a house, simple and small with an old car parked in front. *What is this? Why did my mother create this scrapbook, and why did Bee want me to see it?*

Bee's silence at dinner told me that she didn't want to discuss the mysterious room or the box of hidden treasures, so I didn't press my luck. I cleared the dishes, and just before I started to load them into the dishwasher, the phone rang.

"Get that, dear, please," Bee said from the hallway. "I'm afraid it's lights out for me. I'm exhausted."

"Sure," I said, picking it up. "Hello?"

"Emily?"

"Yes?"

"It's Evelyn."

"Oh, hi, Ev—"

"No, no, dear, Bee must not know that I'm calling you."

"OK," I said cautiously. "What's going on?"

"I need your help," she said.

"With what? Are you OK?"

"Yes—well, no. I need to speak to you. In person."

I paused for a second. "Do you want me to come over?"

"Yes," she said. "I'm just up the beach, honey. The big house with the wisteria arbor in front, about six houses past Henry's. It's a bit chilly out, dear, so wear a coat."

I didn't tell Bee I was going out, a decision I regretted once I got to the beach. The tide was coming in, which made the water seem menacing, as though it was stalking me, extending its frothy hooks onto the shore and making eyes at my feet. I imagined that bats were flying overhead, even though they were probably just seagulls nestling into the treetops for the night. I zipped my coat up and told myself to look straight ahead. I passed Henry's house, which was dark, then started counting. *One, two, three.* The homes looked cozy nestled up against the hillside. *Four, five, six, seven.* I wondered if I had misinterpreted her directions. *Eight, nine.* I looked up and saw Evelyn's home in the distance. The wisteria looked bare and vulnerable clinging to the arbor, but somewhere deep inside its branches was the promise of spring, and when I looked closely, I saw a few pale green shoots emerging from the trunk. I turned to walk up the steps, and when I did, I saw Evelyn on the front porch, sitting in a rocking chair. I could see that she was in a nightgown. Her hair, usually carefully styled, looked matted and messy.

"Thank you for coming," she said, reaching for my hand.

"Of course," I replied, squeezing in response.

Her face looked ashen. She appeared weaker, more frail than she had only days ago.

"It's the cancer," I said. "You're—"

"Isn't it a beautiful night?"

I nodded.

She pointed to a rocking chair next to hers, and I sat down.

"I'm going to miss this island." Her voice was distant, far away.

I swallowed hard.

She looked out to the shore. "Did you know that your aunt Bee and I used to go skinny-dipping out there? We'd strip right down and just dive in." She turned to me. "You should try it. There's absolutely nothing like feeling Old Man Puget Sound on every inch of your skin."

Laughing would have been the appropriate response, but I couldn't summon anything but a half smile. What do you say to someone who is reminiscing about her life for perhaps the final time?

"You will take care of her, won't you, Emily?"

"Of course I will," I said, looking into her eyes. "I promise."

She nodded. "Bee isn't an easy person to get along with, you know. But she's as much my home as this island is."

I could see tears welling up in her eyes. "She told me, after my husband died, that I wasn't alone—that I'd never be alone. And as long as Bee has been in my life, that has been true."

I nodded.

"It's not right that I'm leaving her. It's just not right." She stood up and walked to the edge of the porch, throwing her feeble fists into the cold air as if threatening the island, challenging it.

I jumped up and put my arms around her, and she turned and buried her face in my shoulder.

She wiped away the tears on her cheek and sat down. "I can hardly bear the thought of leaving her."

I leaned in so she could see my face better. "I will look out for her. Don't you worry."

She sighed. "Good. Will you come in for a moment? I have something to give you."

I nodded, following Evelyn through the front door. The warm air inside felt good on my face.

Evelyn's living room looked like the quarters of a sick woman, as it should have. Magazines, books, mail, and piles of paper covered the coffee table alongside a collection of water glasses and dishes encrusted with old food.

"I'm sorry about all of this," she said quietly.

I shook my head. "Please, don't apologize."

"I think I left it in the other room," she said. "It will be just be a minute."

I wasn't sure what *it* was, but Evelyn looked as though her life depended on finding it.

"That's fine," I said. "I'll wait here."

I knew I didn't have much time, so I worked fast, first collecting the dirty dishes and loading them into the dishwasher. I threw away the tissues that had been piled high in a heap, and after I'd moved a mound of mail to the kitchen table to be sorted, I gave the table a quick wipe down. *There.* Then I sat down on the couch near the window. My eyes found their way to a nearby bookcase, where shelves displayed trinkets and framed photos.

Next to a glass vase filled with sand dollars, there was a photo of Evelyn on her wedding day—so beautiful and elegant with her tall husband standing by her side. I wondered what he was like, and why they'd never had children. There were photos of dogs—a Jack Russell and a dachshund that looked as if he had been fed pie for dinner every night. But then I saw a portrait of a woman, and I recognized her instantly. She was the same woman in the photo at Henry's house. In this shot she was smiling, standing next to someone else. I squinted to get a better look. She was standing next to Bee.

I heard a sound behind me, and turned to see Evelyn. I hadn't heard her enter the room.

"Who is she, Evelyn?" I asked, pointing to the photo. "I saw her in a photo at Henry's house. Bee wouldn't tell me. I have to know."

Evelyn sat down, clasping something in her hands. "She was once Henry's fiancée," she said.

"And your friend?"

"Yes," she said. "A very dear friend."

She sighed and walked toward me, and when she did, I could see the deep fatigue—the finality—in her face.

"Here," she said, handing me an envelope that had been carefully folded in half. "I want you to give this to Bee."

"Now?"

"No," she said. "When I'm gone."

I nodded. "Of course."

"Thank you, Emily," she said, squeezing my hand again. "You

are special, you know. All of this"—she paused and swept her hand out toward the sound—"all of this was meant to be. You were meant to be here. You have such purpose, my dear. Such purpose."

I hugged her, wondering if it might be the last time.

"Are you going to go through with it?" Rose asked me when I returned to the table and told her the two paths Elliot's letter had laid out: Meet tonight and start a new life together or say good-bye to him forever.

We both knew that the stakes were high. I clutched the envelope as if it were his hand. I could see the whites of my knuckles, and my nails were digging into my palm. It was as if I had somehow believed that if I let go, I'd let go of Elliot, and I couldn't bear to see him go. Not again. Not another time.

"I don't know," I said, and I truly didn't. How would I sneak out? The baby didn't fall asleep until after eight, and how would I explain to Bobby that I needed to leave? Stores weren't open that late, so I couldn't lie and say I needed eggs or milk. Plus, even if I found a way, what would I say when I got there, when I faced Elliot? And what would I do? This is the part that scared me most. What in the dear Lord's name would I do?

"Esther," Rose said in a practical voice. "I want you to know that I will support you in whatever choice you make."

Bobby caught an early ferry home and surprised me at five with a bouquet of daffodils from the Pike Place Market. "I thought you'd like these," he said. "I remembered that daffodils were your favorite."

I didn't tell him that he'd gotten it wrong, that my favorite flowers were tulips. Instead, I hugged him and thanked him for the gift.

"I bet you've forgotten," he said, "being so busy with the baby and all, but I haven't."

I gave him a puzzled look. It wasn't my birthday, or Mother's Day.

"Forgotten what, Bobby?"

"Happy anniversary!" he said. "Well, I mean, happy anniversary a day early. I got so excited I couldn't wait. I'm taking you out tonight so we can celebrate properly."

Of all the nights to surprise me, why did it have to be this one? Fate, the wretched witch that she was, had just slapped me with her cruel, cold hand.

"But what about the baby?" I said, eager to find a hole in his plan. She reached her little hand up to my necklace, grabbed the starfish on the chain, and cooed. I rewarded her with a kiss on the cheek.

"I've already made arrangements," he said. "My mother is coming over."

The timing couldn't have been worse. Elliot would be waiting for me tonight, and I would be with Bobby.

Bobby took me to the Crow's Nest, a beautiful restaurant perched high on a cliff overlooking the sound. Elliot and I had dined there many times, but this was a first for Bobby and me. You see, Bobby was frugal. Spending money on dinners out just wasn't something he did. So when he held open the big knotty pine doors to the restaurant, there was an air of pride in his swagger. "Only the best for my Esther," he said as we made our way inside.

We were seated at six, but the food didn't arrive until at least seven thirty. No matter how fast I tapped my foot, how tightly I clenched my teeth, or how many times I glanced at the clock, the evening just inched along.

Bobby didn't notice my mood. He was too busy questioning the waiter: "Is the duck cooked in a wine sauce?" "Are the oysters fresh?" "Do the potatoes come mashed?" "Could we substitute salad for soup?"

I tapped my finger against my leg under the table, trying to hide my frustration, and out of the corner of my eye, I saw someone looking my way. I glanced up at the bar, where Billy, my old high school boyfriend, was seated, holding a drink and looking a little bleary-eyed. Billy had proposed to me just before Homecoming our junior year. He gave me a ring, and I said yes—well, actually, I said maybe. I loved Billy, and we had grand times together, but that was before Elliot came into my life. Frances always said that Billy never got over me, and there was a look in his eyes that evening that told me she was right. Yet he never hated me for my decision—not for a minute. That night, I even got the feeling that he felt sorry for me.

He waved from the bar, where he was sitting with another man. They were both in suits. I waved back.

"Who's that?" Bobby asked.

"Just Billy," I said, gesturing toward the bar.

Bobby turned to smile at him too, a gesture with a singular purpose: to underscore the fact that I was his. I sometimes got the feeling that Bobby was less in love with me than he was with the idea of me. I was his trophy, one he liked to polish up and take out and parade around every now and then.

"Esther," he said after our dinner arrived, and after he'd downed two glasses of beer, "I was just thinking that maybe"—he lowered his voice—"maybe we should try for another baby."

I spilled my water in my lap just as I heard the word "baby."

"What do you say, sweetheart?"

"Well, isn't it a little too soon?" I said. "I mean, she's just four months old."

"Give it some thought," he said.

I nodded.

We finished our dinner, and Bobby suggested dessert. "I've been feeling like baklava ever since Janice brought some over to my office last week," he said.

"Why was she at your office?"

"She had an appointment on the floor below," he said, wiping a few breadcrumbs from his lips. "She stopped in to say hello." He picked up the menu and lowered his glasses on his nose. "Do you feel like dessert, sweetheart?"

No, I didn't feel like anything except leaving. I looked at my watch: It was nearly nine thirty. Elliot hadn't specified a time, but it was getting late, almost too late. If I was going to go, I needed to go soon.

"No," I said. "I'm actually feeling a bit tired. I think we should call it a night."

Bobby paid the bill, and as we left, I deliberately dropped my purse beneath our table. It would be my alibi.

Once at home, Bobby thanked his mother and walked her to the door, while I checked on the baby, sound asleep in her crib. I felt the passage of every minute, every second. Then, Bobby undressed and got into bed, waiting for me to follow.

"Rats," I said. "I left my purse at the restaurant."

"Oh no," he said, standing up and reaching for the trousers he'd laid over the chair. "I'll go get it for you."

"No, no," I said. "You have to get up so early for work in the morning. I'll go. Besides, I forgot to drop something by Frances's house, and I can do that on the way back." Brilliant, I thought, as my heart raced. I'd just bought myself another thirty minutes.

"But, Esther, it's so late," he said. "A woman shouldn't be out on the road at this hour."

Bobby believed his lot in life was to protect me, and that my lot in life was to be protected.

"I'll be fine," I said.

He yawned and climbed back into bed. "OK," he said, "but don't be long. Wake me when you get home so I know you're all right."

"I will," I said.

But I knew I wouldn't. I would be gone much too long for that, and as I closed the door to the house, I could hear the sound of his snoring down the hall.

I drove the Buick fast that night, too fast, past the restaurant, past Frances's house, and down the long road that led to Elliot's. I looked in my rearview mirror a few times, just to be sure no one was following me.

It was after eleven when I parked my car on the street in front of Elliot's property. I smoothed my wool twinset and ran my fingers through my hair, chastising myself for not brushing it before I left, or even looking in a mirror, for that matter. The trail that led down to the beach was dark, but I had memorized every step.

The full moon lit up the sky and beamed down on the beach I knew so well—the beach where we had made love for the first time, and the last. I looked around, expecting to see him sitting on a log or lying on a blanket in the sand, the way he used to wait for me so many years ago. He'd hand me a bit of beach glass or some beautiful shell he'd found to add to my collection and we'd fall into each other's arms.

But he wasn't there. I was too late.

The house lights were dark. Could he have already gone? I gasped at the thought. Our timing had always been dreadful, so why did I expect anything different on this night? Still, the pain surged out of my heart like an electric shock. I turned back to the trail, and I would have raced up the embankment to my car had it not been for the glimmer of light purple petals underfoot. I shook my head. Wood violets? I hadn't seen them since I was a girl, when they appeared one summer in my grandmother's garden. I'd never noticed them on Elliot's property. What were they doing here?

Many on the island, me included, believed that these flowers had mystical powers, that they could heal wounds of the heart and the body, mend rifts in friendships, even bring about good fortune. I knelt down and ran my hand along the carpet of dusty purple nestled into pale green leaves.

I stood up suddenly when I heard distant music floating through the night air. I recognized the melody in an instant; Billie Holiday's voice was unmistakable. "Body and Soul."

My eyes searched the front porch for Elliot, but all I could make out was a fishing pole angled against the railing. The scene was as I remembered, a vision frozen in time.

And then, out of nowhere, arms wrapped around me. I didn't flinch or pull away; I knew his touch, I knew the smell of his skin, I knew the pattern of his breathing—I knew it all by heart.

"You came," he said into my neck.

"How could I not?" I said, turning around to face him.

"Have you thought of me?"

"Every second of every day," I said, allowing myself to fall into his arms completely. His pull on me was magnetic.

He kissed me with the same fire, the same ferocity that he had years ago. I knew, as he did, that whatever was between us was still there, just as strong as it ever was. Just as real.

I heard a rustling sound coming from the trees near the trail that wound up to the road. But I didn't stop to look or worry—not tonight, not when Elliot was taking my hand and leading me up to the house.

We walked through the door and into the living room. He pushed the chair to the side, and then the coffee table, and laid me on the bearskin rug by the fireplace.

As he unbuttoned my dress, I didn't think about Bobby, the man I should have been with on this day of my wedding anniversary, or my baby asleep in her crib, or the lie I'd told to get there. I just felt the warmth of the fire on my face, and Elliot's breath on my skin. It was all I wanted to feel.

March 8

I tried not to overthink Jack's words. *But didn't he say he'd be back from Seattle today?* I stared at the clock a dozen times before breakfast that next morning, wondering. I thought about the way Elliot had kissed Esther. I wanted to be loved with the same passion, the same fire that Elliot seemed to impart so naturally, so perfectly.

The phone didn't ring at eleven a.m.; nor did it ring at noon. *Why isn't he calling?*

I went for a beach walk at two, but the only sound my phone made was a chime alerting me to a text message from Annabelle.

By five, Bee began mixing a drink and asked if I wanted one too. I set the phone down and said, "Make it a double."

After about an hour, Bee was back in the lanai, working her magic with the liquor bottles, but this time she didn't offer me another. "Get dressed, dear," she said. "Greg will be here soon."

I had almost forgotten about the plans I'd made with Greg. I walked to my room quickly to dress, choosing a long-sleeved blue knit dress with a deep V neckline. I liked the way it felt against my skin.

Greg arrived at seven, just when he'd said he would, looking freshly scrubbed in a pair of clean jeans and a crisp white shirt. His golden skin almost glowed against it.

"Hi," he said as I walked out to his car. "Ready for Chinese?"

"Sounds wonderful," I said. "I'm starving."

We drove into town, past the Town and Country Market, and parked where several restaurants and cafés dotted Main Street. It was a warm evening, at least by Bainbridge Island standards, and a handful of people were sitting outside, eating alfresco.

Inside the restaurant, Greg gestured to the hostess. She looked like someone I had known in high school: Mindy Almvig, with her dangly earrings and spiral perm. "I called in an order about forty-five minutes ago."

"Yes," she said, smacking her gum. "It's ready." The place smelled delicious, of Szechuan sauce and spring rolls fresh from the fryer.

He paid, and then picked up the rather enormous paper bag. We climbed into the car, and I noticed a little restaurant nearby. Diners were seated outdoors under heated lamps. And that's when I saw *Jack*.

He was with a woman, that much was clear. I couldn't see her face from my vantage point, just her *legs*, which were barely covered by the short black dress that clung to her thighs. They were drinking wine and laughing, and as Jack turned toward the direction of our car, I pulled the sun visor down and turned in the other direction.

Who is she? Why didn't he mention that he's involved with someone else? Maybe she's just a friend. But if she was a friend, why didn't he say something about her?

Greg drove for about a mile before he pulled up into a gravel-covered driveway. His home, a yellow farmhouse, complete with a white picket fence, frankly shocked me. *Greg with a picket fence?*

"Here we are," he said.

"I'm so surprised," I said.

"You're surprised?"

"Yeah, I mean, it's so *cute*. It's so Martha Stewart meets Old Mac-Donald. I guess I never imagined you living somewhere like this."

He smiled and pulled the keys out of the ignition. I saw the edge of a tattoo I'd never noticed peeking through his sleeve.

The house's interior was much too decorated for Greg to have accomplished it himself. Everything matched—the pillows and the sofa, the rug and the wall color. There was a wreath on the front door. A *wreath*. This was the work of a woman. What man chooses an ottoman covered in green toile fabric?

Yet, upon closer examination, I could see that if there had been a woman in his life, she hadn't been around for a while. There were dishes piled in the sink. The counters hadn't been wiped down, and there was a basket of laundry at the foot of the stairs.

"So, this is it," Greg said, a little embarrassed, as if my being there had allowed him to see the place in a new light.

The bathroom door was open, so I took a quick peek: The toilet seat was up and there was a roll of toilet paper on the floor, not in the dispenser where it belonged. Here was the home of a single man.

"There," Greg said, placing two napkins, plates, and sets of chopsticks on the coffee table next to the wine he'd poured for us. "Dinner is served."

It wasn't exactly dinner at Jack's house—no linen napkins or gourmet cuisine—but it was Greg-style, and after the scene in town, it made me appreciate Greg a little more than I had. At least he was being real.

"How long have you lived here?" I was eager to satisfy my curiosity regarding the female in his life—or his former life.

He looked up at the ceiling as if trying to calculate the years. "About nine years," he said.

"Wow, that long? Have you always lived here alone?"

"No, I had a roommate for several years," he said. He didn't offer whether the roommate had been male or female.

"Well, you've really done a nice job with the place. It's lovely."

Greg helped himself to more chow mein. "I just keep thinking about running into you at the market the other day, out of the blue like that."

I swallowed a bite of dim sum. "Me too. Honestly, you were the last person I expected to see that morning."

He turned to face me. "I always hoped we'd see each other again."

"Me too," I said. "I used to play this little game with myself. Whenever I'd come across one of those Magic 8 Balls, I'd shake it and ask, 'Will I ever kiss Greg again?' And you know what? I never got a no. Not even once."

Greg looked at me with a teasing face. "And what else do you consult your Magic 8 Ball about?"

I grinned and sank my teeth into another spring roll, deciding not to tell him that I'd actually consulted the 8 Ball at Annabelle's apartment the day before my divorce went through.

We finished our dinner and Greg kept my wineglass filled so efficiently, I lost track of the number of glasses I'd drunk.

It was dark outside, but under the light from the moon I could make out a patch of flowers through the French doors in the back. "I want to see your garden," I said. "Can you give me a tour?"

"Sure," Greg said. "It's my little piece of heaven."

I felt a bit woozy as I stood up, and Greg must have noticed because he held my arm as we walked out onto the slate stone patio.

"Over there, those are the hydrangeas," he said, pointing to the far left corner of the yard. "And here is the cutting garden. This year I have daylilies, peonies, and dahlias coming up."

But I wasn't looking at the cutting garden. Just below the kitchen window stood a row of tulips, white with striking red tips. They were brilliant nestled against the house's yellow siding, and I walked over to have a closer look. I'd never seen them before, of course, but I felt as if I had. They were identical to the ones Elliot had given Esther in the diary.

"These tulips," I said, a little astonished, "they're beautiful."

"Aren't they?" Greg said in agreement.

"Did you plant them?" I asked, almost accusingly, as though I expected him to have Elliot upstairs, bound and gagged in a bedroom closet.

"I wish I could take credit," he said. "But they're volunteers. They were here when I bought the house. They've been multiplying over the years. There must be three dozen now."

I reminded myself that the diary I was reading was probably only a story, not reality. Yet I couldn't help but wonder if Elliot and Esther had once walked this island, perhaps in this very spot.

"Who did you buy the house from?" I asked.

"He paused to think. "I can't remember her name," he said. "She was an elderly woman whose kids were moving her into a retirement community."

"Where? Here on the island?"

"No, I think it was Seattle."

I nodded and looked back down at the tulips. They were breathtaking.

"Hey," Greg said, "why do you want to know?"

"I don't know," I said, reaching down to pick one of the flowers. "I guess I just have a thing for stories of the past."

Greg looked at me in the way that used to make me wild. "I wish our story had a different ending."

I felt his breath on my skin, inviting, beckoning, but there was that voice again, the cautionary voice. "Let's open our fortune cookies," I said, breaking free from his gaze.

"Nah, I hate fortune cookies."

"Come on," I said, reaching for his hand.

Once we were seated on the couch, I handed one cookie to Greg and kept one for myself. "Open it."

He cracked his open and read the tiny piece of paper in his hands: "'You will find the answer to what you are searching for.' See?" he said. "Totally meaningless. You could read into that a million different ways."

I opened mine and stared blankly at the words: "'You will find true love in the present, by looking to the past.'"

"What does yours say?" Greg asked.

"Nothing significant," I said. "You're right. It's nonsense." I carefully tucked the scrap of paper into my pocket.

Greg inched closer. "What if it isn't nonsense? What if it means something? About us?"

I remained motionless as his hands caressed my face, then I closed my eyes as they traveled down my neck and shoulders to my waist.

"No," I said, opening my eyes and pulling away from his arms. "I can't, Greg. I'm so sorry."

"What's wrong?" He looked wounded.

"I don't know," I said, disoriented. "But I think my heart is elsewhere." What I didn't say was that "elsewhere" meant, plain and simple, *Jack*.

"It's OK," he said, looking at his feet.

"I guess I better go," I said awkwardly as he stood up to get his keys. Before I got into the car, I ran back to the garden and retrieved the tulip I'd picked.

Greg drove me back to Bee's and before I got out of the car he said, "He's a lucky guy, whoever he is."

"Who's a lucky guy?"

"The guy who ends up with you."

Chapter 10

March 9

I could hear the phone ringing in the living room the next morning, ringing so intently and consistently that it jarred me out of a perfectly pleasant dream. *Isn't Bee going to get it?*

On the tenth ring I stood up, groggily, and walked out to the living room.

"Hello?" I said in a tone that let the caller know how I felt about being disturbed at seven forty-five a.m.

"Emily, it's Jack."

My eyes shot open. I recalled writing my cell phone number on a scrap of paper the night I visited his house. *So why is he calling the landline?*

"I'm sorry for calling so early," he said. "I've been trying your cell, but it's going straight to voice mail. Anyway, if it's not too early . . ."

"No," I stammered. "It's not too early." My voice sounded more eager than I'd anticipated.

"Good," he said, "because I wondered if you wanted to meet me for a beach walk this morning."

"Now?"

"Yeah," he said. "You have to see what's happening on the shore right now. Can you meet me in ten minutes?"

As I trudged down to the beach, I could see Jack way ahead—well, a speck that was Jack. We waved as we walked toward each other.

"Morning!" Jack shouted from his vantage point on the shore, which was several hundred feet away.

"Hi!" I yelled back.

When we finally met, he pointed ahead. "The thing I want to show you is around the bend."

"The thing?"

He smiled. "You'll see."

I nodded. "How did your trip to Seattle go?"

"It went well," he said. And that was all. "Sorry I didn't call sooner," he added, without offering an explanation.

We rounded the point, and followed the beach a little farther as it curved around the hillside. Jack stood still for a minute, looking out toward the sound.

"There," he said softly.

"Where?" I said, and then I saw it, a spout of water streaming up into the air, and then something enormous undulating beneath the sea.

I smiled like a child who has just been dazzled by a jack-in-the-box. "*What* was that?"

"An orca," Jack said with pride.

Bee always spoke of orca sightings, but even during all those summers on the island, I had never seen one with my own eyes.

"Look!" Jack exclaimed. There were two now, swimming close together.

"They come through here every year at this time," he said. "I've always loved it. I used to sit here, right here"—he paused and pointed to a boulder about the size of a large stump, embedded in the sand—"when I was a boy and watch the whales go through."

I couldn't take my eyes off of the water. "They're spectacular," I said. "Look at the way they're swimming, with such strength, such purpose. They know where their journey is taking them, even without a map to guide them." Then I paused as a thought struck. "Jack?"

"Uh-huh?"

"You said you were here as a boy. Were you ever here during the summers?"

"Yes," he said, smiling a private smile. "Every summer. The house I live in now, it was my family's old beach house."

"So why didn't I ever meet you during those summers?"

"I wasn't allowed to go down that way," he said, pausing. "Toward your aunt's house."

I grinned. "I wasn't allowed to come up this way, either," I said. "You'd think I would have seen you at least once."

His eyes met mine. "You don't remember, do you?"

"Remember what?"

He shook his head playfully.

"I'm sorry," I said, racking my brain and wishing I could recall something, anything. "I don't."

"You were fourteen—and beautiful, if I might add," he said. "My dog had gotten off his leash, and he ran down in front of your aunt's house. You were lying on a beach towel with another girl. You were wearing a bikini. A pink bikini. And Max, my dog at the time, ran right over to you and licked you on the face."

"That was you?"

"Yes."

"I don't believe it."

"Believe it."

"*Oh gosh,*" I said. "I do remember being licked by that dog."

"Yeah," he said, "you didn't seem too happy about it."

"Oh, and then he ran away with my sandal in his mouth," I said, and as I did, the memories came rushing back.

"Some way to impress a girl, huh?"

I cocked my head to the right and looked at him in a new light. "Oh my gosh, I remember *you*," I said. "You were really skinny?"

"Yes."

"Braces?"

He nodded.

"*That* was you?"

"Yep, in the flesh."

I couldn't help but laugh.

"What?" Jack said, pretending to be hurt. "You mean you didn't find a tall, gangly kid with braces and acne attractive?"

"No," I said. "I mean, no it's not that, it's just that, well, you're just so *different* now."

"No, I'm really not," he said. "I'm exactly the same. Except the acne's cleared up. You haven't changed much yourself. Except you're even more beautiful than I could have imagined you'd be."

I didn't know what to say, so instead I just smiled, a smile that started inside and traveled to my face, where it stayed for the rest of the morning.

"Hey, want to come up to my place?" he said. "I'll make you breakfast."

"I'd love to," I replied. And without thinking, I reached down and grabbed his hand, and he instantly weaved his fingers into mine, as if we'd done this a hundred times before. So what if he had been on a date the night before? So had I. We were even. What mattered now was that we were together.

I sat at the stool at Jack's kitchen island and watched as he ground the coffee beans and then cut five oranges in half and sent them through the juice press. Then he pulled out a bowl and started cracking eggs. I sat there, mesmerized by his movements in the kitchen. He was swift, yet precise. I wondered if Elliot had ever made Esther breakfast.

"I hope you like French toast," he said.

"Like?" I said. "Too small of a word. I *love* French toast."

He grinned and continued whisking. "So," he said, "did your aunt tell you any nasty stories about my family?"

"No. She won't give me any details. Any chance you can fill me in?"

"I'm really the last to know about the skeletons in the family closet," he said. "All I know is that my father warned me early on that we were not welcome at Bee Larson's house. And that scared the hell out of me as a kid. I imagined she was the witch in the Hansel and Gretel story. My sister and I were sure that if we stepped foot on her property, she'd capture us and lock us up in her dungeon."

I giggled at the thought of that.

He nodded. "We used to think her house was haunted."

"Well, it's not hard to come to that conclusion," I said, thinking of the old house's second-story rooms, which were mostly locked, and those creaky wood floors. "Sometimes *I* think it's haunted."

Jack nodded, measured out one teaspoon of cinnamon, and

whisked it into the egg mixture. "I wish I knew more about the circumstances behind all of that," he said. "I should have asked my grandfather."

"Oh, you saw him?"

"Yeah," he said. "He lives in Seattle. I was just over there yesterday. I go over at least once a month and spend a few days with him."

"Maybe you could ask him about it next time you speak to him," I suggested. "Because, Lord knows, I'm getting nowhere with Bee."

"I will," he said.

Jack's talk of his grandfather made me think of my own. I loved how, when I was a child, he'd let me spend hours with him holed up in his study. Seated at my makeshift cardboard-box desk, I'd adoringly watch him work at his big oak secretary, where he paid the bills and I pretended to type letters. Grandpa always let me lick the envelopes before he took them out to the mailbox.

Grandma Jane, on the other hand, had died quickly and suddenly, of a heart attack, and at her funeral, when my mother asked me if I'd share a memory at the church from the pulpit, I told her I wasn't comfortable with public speaking. But the truth was more complicated than that. As I stared at her casket, I looked around. Mother was crying. So was Danielle. Why didn't I feel anything? Why couldn't I muster the sadness that the passing of a grandparent deserves?

"You're lucky," I said to Jack.

"Why so?"

"Because you're close to your grandfather."

"Oh, I know," he said, dipping thick slices of bread into the egg mixture. I could hear the sizzle of the bread hitting the hot butter when he dropped each slice into the cast iron skillet. "You'd really love him too. He's such a character. Maybe you could meet him sometime. I know he'd be crazy about you."

I smiled. "How do you know?"

"I just know."

The coffee machine beeped, and Jack poured me a cup.

"Cream or sugar?"

"Just cream," I said, watching to see if he also poured a cup, but instead he reached for a glass of orange juice.

Annabelle had been doing some unscientific research on couples and coffee preferences. According to her very preliminary findings, if you could even call them findings, people who like their coffee dressed in the same manner have greater success in marriage.

I sipped my coffee, and walked into the living room, where Russ was curled up next to the fireplace. He looked cozy and teddy-bearish, as all golden retrievers do. I squatted down to pet him, and I noticed a small piece of green paper in the corner of his mouth. The rest of what looked like a chewed-up green file folder lay to his right. There were some loose papers scattered around him too.

"Russ," I said, "you naughty dog. What have you gotten hold of?" He rolled over and yawned, and I saw that there were more rumpled papers beneath him, presumably papers he had planned to snack on. I picked up a slobber-drenched page and squinted. Most of the type on the page was blurred and torn, but at the top were the words "Seattle Police Department, Bureau of Missing Persons." I set it down, a little startled, and picked up another, which was a photo-copied news clipping from the Bainbridge Island paper. It looked old—I could tell by the type—and also nearly unsalvageable.

"Emily?" Jack called out from the kitchen.

I nervously dropped the page in my hand. "Uh, I'm just here with, um, Russ. He seems to have gotten into something."

Jack appeared around the corner with a plate of French toast in his hands, but he quickly set it down.

"Russ, go to your bed!" he shouted.

"Let me help you," I said.

"*No*," he said, one decibel below a shout. "I mean, no, sorry, you shouldn't have to help with this mess. I've got it."

I took a step back, wondering if I'd seen something I shouldn't have. Jack tucked the file and its dilapidated and slobbered-on contents under a stack of magazines on the coffee table.

"Sorry about that," he said. "I wanted this breakfast to be perfect."

"No big deal," I said. "Dogs will be dogs."

I watched Jack pile the pieces of French toast one on top of another and then dust the platter with powdered sugar.

"There," he said, holding out a plate for me. "Your breakfast."

I reached for my fork just as the phone in the kitchen rang.

"I'll just let the machine get it," he said. I took a bite and nearly swooned, but my attention drifted when I heard a woman's voice on the answering machine.

"Jack," began the voice, "it's Lana. It was so good having dinner with you last night. I wanted to—"

Jack raced out of his chair and turned the machine off before she could continue.

"Sorry," he said a little sheepishly. "That was, uh, a client. We met last night to discuss a painting."

I didn't like the tone of her voice. It sounded too personal, too intimate. I wanted to ask him twenty questions. No, two hundred questions. Instead I smiled politely and continued eating. I didn't doubt that the woman was a client, but if that was all, what was he so skittish about? What was he trying to hide?

Just as he sat down and took a bite, the phone rang again. "Good grief," he said.

I gave him a look that said, "It's OK, go answer it," but I really wanted to pull the plug out of the wall so that whoever this woman was, she wouldn't call again.

"Sorry," Jack said, running back to the kitchen to answer the phone.

"Hello?"

He paused for a few moments.

"Oh no," he said.

There was a long pause before he spoke again. "Of course. She's right here. I'll get her."

Jack ran back into the dining room and motioned for me to come to the phone. "It's your aunt."

My heart nearly jumped out of my chest as I picked up the phone.

"Emily?" Bee's voice sounded frantic and confused.

"Yes," I said. "Bee, what is it? Is everything OK?"

"I'm sorry to disturb you, but Henry was out on the beach this morning and he said he saw you walking toward Jack's so I, well . . ." Her voice was quivering.

"Bee, what is it?"

"It's Evelyn," she said, sounding lost. "She was here for breakfast this morning. And she . . . she collapsed. I called 911. They're taking her to the hospital now."

I didn't hesitate. "I'll be right there."

"No, no," she said. "There isn't time. I'm leaving right now."

"I understand," I said. "You go. I'll find my way there."

I didn't have to ask if Evelyn had hours or minutes left. I already knew. And I sensed that Bee knew too, instinctively, in the way of twins, or soul mates, or lifelong friends.

I hung up the phone. "Evelyn is in the hospital," I said, shaking my head in disbelief.

"I'll drive you," Jack said.

I glanced at the table and the plates full of perfect French toast that had suddenly lost their appeal.

"Just leave it," he said. "If we go now, we can be there in under a half hour."

Chapter 11

The nearest hospital was thirty minutes away, off the island in Bremerton, a small city to the west. We crossed a bridge to the peninsula, and I instantly felt the island's aura dissipating, like coming back down to earth from some otherworldly stratosphere.

When we arrived, Jack and I ran to the reception desk and asked Evelyn's room number.

The white-haired woman behind the counter took so long, I wanted to jump over the desk, commandeer her computer, and find the information myself. The tapping of my finger on the counter probably told her as much.

"Yes," she said, "here she is: sixth floor."

When we got to her room, Jack stood back. "I'll wait outside," he said.

I shook my head. "No, come in." I wouldn't let him feel like an outsider, like he was shunned. Not any longer. Whatever reservations Bee had about his family would end with this generation, I decided.

"Nah," he said. "It's OK. I'll be here when you need me."

I didn't push him, and instead nodded and opened the door to the room. Inside, Bee was sitting at Evelyn's bedside, holding her hand.

"Emily," she said, "we don't have much time left."

"Oh, cut it out, Bee," Evelyn said. I was glad to hear the life, the spunk, was still in her voice. "I will not let you carry on like this, sobbing like a baby. Will someone get me out of this awful gown and into something decent, and for the love of God, someone get me a cocktail."

I could see why Bee loved her so much. I loved her too. "Hi, Evelyn," I said.

She smiled, and when she did, I could see the exhaustion in her eyes. "Hi, dear," she replied. "I'm sorry, your geriatric friend has probably pulled you away from an exciting date."

I smiled. "I actually brought him with me."

Bee looked up at me, concerned, as if the thought of Jack being near her caused her great consternation.

Evelyn ignored Bee's mood. "You light up when you talk about him."

No one had ever said I lit up around Joel. In fact, it had been just the opposite. People always told me I looked tired, worn down, when we were out together.

"Enough about me," I said. "How are you feeling?"

"Like an old lady with cancer," she said. "But a martini would help."

Bee sat up, as if she knew exactly what she had to do. "Then a martini it is," she said, standing. "Emily, will you stay here with Evelyn? I'll be right back."

"I'm not going anywhere," I said reassuringly. I thought it was sweet that she was going to try to fulfill her dying friend's wish, but I wasn't sure how she would pull it off. Drive to a liquor store? Buy a shaker? And then there was the business of smuggling the ensemble in past the nurses.

Once Bee had left, Evelyn leaned in. "How's your reading coming?" she said. There were so many wires and monitors hooked up to her that it felt strange to talk about anything other than her illness, but I sensed that she wanted none of that.

"I'm absolutely enthralled," I said.

"How far are you into the story?"

"Deep," I said. "Esther has just gone to meet Elliot at his house."

Evelyn closed her eyes tightly, and opened them again. "Yes," she said.

A nurse entered the room and fiddled with an IV line. "Time for more morphine," she said to Evelyn.

Evelyn ignored her and continued to stare at me intently. "So what do you think?"

"About what?"

"About the story, dear. The love story."

"How do you know this story, Evelyn?"

She paused and smiled, looking up at the ceiling before her eyelids got heavy. "She was always such an enigma."

I gasped. "Evelyn, who?"

Her breathing was labored and slow and it occurred to me that the intravenous medicine had kicked in. "Esther," she said softly. "Oh, how we loved her. We all loved her."

Evelyn's eyelids looked heavy, and I stifled my urge to quiz her further.

"You will make it right, dear, I know you will," she said weakly, slurring her words. "You will make it right for Esther, for all of us."

I reached for her hand and laid my head on hers, watching her chest rise and fall with each strenuous breath. "Don't worry, Evelyn," I said. "You don't have to worry anymore. Just rest."

Bee returned about thirty minutes later, looking exhausted

herself, with a brown paper bag in hand. "Evelyn, your martini. I will make it now."

"Shhh," I said. "She's sleeping." I made room for Bee to take her rightful place by Evelyn's bedside, to soak up every last second with her best friend.

Jack had been in the waiting room for at least an hour, and when I walked out to see him, he stood up nervously. "Did she . . . ?"

"No," I said. "Not yet. Bee is with her now. But there isn't much time."

"Is there anything I can do?"

He walked toward me, and his eyes searched my face. Right there in the waiting room he wrapped his arms around me and held me tight, tighter than anyone had held me before. I looked out the window, over his shoulder, and the view wasn't much—large stretches of pavement with an occasional clump of dandelions courageously poking up out of the asphalt—but a boarded-up movie theater caught my eye. The marquee read E.T., and I wondered if it had remained like that since the 1980s.

I looked up at Jack, and this time I really looked at him, deep into his eyes. He pulled me close and kissed me. Even though everything felt unsettled and unanswered, at that moment, I couldn't deny the fact that everything also felt right.

Evelyn died a few hours after I left the room, but not before Bee had made her that martini. In mere minutes, she had shaken over ice gin and vermouth, garnished with an odd number of olives for luck. Evelyn had opened her eyes briefly and shared a final drink with her best friend. It was a parting act that suited them perfectly, and when we were home that night, Bee made another round, and we toasted Evelyn's memory.

I asked Bee if she wanted me to stay up with her, if she wanted a shoulder to cry on, but she said no, that she just needed sleep.

I did too, but not with Evelyn's words ringing in my head. *How did she know Esther? How did the diary end up here, in Bee's guest room? And why did Evelyn think these pages were meant to be found— meant to be found by me?*

Chapter 12

March 10

I didn't want to get out of bed the next day, but I couldn't sleep, either, so I turned my attention to the diary.

Bobby was asleep when I got home from Elliot's. I knew when I walked in the front door, because I could hear him snoring, just as I had left him. I undressed and pulled back the bedspread inch by inch, praying I wouldn't wake him. I stared at the ceiling for a long time, thinking about what I'd done, thinking about where I'd go from here, but no answers came. And then Bobby rolled over and flung his arm over me, pulling me close. I knew what he had in mind when he started nuzzling my neck, but I rolled over and pretended to be asleep.

The next morning, when Bobby had left for work, I wanted to call Frances and tell her everything. I longed to hear her voice, and her approval. Instead, I called Rose in Seattle.

"I saw him last night," I said.

"Oh, Esther," she said. Her tone was neither judgmental nor encouraging. It reflected the worry and excitement and terror I felt about the decisions that lay ahead. "What are you going to do?"

"I don't know."

She paused for a minute. "What does your heart tell you?"

"My heart is with Elliot. It will always be with Elliot."

"Then you know what you need to do," she said simply.

Bobby came home that night, and I made him his favorite meal: meat loaf, boiled potatoes, and string beans with butter and thyme. On the surface, it was as if nothing had changed. We were a happily married couple having a nice anniversary dinner. But I carried a heavy weight on my shoulders, the weight of great guilt.

With every glance from Bobby, every question, every touch, my heart came closer to bursting. "What's different about you?" he asked at dinner.

"Nothing," I said quickly, worried that he could see right through me.

"It's just that, well, you seem different," he continued. "More beautiful than ever. March becomes you."

I felt as though I could no longer carry on and decided that I needed to go to the priest and air my secrets in a confessional booth.

So, I dressed the baby in her Sunday clothes and we drove to Saint Mary's. My heels clicked on the wood floors as I walked through the church to the row of confessionals along the right-hand wall. I walked into the first one and sat down, bouncing the baby on my lap.

"Father," I said. "I have sinned."

"What is it, child?"

I suppose he expected me to say something like "I have gossiped" or "I have coveted my neighbor," or something generally benign. Instead I opened my mouth and said the unthinkable.

"I've slept with a man who isn't my husband."

There was silence on the other side of the booth, an uncomfortable silence, so I spoke up again.

"Father, I love Elliot Hartley, not my husband, Bobby. I am a horrible woman for it."

I listened for a sign that the priest was there, that he was listening. I wanted him to tell me I was forgiven. I wanted him to tell me to do a thousand Hail Marys. I wanted him to lift the weight off my shoulders, because it was getting too heavy for me to carry.

Instead he cleared his throat and said, "You've committed adultery, and the Church does not condone such behavior. I suggest you go home and repent to your husband and pray that he forgives you, and if he does then God will forgive you."

Aren't all sins the same in God's eyes? Isn't that the message I'd heard in Sunday school since childhood? Instead, I felt like a heathen, unable to work my way back to heaven.

I nodded and stood up, holding the baby over my shoulder, and walked out feeling great shame, with an even heavier burden to carry. The big brass doors closed loudly behind me.

"Hello, Esther." It was a woman's voice behind me in the parking lot. I turned around and saw that Janice was walking toward me, with a strange smirk on her face, but I just kept walking.

Another day went by. Bobby came home from work and I thought about telling him, but I couldn't bring myself to say the vulgar words I'd need to say to explain myself. No matter how I spit it out, there was the fact that I'd given myself to someone else. Bobby was always so sunny, always so cheerful, even when I wasn't. He was too good a man. I couldn't bring myself to shatter him. I wouldn't do it.

And then the next morning, after Bobby had gone to work, I got the call—the call that made me question every choice I'd made to this point, every emotion I'd felt.

"Mrs. Littleton?" the female voice said on the other end of the line.

"Yes," I said.

"This is Susan from Harrison Memorial Hospital; I'm calling about your husband. He's in the hospital."

She told me that Bobby had collapsed just before walking onto the ferry that morning, and an ambulance had rushed him to the hospital in Bremerton. When I heard her say the words "heart attack," my own heart cracked a little—cracked with regret, the way it does when you have been cruel to someone whom you should have loved. Bobby didn't deserve this. He didn't deserve any of this, and I decided to make it up to him.

What would I do with the baby? I couldn't bring her to the hospital, not today, not under these circumstances. So I knocked on Janice's door, as a last resort, and handed the baby over, wrapped in pink blankets. I didn't like the way Janice looked at her, with the disquieting sense that she'd take my child, take my home, take my place in Bobby's bed if she had the chance.

"Where are you going?" she asked, with that familiar look of disapproval in her eyes.

"Something very important has come up," I said. "It's an emergency." I didn't dare tell her it was Bobby. She'd be at his bedside before I could blink an eye.

"Of course," she said. "And Bobby, when will he be home?"

"Not for a while," I said, running to the car. "Thanks for watching the baby. I really appreciate it."

I drove to the hospital and when I arrived, I backed into another car in the parking lot, but I didn't stop to check the damage. None of that mattered. Bobby needed me.

"I'm looking for Bobby Littleton," I practically barked to the receptionist. She directed me to the sixth floor, where Bobby was getting ready for surgery, and I made it to the room just in time.

"Oh, Bobby!" I cried. "When they called me I was beside myself."

"They say I'm going to make it," he said, winking at me.

I leaned over his bed and wrapped my arms around him. I lay like that until the nurses tapped my shoulder and said, "It's time." I didn't want to let go, and as I watched them wheel him away, I was haunted by the fear that I had caused all of this.

Waiting for him to come through surgery was agony. I paced the floors relentlessly; I was sure I'd walked at least three miles. Occasionally I'd look out the window, to the theater below to see what was playing. On the marquee was BLUE SKIES, WITH BING CROSBY. I watched couples, mostly teenagers, walking arm in arm, and I wished I were one of them. I wanted to turn back time and get it right, without any of the regret, without the pain.

I gazed out the window a little longer, watching couples file in for the show.

And that's when I saw Elliot.

His tall frame stood out in the crowd, in any crowd. And he wasn't alone. There beside him was Frances.

"Mrs. Littleton," the nurse said from the doorway.

"Yes?" I said, forcing myself to turn away from the window. I felt trapped between two worlds. "Is he OK? Tell me he's OK."

She smiled. "That husband of yours is a fighter. He came

through surgery just fine. But his recovery will be tough. He'll need your around-the-clock care."

I nodded.

"Speaking of which," she said, "I'll just need to see your ID, for the discharge paperwork."

I reached down to the place where my purse always hung on my arm, but it wasn't there. Then I remembered that I'd never retrieved it from the restaurant the night I'd gone to see Elliot. All of it seemed so unfathomable now.

"I'm sorry, I must have left my purse at home," I lied.

"That's OK, dear," she said, smiling. "We can do without."

"Thank you," I said. "Can I see him now?"

"Yes," she said. "But he's quite groggy. Just keep that in mind."

I followed her back to the post-op area and there he was, eyes closed.

"Hi, Bobby," I said, caressing his hand.

He opened his eyes and smiled at me. "Told you I'd be all right," he said.

Unlike me, Bobby never broke a promise.

It was at least ten before Bee and I made our way to the breakfast table. The air was thick with sorrow.

"Good morning," she said in a weak voice. She was still in her nightgown and robe. I'd never seen her in pajamas, and the garb made her look much older.

"I'll get the paper for you," I said, walking out to the front porch and finding the *Seattle Times* embedded in the mud below a rosebush next to the house. Thank goodness for the plastic bag that covered it.

"The funeral is the day after tomorrow," Bee said. She didn't look at me when she spoke, and it occurred to me that she might have been just saying the words aloud to try them on for size, perhaps to see if Evelyn's passing wasn't just a bad dream.

"Can I help with anything?" I asked.

Bee shook her head. "No. Her husband's family is taking care of everything."

I made scrambled eggs as Bee sat there staring out at the water. I thought of Joel when I did, and of the morning he'd told me about Stephanie. I had dropped a plate, a detail that I had forgotten until now. It was a piece of our wedding china—Waterford, white, with a big silver rim, so expensive that the salesgirl at Macy's squealed a little as we added twelve place settings to our registry. What once was a treasure lay shattered on the floor in jagged pieces.

"It's funny," I said to Bee, turning the eggs in the pan with a spatula.

"What, dear?" she replied quietly.

"I broke a plate."

"You broke a plate?"

"Yeah, at home, when Joel told me that he was leaving."

Bee just stared ahead, motionless.

"And I didn't care. Now, as I think back on that morning, I seem to be more disturbed about the plate than I am about Joel."

The corners of Bee's mouth turned up ever so slightly, forming the haziest smile. "Progress."

I smiled to myself, and presented Bee with a plate. "Eggs and toast."

"Thank you," she said. But she didn't eat that morning. Not even a bite. "I'm sorry," she said. "It's not your cooking, it's just . . ."

"Don't worry," I replied. "I know."

"I'm going back to my room to lie down."

I nodded and felt a lump in my throat as I watched her walk down the hall, one foot in front of the other.

I decided to get dressed and tidy the house for Bee. There's nothing more depressing than unwashed dishes or a living room piled high with newspapers. By eleven, the place was shining. The phone rang as I polished the kitchen, and I stopped to admire how it shone before I answered.

"Hello?"

"Hi, Emily, it's Jack."

"Hi," I said, loving the sound of his voice.

"I just wanted to check and see how things were going over there. How's your aunt?"

"She's holding it together," I said.

"How about you?"

"I'm doing OK," I replied.

"I'd love to see you again," he said, "whenever you feel you can break away."

"Well, Bee's asleep now. I guess you could come over."

"Are you sure?"

"Yeah," I said.

Jack arrived about a half hour later. He seemed in awe of the house—cautiously in awe.

"It's so beautiful," he said, looking around. I've never been inside. I've always wondered what it would be like in here."

"You probably imagined monsters and ghosts, right?" I said.

"And gremlins," he replied.

We walked into the lanai, and I closed the door, so Bee wouldn't be disturbed, but really so that if she came out of her bedroom, she wouldn't be startled to see Jack.

"Maybe we should just hide in the closet," he said with a mischievous grin.

"Maybe we should," I said in a sly voice, as we sat down on a small sofa facing the sound.

He reached for my hand, and I leaned my head on his chest. We sat there together for a minute, in silence, watching a robin with a fluffy brown chest pry a twig out of the grass and fly up to the top of a nearby tree.

"It's a perfect place to write, this island, isn't it?" Jack said.

I nodded. "It's certainly a storied place."

"I was just thinking," he continued, "you said you were looking for inspiration for your next book . . . have you considered writing a story about this island? Setting it right here on Bainbridge?"

I sat up and looked at his face, thoughtful, contemplative. He loved the island as much as I did; his paintings were proof. But there was something deeper, something unsaid, that punctuated his words just then, and I studied his eyes for a clue.

"There's a story in my heart," I said, watching the old cherry tree taking the brunt of the north wind and putting up an admirable fight. I used to climb its branches as a girl, sitting up there for hours eating its equally sweet and tart Rainier cherries and imagining stories about other little girls who had sat in its branches years before me. I shook my head. "I guess I'm afraid."

Jack turned his gaze from the window to me. "Afraid of what?"

"Afraid that I won't be able to tell the story with the kind of beauty and conviction that it deserves," I continued. "My first book . . . was different. It's not that I wasn't proud of it, because I was. But . . ."

Jack looked at me as if he knew exactly what I was trying to say. "It wasn't from your heart, was it?"

"Exactly," I said.

"Have you found what you're looking for here?" Jack asked, his eyes fixed on the birds out the window.

I thought of the diary in the drawer of the bedroom and realized that I may not have found what I thought I was looking for, but I had found something better, both in its pages and in Jack's arms.

I laced my fingers through his. "I think I have," I said softly.

"I don't want you to ever leave," he said. His voice sounded strong and sure.

"I don't want to either," I said.

And we sat that way for a long time, watching out the window as the waves hit the shore.

Jack invited me to join him for dinner at a café in town. I wanted to, but I couldn't leave Bee. Not on this night. He understood.

"I'd offer to cook," I said to Bee once she'd emerged from her bedroom, "but I'm afraid I wasn't blessed with the culinary gene."

"Nonsense," she said. "I didn't learn to cook until I was sixty. It comes later in life."

I nodded, glad to hear that some things do get better with age. "So how about takeout, then?" I suggested. "I can go pick something up."

"Well," she said, "Evelyn and I used to like that little bistro across from the market. Their roast chicken was her favorite."

"Done," I said. I was happy to see that she was getting her appetite back, even happier that I could do something to help.

On the drive into town, I kept the window down so I could take in the island: its green canopy and the damp, crisp air that smelled of seawater and fir trees. I parked in front of the bistro and walked inside.

It was a lovely little spot, with emerald green walls and dark mahogany trim. Each table looked inviting, as if this was the kind of place where you'd order a bottle of wine and savor it slowly until closing time. I wondered if Esther had dined here.

"I'd like to make a to-go order," I said to the hostess. She handed me a menu, and I quickly made our selections.

"It'll be about thirty minutes," she said.

"That's fine," I replied.

I walked outside, crossed the street, and sat down on a bench that faced the water. You could see ferries coming in from this perch, and in the far distance you could also see the Seattle skyline.

I was struck with a sense of familiarity when I sat down, and it took only seconds to piece it together: I'd sat here before—with Greg. He'd taken me out to dinner at a Mexican restaurant that last summer, when I was sixteen, and then we walked across the street and sat right here. It was dark by then, and private, and we kissed for what felt like forever before he drove me back to Bee's. My mother scolded me for being ten minutes late, but Bee just smiled and asked if I'd had fun. I had.

When thirty minutes had come and gone, I walked back to the bistro to pick up my order. "Here you are," the hostess said, handing me a large paper bag. She had an engagement ring on her finger—a solitaire, all shiny and new. It made me remember my wedding ring, Joel's grandmother's ring. I threw it at him a week after he told me about the affair, when he'd come home to collect some of his things. And at that moment it occurred to me that the ring may still be there, lying on the hardwood floor under the bedroom dresser. I didn't know if it was, and I didn't care.

"Thanks," I said, tucking my left hand in my pocket.

"Jack called while you were out," Bee said. There was neither approval nor disapproval in her voice.

I smiled and dished up dinner for us both. We ate in silence, listening to the crackling of the fire.

"I'm heading to bed," Bee said a few minutes before nine.

"OK," I replied.

She walked back to her bedroom and closed the door, and I picked up the phone.

"Hi," I said to Jack.

"Want to come over?"

"Yes," I said.

I grabbed a piece of notebook paper and scrawled out a quick note to Bee:

Going to visit Jack. Will be back late.

Love,

Em

I could see him from the beach, leaning in the doorway on the front porch in a white T-shirt and jeans.

"Thanks for coming," he said, smiling, as I made my way up the steps.

I felt shy, and I think he did too.

We walked inside and he helped me unbutton my coat. As he fumbled with the buttons, I felt my breathing pick up its pace. There was electricity in his touch.

He pointed to the living room, where two glasses of wine were waiting on the coffee table.

I sank into the sofa and he eased in right next to me.

"Emily," he said, running his fingers through my hair, softly, hypnotically. "I want to tell you something."

I sat up straighter. "What?"

Jack looked around the room, as if he needed a moment to collect himself. "Four years ago," he began, "I was married. Her name was Allison."

I searched his face.

"She died three days before Christmas. A car accident. She was passing the market when she called me from the road on her cell phone. She asked me if I needed anything. I said no. For a long time I was tormented by the thought that if I'd just asked her to buy some apples, bread, a bottle of wine—anything—it would have bought her a few more seconds. That it would have saved her life."

"Oh, Jack, I'm so sorry."

He put his hands to my lips. "You don't need to say anything. I've come to terms with it. I just thought you should know. It's a part of who I am."

I glanced up to the mantel, where the photo of the woman was. "Is that her?" My heart clenched. *Is he really ready to love again?*

He nodded. "That day at Henry's," he said, "I felt something—something I haven't felt since . . ."

I squeezed his hand in mine. "Me too."

March 11

I woke up the next morning with the unmistakable feeling that someone's eyes were on me. I looked up and saw that they were Jack's.

"Morning," he said.

I looked around and realized I was at his place. I must have fallen asleep on his shoulder.

"I could watch you sleep forever," he said, nuzzling my neck.

I rubbed my eyes, kissed him gently, and frantically looked for a clock. "What time is it?"

"Seven thirty," he said.

I thought of Bee, and knew I couldn't stay any longer. She'd be wondering and worrying.

Jack reached for his coat, and I found mine. "Let me walk you home," he said, reaching for my hand.

"I don't want to go," I said, pulling him back toward me.

He grinned. "Then stay."

For the first time in a long time, I felt like my heart could burst. In a wonderful way.

An hour later, I quietly slipped through Bee's front door. The door to her bedroom was still closed, and the note I'd left for her was still on the table, so I tucked it into my pocket. I hammered out a few more paragraphs on my laptop, which were mediocre at best. So when I lost the will to write, I read.

Bobby didn't mean to be a burden, but he was. Day after day, I spoon-fed him, gave him sponge baths, even helped him use the toilet. And one morning, he couldn't wake me in time to take him to the bathroom. It all happened so fast.

"I'm so sorry," he nearly cried in humiliation.

"It's OK," I said. "Let's get you to the bathroom to clean you up, then I'll change the sheets."

This was my punishment, I told myself, the price I would pay for the choices I'd made. I knew I deserved every second of it, every grueling second.

I still hadn't told Bobby, and I decided that I'd take it with me to my grave. As much as my heart belonged to Elliot, our love would be for another time, another life.

I'd heard the Vera Lynn song "We'll Meet Again" on the radio that morning, and the words haunted me. I was sure we would meet again, that we would love again—but when? Months later? Years later?

And when I heard a knock at the door one afternoon, several days after Bobby had come home from the hospital, Elliot was the last person I expected. There he was, standing on my doorstep—the doorstep of the home I shared with Bobby. As much as I'd dreamed of seeing him, as much as I'd relished that moment, seeing him there felt strange and wrong. I shuddered at the sight of him, out of place and context: unshaven, pale, eyes darting around nervously.

"I heard about Bobby," he said. "I'm sorry."

"How can you say that?" I said, looking around to determine if any neighbors were watching. "After what you did?" I lowered my voice to a whisper. "After what *we* did?" I suddenly felt overcome with emotion. Anger. Sadness. Regret. It made no sense that I would blame Elliot for Bobby's accident, but I did.

Elliot just looked at his feet.

"Why did you come?" I whispered, regretting what I had said and wishing, for a moment, that I could take him into my arms.

"I had to see you," he said. "It's been a long time."

"Elliot, you can't just show up here like this." He looked thin—thinner than I'd ever remembered him looking—and

tired. There were little wrinkles extending from the corners
of his eyes to the top of his cheeks.

"Esther, do you really think this is easy for me?"

The thought hadn't occurred to me. I always felt that he was
the free one, while I was trapped. I looked up when I heard
Bobby's voice calling from inside. "Esther, is that the postman?"
he said. "Will you give him the letters I have here by my bed?"

"It's just a . . . a neighbor. I'll be right there." I turned back
toward the doorway. "Elliot, I have to go," I said quickly.

He looked desperate. "But when will I see you again?"

"I don't know if we should see each other again," I said. It
was the hardest thing I would ever have to say, but it was even
harder watching the effect of those words on him. They were
like knives jabbed deep into his heart.

"You can't mean that, Esther," he said. "Run away with
me. We can start a new life together. You can take the baby.
I'll love her like my own. Tell me you'll come with me. You
just have to come with me."

I could hear Janice next door, opening her door, and when
I glanced toward her front porch, I could see that she had
poked her head out to watch the scene unfold between Elliot
and me.

I shook my head. "No," I said, wiping a tear from my eye.
"Elliot, I just can't."

He took a step back and looked at me with a sudden intensity, as if trying to memorize my face for the final time, before
turning toward the road. I didn't care that Janice was staring.
I watched Elliot until he was out of sight. I couldn't bear to
take my eyes off of him.

Days passed, and then weeks. Bobby was still laid up, and I
continued to care for him. But one morning, I woke up feeling

very ill. I had the chills and nausea, and ran to the bathroom to be sick. I spent the next few days in bed, and on the third day, Bobby encouraged me to go see the doctor.

After an examination and some tests, Dr. Larimere returned with a grin on his face. "Mrs. Littleton," he said, "looks like you've got a case of the influenza that's been going around this town."

I nodded. "Good, so it's nothing serious, then?"

"No, ma'am," he said. "But there is something else." He reached for a typed page inside my medical chart. "These results just came back from the lab. I'm pleased to tell you that you're expecting a child."

"What?" I said. It had never occurred to me that I could be pregnant. "This can't be," I said, in shock.

"It can," he said.

I shook my head. "How far along am I?"

"Still very early," he said, still grinning. "But, nevertheless, with child. Now, you better get home to that husband of yours and tell him your good news. That is bound to cheer up a man in his condition."

All I could do was stare straight ahead.

"Mrs. Littleton," the doctor finally said. "Is something wrong?"

"I'm fine," I said, forcing a smile and walking toward the door. But I wasn't fine. Nothing would be fine from this point forward because of one simple fact: This baby wasn't Bobby's; it couldn't have been. It was Elliot's.

Chapter 13

March 12

I decided to call Annabelle before Bee and I left for Evelyn's funeral. So much had happened here that I'd forgotten about all I'd left behind in New York, including Annabelle.

"Annabelle?"

"Hi, Em!"

"I miss you," I said. "I'm sorry I haven't called. So much has been going on here."

"Is everything OK?"

"Sort of," I said. "But first, how are you?"

"Good," she said without much fanfare, and then she dropped a bomb. "It's official. I'm finally going to face my narcissist romantic nature and admit it: I am falling for Evan again."

"Annabelle, really?"

"Yes," she said. "We had dinner and talked, and I think we're getting back to where we were."

"I'm so glad to hear that," I told her. Annabelle deserved to find love more than anyone I knew, maybe even more than I.

"And what about the whole jazz thing?"

She laughed. "I'm working on him."

I filled her in on Greg and Jack, and Evelyn.

She seemed particularly saddened by the news of Evelyn, but then, Annabelle cries during Kleenex commercials.

Bee motioned to the clock. It was time to go. She was a pall-bearer and didn't want to be late, which meant arriving an hour early just in case of traffic, even though there was never traffic on Bainbridge Island.

"Sorry, Annie, I've got to go," I said. "We're leaving for the funeral now."

"No worries," she said. "Just call me when you can."

The funeral was to be held at Saint Mary's Church, which made me remember Esther's ill-fated confession. Saint Mary's is more of a cathedral than a church, with its ornate detailing, gold-plated finishes, and cherub-painted ceiling. There is a lot of money on the island, and it shows.

Bee told me to go ahead and take a seat, that she'd join me later, once she'd helped carry Evelyn's casket to the front of the church. I could see tears in her eyes as she looked around the sanctuary, but her gaze stopped at the sight of Jack escorting an older man into the church.

I waved, but Bee looked away quickly and joined her fellow pallbearers.

Evelyn had chosen to be buried in a small cemetery on a quiet corner of the island, and when we arrived, I could see why. The place didn't feel like a cemetery. It was more akin to a park, one you'd want to return to, maybe with a picnic blanket and a good book, or a date and a bottle of wine. A sliver of the Seattle skyline, including the Space Needle, completed the view.

At least two hundred people attended the funeral, but just a handful of close friends and family came to the burial, roses and tissues in their hands. Henry was there too, as was Evelyn's late husband's family, and some of her nieces and nephews.

The priest said a few words, and then the cemetery staff slowly eased the casket into the ground. Everyone gathered around to throw in a rose or two and say their farewells, which is when I noticed Jack in the distance. He wasn't gathered around Evelyn's grave like the rest of us. Instead, he stood near a headstone a few hundred yards away with the older man he'd been with at the church. His grandfather? I couldn't make out his face to check for a family resemblance. I watched as the older man handed Jack something. I squinted, trying to make out the shape in Jack's hands, and could see that it was a black box, small enough to tuck into his jacket pocket, which he did. Jack looked in my direction, and I quickly turned my gaze back to Evelyn's grave, which is when I realized that Bee wasn't standing by my side, where she had been moments ago. Worried, I tiptoed away from the mourners and found her in the car, slumped over in the passenger seat.

"Bee?" I said, knocking on the window.

She rolled down the window. There were fresh tears on her face. "I'm sorry, dear," she said. "I just can't. I can't."

"I know," I said. "You don't have to be brave. Evelyn would have wanted you to just be you."

I reached in my coat pocket and pulled out the envelope Evelyn had asked me to give to Bee. "Here," I said. "This is from Evelyn."

Bee's glossy eyes brightened for a moment and she clutched the letter to her chest. I knew she would wait to be alone before she opened it.

"Hand me your keys," I said. "I'll drive us home."

Bee leaned back in her seat as I drove the car to the four-way stop, turning right onto the main thoroughfare that connected the north and south sides of the island. Few cars were out today, and the solitude matched the loneliness of the day, but then, behind us, I heard a police siren, and then another. I slowed the car and pulled over as, one by one, along with an ambulance, they filed into the entrance to Fay Park.

"I wonder what's going on?" I said, turning to Bee. I couldn't recall ever seeing an ambulance, or a police car, on the island.

Bee looked out the window in silence.

I pulled back onto the road, but a police officer motioned for us to stop, and I rolled down the window.

"Sorry, ma'am," he said. "We're redirecting traffic. The detour route is along Day Road. Just pull a U-turn and take your next right. There's an investigation in progress."

I nodded. "What happened?"

"A suicide," he said. "A young one. Probably no older than twenty. She jumped right off that cliff in the park."

I gasped. "How very sad," I said before turning the car around.

We drove for a few miles in silence. I wondered about the woman who had ended her life just moments before. *What was she running from, and whom did she leave behind?* When we finally turned onto Hidden Cove Road, Bee stirred in her seat. "Always the young women," she said distantly, her gaze cemented out the side window.

* * *

That afternoon we walked on the beach, we listened to music, we looked at old photos of Evelyn. We sulked. It was a day for remembering, and for me, reading. And by the next morning, we would both be ready to face the world again, each in our separate ways. I wondered if Esther would be too.

"You need a reprieve," Bobby told me one day. "The way you've cared for me these past weeks, you've been a martyr. Why don't you call up Frances and Rose and plan a lunch out or a shopping trip to Seattle? I can have my mother help with the baby.

It was a generous offer, and one I was eager to accept. I called Rose.

"Hi," I said. "What are you doing later today?"

"Nothing," she said. "Want me to come over on the next ferry?"

"I'd love that," I said. "Bobby said I could have a girls' day, a day off. I was thinking we could have lunch. And there's the street fair on Main."

"We can't miss the fair," Rose said. "I'll call Frances and invite her to join us."

"I don't know," I said, hesitating. "It's been a while since we've talked."

"Well," she said, "there's no time like the present. I'm calling her. You two will put this all behind you."

I hoped she was right.

I was glad that Rose showed up at the restaurant first. I didn't think I could bear to be alone with Frances.

I hadn't told Rose about the pregnancy yet—or anyone,

for that matter. But my condition would be obvious before too long.

Frances walked in and sat down at the table. "Hi," she said blankly to both of us.

Then she turned to me. "Sorry about Bobby."

"Thanks," I said. It was all I could say.

"Look," Rose said, breaking the silence at the table. She pointed out the window at a pair of schoolgirls with painted faces, sharing a brown paper bag of roasted peanuts. Their arms were linked together as they skipped down the sidewalk outside the restaurant. "The fair! Let's go have some fun. Just like old times."

The traveling fair made its way into town every year, usually in April, when the winter chill was a distant memory, but this year it had come early, catching us all by surprise. Every year since we were young, the three of us had reenacted our own traditions, eating cotton candy, riding the Ferris wheel, and having our fortunes read. This year we skipped the Ferris wheel and the cotton candy, and headed straight for the fortune-teller's booth.

But something, or rather someone, stopped us first.

"Esther," a man's voice called out from the crowd behind us. I turned around. It was Billy.

"Oh, hi," I said.

"Hi," he said, smiling, staring into my eyes a little too long. "Your purse," he said, handing it to me. "You left it at the restaurant a while back. I've been hoping I'd run into you so I could return it to you."

He looked hurt, but I wasn't sure exactly why.

"Thank you, Billy," I said, with a tone of apology in my voice. It had been years since we'd dated, but every time I saw him, I was reminded of something Frances had said, about the sight of me breaking his heart all over again.

"Are you coming, Esther?" Rose called out. She and Frances were standing in front of the fortune-teller's tent. I nodded and said good-bye to Billy.

Inside the tent, which was draped in exotic tapestries, a fiftyish woman with dark hair and olive skin approached us. I didn't recognize her from previous years. "How can I help you?" she said, in a foreign accent.

"We'd like to have our fortunes read," I said.

She nodded and then led us through an entryway lined with strings of beads. "Fifty cents each, please," she said. It always seemed like a lot of money, but we paid it year after year in hopes of leaving with a single grain of truth.

The three of us sat down on the cushions that were scattered over the floor. The woman spread out three cards before us. "Who wants to go first?"

Rose raised her hand.

"Good," she said, "Choose a card, please."

Rose chose a blue card depicting an elephant. The woman gestured for her to extend her hand, which she studied intently for at least a minute. Then she looked up and smiled, and simply said, "Yes."

She added the card Rose had chosen to a stack to her right, and then dealt out three more. "Aha," she said. "Just as I expected. A happy life, prosperity, and joy. I see no rain clouds in your future—in fact, not even a drop of rain."

Rose smiled knowingly. "Thank you," she said.

"Next?"

Frances nodded. "I'll go. Better to get this over and done with." She had always been uncomfortable with the idea of fortune-teller readings, yet she went with us year after year.

"Pick a card, please, dear," the woman said.

Frances reached for a purple card with a bird on the front. "This one," she said cautiously.

"Yes," the woman said, examining Frances's hand. She ran her finger along the length of her palm.

"What is it?" Frances asked impatiently, retracting her hand. "What do you see?"

"My vision is not clear," she said. "I need to consult the cards to be sure."

She added them to the deck as she had done with Rose's card and then dealt three more in front of Frances.

After she flipped them over, the woman's expression clouded. "You will live a long and full life," she said. "But your love line, there are problems there. I've never seen anything like this."

"What do you mean?" Frances said.

"It seems there will be two great loves in your life."

Frances's cheeks flushed. Rose and I giggled.

"But wait," she continued, "there is deep grief, too. And someone at the center of that grief."

"Stop," Frances said. "That's enough. That's all I want to hear."

"Are you OK, dear?" Rose asked.

"Yes," she replied stiffly, rubbing her palm as if to rub off the fortune she'd just been read.

"I guess that leaves me," I said, turning to the woman.

Before she even offered me a card, she looked into my eyes and then frowned.

"I'll pick that one," I said, pointing to the pink card with the dragon on the front.

The woman looked worried, as though I'd just committed a cardinal sin of fortune-telling, but she reached for my hand anyway.

My examination took the longest of all. I waited patiently

as she ran over the lines of my hand again and again, as if trying to piece something together. After several minutes, she let go of my hand suddenly, as if something had startled her. Then she consulted the cards, laying three out before us.

She stared at them for a long time, and then she finally opened her mouth. "I'm sorry," she said. "I will give you a refund."

"No," I said. "I don't understand. Why can't you tell me what you see?"

She hesitated and then said, "I can't."

I leaned in and grabbed her hand. "I need to know," I said with such intensity that I think it startled Rose and Frances. "I have to know."

"All right," she said, "but maybe you will not like what I say."

I said nothing and just waited, waited for her to tell me this thing, this terrible thing that was my fortune.

"There is little time," she said. "You must follow your heart." She paused to think of the right word. "Before it is too late."

"What do you mean, before it's too late?"

"There is trouble here for you. Trouble for your life line."

We all knew exactly what she meant. But Frances was the only one to react.

"Enough," she said. "We're getting out of here."

"Wait," I said. "I want to hear the rest."

The woman looked at Frances, and then back at me. "You must write."

"Write what?"

"Your story."

Frances threw up her hands and walked out of the booth, leaving Rose and me there to make sense of this woman's cryptic message.

"What story?"

"The story of your life," she said.

I shook my head. "Why?"

She nodded. "It must be done. You must write it. Your words, dear, will have great importance for . . . the future."

I sat up in bed and read that last line over again.

Could this be the sort of eerie hint that Evelyn gave me—that these pages are meant to be in my hands? But how could any of this have anything to do with reality, with here and now? Why would a story from the 1940s, from someone I know nothing about, have any relevance to my life? How could it? None of it made sense, yet somewhere in my heart, I was beginning to feel that maybe it did.

Chapter 14

March 13

By the following day, Bee was doing better. She was sleeping less, eating more, and laughing a little. And when I suggested that we play a game of Scrabble, she didn't just say yes; she said, "And you think you can beat *me*?"

I was glad to see the spark in her eyes again, even if she did beat me with the word *tinware*. I said it was a made-up word, and she swore it wasn't.

I countered. "Cookware, glassware, silverware—real words. But tinware?"

She pulled out a dictionary, and sure enough, she expanded my vocabulary.

"Want to play another round?" I asked.

"No," she said. "I'd just beat you again."

"I'm glad to see you smiling."

She nodded. "Evelyn wouldn't have wanted me to carry on like I was. I can hear her now: 'For the love of God, get yourself out of bed, get yourself dressed, and stop feeling sorry for yourself.'"

"Yep," I said. "That sounds like her."

She slipped off her reading glasses and reached into the drawer of the coffee table. "Before I forget," she said, "I have something for you—from Evelyn."

"What do you mean?" I said. "She gave you something to give to me?"

Bee shook her head. "I was over at her house this morning," she said. "Her family is cleaning out her belongings. They found this."

She handed me a 5 x 7 manila envelope with my name on it. It was sealed with a piece of masking tape.

I looked at Bee, puzzled. "What is it?"

She shrugged. "I don't know, dear. Why don't you open it?" Then she started walking down the hallway to her bedroom and closed the door.

Inside was a familiar photo. The black-and-white scene was almost identical to the one that hung in the hallway of my childhood home—Bee on a beach blanket, surrounded by friends. Yet the photo had clearly been snapped after the one I'd come to know so well. This image had been captured seconds later, because the woman next to Bee, the one who had been whispering in her ear moments before, faced the camera now. You could see her face, her smile, those beautiful, piercing eyes. I knew in an instant that she was the same woman in the portraits at Henry's and Evelyn's. Attached by paper clip was a note, which I carefully unfolded:

Dear Emily, I thought you'd like to have a photo of Esther. Lots of love, Evelyn.

I took a deep breath and blinked hard, walking back to my bedroom. *I knew it was her.* I set the envelope down, but realized there was something else inside. I reached my hand in and pulled out a delicate gold chain punctuated by a simple gold starfish. *Esther's necklace.* My heart ached as I held it in my hands.

We didn't talk about the fortune-teller visit after that day—not I, not Rose, and certainly not Frances. But I took her advice to heart and wrote my story, every word of it.

For a while, things started to feel normal again. Bobby's health improved, my guilt subsided, and if I couldn't force myself to stop loving Elliot, I could force myself to stop thinking about him, and that's what I did. And maybe Frances did too. She offered me a room in her house, if I wanted to leave Bobby and start over. But I said I'd manage. I thought I had it figured out—that is, until the night that everything changed.

Bobby hadn't told me that Father O'Reilly was coming. And when I answered the door, I felt my palms moisten. The last time we'd talked, I'd told him about my infidelity, and he'd told me to tell Bobby, which I hadn't done.

"Hello, Mrs. Littleton," he said in a clipped tone. "I'm here to see your husband."

I wanted to tell him to go home, back to the parish, but I let him in instead, fearful of what he might say once he was inside.

"Father O'Reilly," Bobby said from the sofa. "I'm so glad you could come." Bobby explained to me that the priest had promised to pray for him, offering a blessing upon him in his recovery.

"Yes, it's so good of you to come," I said, forcing a smile.

"Esther," said the priest, "if you wouldn't mind, I'd like some private time with Bobby."

I nodded and walked reluctantly down the hall to the bedroom.

After a few minutes, I heard the front door close and the

engine of a car. I took a deep breath and ventured back out into the living room, ready to face my husband, my infidelity. "Bobby?"

He looked up from the couch and smiled at me. "Hello, love," he said, motioning me to come sit by him. "Father O'Reilly just left. What a kind man to come over and pray with me."

"Yes," I said, relieved.

Then there was a knock at the door.

"I'll get that," I said.

I looked at the clock. "Who would be calling after eight?" I said to Bobby as I unlatched the door and opened it slowly to find Janice, our neighbor, standing on the porch. Her eyes were red. She'd been crying.

She shook her head. "He didn't tell him, did he?" Her voice sounded desperate, unpredictable.

My heart started beating faster. I remembered seeing Janice at the church. Could she have overheard my confession somehow? No. Impossible. "I don't know what you mean, Janice."

"Of course you do," she said. Her eyes were wild now, and her voice louder. "Don't just stand there with that pretty face and play dumb. You were unfaithful to your husband. I know because I saw you that night on the beach at Elliot Hartley's house. He had his hands all over you. It was unchristian."

I turned around to look at Bobby, who was listening to the entire exchange from the sofa, a few feet away. He was standing now. "Esther, what is Janice is saying? Tell me this isn't true."

I looked at my feet. "Bobby," I said. "I . . ."

"How could you?" he demanded. He looked visibly shaken.

I ran over to Bobby. "I wanted to tell you, but then you

were sick, and I . . . Bobby, I never meant to hurt you. I didn't want to hurt you."

"After I loved you, after I gave you everything you could ever want, you go and give yourself away like a cheap whore?" The words stung, but his tone, angry and desperate, hurt more.

I approached the couch and reached my hand out to him, but he pushed it away. "All I ever wanted was for you to love me the way I loved you. How could you betray me like this, Esther? How could you?"

Bobby sat down and buried his head in my lap. I began to stroke his neck, but he stiffened at my touch. "No," he said, suddenly sounding angry. "I won't take your pity. I won't take it. If you want to be with that son of a bitch, go, get the hell out of here. I don't want to be married to a whore! A lying whore."

My hands were trembling, and I realized that Janice was still there, watching the scene unfold, in all of its ugliness, from the doorway.

Bobby stood up and started pacing the floor. For the first time ever, I was afraid of him, afraid of what he might do. He grabbed my elbow and pulled me back toward our bedroom. I clenched my fists tightly as he pushed me onto the bed. I watched as he threw a suitcase on the floor, before opening up my closet and piling some of my dresses inside. "You'll need these," he said, "to look extra special for him."

Then he went to the dresser and pulled out my nightgowns. "And these," he said, "for romantic nights." He closed the suitcase and walked it toward me, dropping it on the floor, where it nearly landed on my feet. "Here," he said. "Go."

"But Bobby," I said, starting to cry, "I never said I was leaving. I never said I wanted to leave you."

"You did when you slept with Elliot Hartley," he said.

"But the baby!" I said. "Our baby? I won't leave her."

"I'll raise her myself," he said, "and when she's old enough to understand, I'll tell her that her mother was a whore, a whore who left her husband and child for another man."

There was that word again—that horrible word.

"No, Bobby!" I cried, but he grabbed my arm and dragged me, and the suitcase, to the front door. I reached for my purse, with my diary safe inside, and was able to grab it before Bobby forced me out onto the porch.

"Good-bye, Esther," he said. And then he slammed the door and locked it.

I could see Janice watching from inside my house as I walked out to the driveway, but even though I was trembling, I didn't give her the satisfaction of crying in front of her. I would save that for later. All I could think about was my next move: Where was I supposed to go? What was I supposed to do? I looked out at the lonely road. Should I go back to the door and plead with Bobby to take me back? Beg him for a second chance? When I saw his face buried in Janice's shoulder, I knew the answer was no. So I opened the door to the Buick, tossed my suitcase in the backseat, and started the engine. My heart ached as I pulled out of the driveway; for my daughter, for Bobby, for a life I had failed. The only thing I could do was to drive. And as I revved up the engine and pulled onto the road, I glanced in my rearview mirror one final time, knowing it would be my last look at that little blue house, where a baby was fast asleep and a husband who once loved me grieved by a warm fire. I felt ashamed and lost.

There was only one place left for me to go. I just hoped Elliot would be waiting when I arrived.

I sped along the road, ignoring stoplights and street signs, past Fay Park, past the winery, and down the road that led to Elliot's house. I parked, and walked down the driveway, and when I arrived at his doorstep, I knocked. Even though I'd refused him before, surely he still loved me, I told myself. Surely he would welcome me with open arms when I told him I was carrying his child?

But there was no answer. I waited there for a while, just in case he'd been on the phone, or asleep. But there was no Elliot, just the sound of the wind blowing the screen door open and then slamming it again with such force it frightened me.

I thought about sleeping in the car, right here in his drive-way, waiting for him to come home, but it was cold, and I didn't have a blanket. I remembered Frances's offer to stay with her, so I started the engine again.

She lived just down the beach. I could have walked, but not with a suitcase. And the wind was too cold. I drove down the long driveway and was relieved to see that the lights were on, and when I stepped out of the car, I could hear music playing inside.

I left the suitcase in the car and walked to the front door. I peered in the window, and could see Frances talking to someone in the living room. She looked excited, animated, more so than she usually was. And then I could see why: Elliot was with her.

Frances was fiddling with the record player when Elliot walked toward her, reaching for her hand. I stood in the cold, watching through the window, as the two of them danced and laughed, and sipped their martinis. I rubbed my eyes, hoping that what I was seeing was just a figment. Of course, deep down I'd suspected something, but seeing it there, right before my face, I blinked hard. This couldn't be happening.

Part of me wanted to open the door, storm into the house, and make them feel the shame and desperation I felt. I ran my fingers along the copper doorknob, and opened the door slowly, before closing it again, a little louder than I had intended. No. This was all too much for me. It was time to go—far away from here. I ran back to the car, driving away so quickly that the tires skidded and squealed. I took one last look behind me and could see Frances and Elliot outside in front of the house, waving at me to stop, to come back. But it was too late. It was all too late.

I drove to Fay Park, where I parked the car and sobbed like I'd never sobbed before. In one night, I'd lost a husband, a child, a lover, and a friend. And all I had to show for it was a suitcase stuffed with mismatched clothes, and a baby growing inside of me.

I thought about my diary, this book I was working on at the suggestion of a fortune-teller. But for whom? And for what? And after reading through the pages, what have I learned? That I've failed at love and at life? I had an urge to set a match to it. But I stopped myself. Maybe it did have some value, as the fortune-teller had explained.

I knew I had serious decisions to make that night. One involved Bobby and the baby. There would be no final good-bye to Bobby—he'd made that much clear—but I longed to hold my sweet daughter once more, to tell her I loved her and to promise her that there was no other way.

And this is where my story ends. I loved and lost. But at least I loved. And on this dark, lonely night, when it's all come crashing down, that small fact gives me comfort.

What is next for me? In my heart, I know what needs to be done.

I turned the page, but it was blank, and so was the next page. *What? Why does it end so suddenly? This isn't how it's supposed to end.* Actually, it wasn't an ending at all. It was a nonending.

I opened up the drawer to the nightstand, hoping a loose page might have detached from the spine, but there was nothing but a layer of dust.

I felt a sense of loss as I closed the diary, stroking its worn velvet cover once more before carefully setting it back into the drawer where I'd first found it. Life already felt lonelier without Esther in it.

March 14

"I miss you," Jack said over the phone the next morning.

"I miss you too," I replied, wrapping the curly phone cord between my fingers, wishing it was his hand interlaced with mine. "I've been so tied up here with Bee and the aftermath of Evelyn."

"It's OK," he said. "I was wondering if you wanted to join me today, for a picnic. There's a place I'd like to show you."

A picnic. It was cute. In all my life, no man had ever asked me to go on a picnic. I looked outside at the gray clouds rolling in, and the choppy water, which actually appeared to be quite angry as it churned and splashed against the bulkhead. It certainly wasn't picnic weather, but I didn't care.

"What can I bring?" I said.

"Just you."

After breakfast, I retreated to the lanai with my laptop, closer to the start of something—a story, a spark—than I had been in years. I stared at the screen for a long time, and let my mind turn to Esther, which is where it wanted to go. *Did she drive off into the sunset and start a new life in Seattle, never to return to Bainbridge Island? Did she turn the car around and go back to face Frances and Elliot, and did she forgive them—did she forgive* him? *And what about Frances?* As much as I wanted to believe that this story had a happy ending, something in me feared it didn't. There was darkness lurking that final night. I could feel it through the pages.

I didn't type a single word that morning, and that was OK with me. There was a story brewing in my heart, one I knew would take time to develop. I'd wait for it. I'd be patient.

Before noon, I dressed for my picnic date with Jack. He didn't say whether we were supposed to meet on the beach or whether he'd be picking me up, but then I heard the doorbell ring, followed by Bee knocking on my door. "Jack's here," she said without making eye contact.

"Thanks," I said. "I'll be right out."

I put on a sweater, and grabbed my jacket, just in case, then walked out to the living room, where he was waiting. He didn't look nervous at all standing there with Bee, and I was glad for it.

"Hi," I said, grabbing my bag from the coffee table.

He reached for my hand. "Ready?"

"Yes," I replied.

"Oh," he said, pulling out something he had tucked under his arm. It was a package, wrapped in brown paper and tied with twine, the way packages looked in old black-and-white movies. Nobody uses twine anymore. "I almost forgot," he said, looking at Bee. "My grandfather wanted you to have this."

Bee looked startled, embarrassed, even, as Jack handed her the package. She held it in her hands as though there was a fairly good chance that it contained explosives.

I desperately wanted to know what was inside, but Bee

deliberately set it down on the coffee table and said, "Well, don't let me keep you two."

In the car, I asked Jack about the package. "Do you have any idea what your grandfather gave Bee?"

"No," he said. "He wanted to deliver it himself, that day at the funeral, but he didn't find a chance to talk to her."

"It was a hard day for her," I said, remembering how she'd retreated to her car at the cemetery. "I'm sorry I missed the chance to meet your grandfather."

"He wanted to meet you too," he said, grinning. "It was all he talked about on the way home. He thought you were quite beautiful. I'd love to bring you out to see him."

"That would be great," I said, "but when?"

"I've got a meeting with a client tomorrow, but how about the day after that? I'm supposed to go visit him that afternoon. You could come with me."

"Yes," I said, smiling. "It's a date."

Jack drove to the far west side of the island, where I'd never been before, even on all of my summer visits. He pulled into what looked like a parking lot, but there were thorny blackberry bushes on all sides, and just enough gravel to park two or three cars. He grabbed a picnic basket out of the trunk. It was one of those old-fashioned wicker ones, red and white gingham with dark red trim. *Perfect*.

"Want to guess where I'm taking you?" he said, grinning mischievously.

"Honestly," I replied, "I have no idea." Branches tugged at my clothes as we pushed through the overgrown brush.

"I should have brought my machete," Jack joked. "I guess nobody comes down here anymore."

"Down where?"

"You'll see."

Darkness descended as we walked beneath a thick canopy of trees. But then, just ahead, I could see a patch of light.

"Almost here," Jack said, turning to me and smiling, as if to reassure me that our jungle walk would soon be over. But I didn't mind it, actually. It was a beautiful scene worthy of a painting—untouched old-growth trees deeply rooted in a carpet of light green moss.

He pushed aside some bushes and motioned with his arm for me to go ahead of him. "You first."

I burrowed through the small opening that Jack had created for me and emerged before an inlet enclosed by rocky hillside. The water was the color of emeralds, and I wondered how this was possible, given that the sound was so decidedly gray. A small plume of water—a waterfall, but not a loud, forceful one, just a trickle—was winding down one side of the cliff, making its descent into the pool below. Birds chirped in stereo.

There was a small patch of sand free of barnacle-covered rocks, like the beach in front of Bee's, and that's where Jack spread a blanket out. "What do you think?" he asked proudly.

"It's unbelievable," I said, shaking my head. "How in the world does water get that color?"

"It's the minerals in the rock," he replied.

"How did you find this place?"

"This is the lagoon that my grandfather used to take girls to," he said, grinning. "He took me down here when I was sixteen—a family rite of passage. He told me to swear never to tell a soul about it, unless that soul happened to be female."

"Why all the secrecy?" I asked.

He shrugged. "He and a friend discovered it when they were boys, and they never told anyone about it. I guess they wanted to keep it to themselves."

I nodded and looked back out at the striking water. "I can see why."

Jack peered into the picnic basket and I sat down next to him. "I love your family stories," I said. "I wish mine weren't so secretive about theirs."

"Oh, mine have secrets too," Jack said quickly. "There's something I'm trying to figure out, actually."

"What?" I asked, perplexed.

"Well, I found some old newspaper clippings in a box in the attic shortly before my grandmother died," he said.

"What newspaper clippings?" I remembered the file I'd seen Jack's dog get into earlier in the month.

"Hey, look," Jack said, pointing to the sky, very obviously changing the subject. I didn't protest. Whatever it was about his family's history, I had a feeling he'd tell me in time.

Dark clouds hung all around us, but right overhead, there was a ray of sunshine beaming down, as if it had appeared just because we were having a picnic.

"Hungry?" he said, turning to the basket.

I surveyed the spread. "Yes!"

He set out two plates, forks and knives, and napkins, and then pulled out several plastic containers. "OK, we have potato salad, and fried chicken, coleslaw, and fruit salad with mint—it grows like a weed in my garden—oh, and corn bread."

It was a feast, and I ate unabashedly, filling my plate and then filling it again, until I settled into the blanket and sighed.

Jack poured wine, rosé, for both of us, and I wedged my back against his stomach, so that I could lean back fully into him, as if he were my personal armchair.

"Jack?" I said, after we sat like that for several minutes.

He pulled my hair back a little and kissed my neck. "Yes?"

I turned around to face him. "The other day," I said, "I was in town, and I saw you with a woman."

His smile vanished.

I cleared my throat. "At the bistro. The night you said you were going to call me."

Jack said nothing, and I looked down at my hands. "I'm sorry, this is all coming out wrong. I'm sounding like a jealous wife."

He reached for my hands. "Listen," he said, "You don't sound jealous at all. And let me reassure you, there is no one else."

I nodded, but my face told him the explanation wasn't exactly satisfying.

"Listen," he said. "She's a client. She's commissioning a painting for her mother. That's all there is to it."

I remembered the woman who'd left a message on his answering machine, and how he'd acted afterward. Jack had secrets, indeed. But I decided to trust him anyway. When he opened his mouth again, I reached my hand up to his lips, then I pushed him to the ground, climbed over his chest, and kissed him like I'd wanted to kiss him for a long time.

His hands reached up and unbuttoned my shirt, and as it slid down my arms, I felt his warm hands on my torso, fumbling with the zipper of my jeans until he got it.

"Let's go swimming," he whispered in my ear.

"Now?" I said, feeling cold just thinking about it.

"C'mon," he said, "I'll keep you warm."

I grinned and watched him strip down to his boxers as I slipped off my jeans. He grabbed my hand and led me down to the water's edge, where I cautiously put one toe in.

"Brrr," I muttered. "It's way too cold. You can't be serious."

But Jack just wrapped his arms around me, his front glued to my back, and we slowly walked in together. With each step, it became less cold and more inviting, and when the water reached my chest, and Jack's waist, he turned me around and pressed me against his body, so that I could feel every part of him, and he could feel every part of me.

"Are you cold?" he said softly.

"I'm perfect."

It was dark by the time Jack drove me home, and my hair was still damp and caked with salt water when I walked in the door. Bee looked up from her book.

"He took you to the lagoon, didn't he?" Her tone wasn't angry or upset, just matter-of-factly, the way one might say, "It was cold today, wasn't it?"

"Yes," I said. "How did you know?"

Bee just smiled and set her book down. "You look like you need a hot bath. Come, I'll get one ready for you."

Chapter 15

March 15

I was still at the breakfast table reading the paper and eating bites of waffles, which I'd slathered in far too much maple syrup, when Bee walked in from the garden, her cheeks pink from the cold air, with a bundle of freshly clipped sage in her hand. "Morning," she said.

This was the morning I decided it was time to clear the air—to tell Bee about the book. To ask her what she knew of Esther.

"Bee," I said weakly, "there's something I need to talk to you about."

She set the sage down by the sink and turned on the water. "Yes, dear?"

"There's someone I need to ask you about," I said, "a woman." I paused to collect my thoughts. "A woman who lived on this island in 1943. Her name was Esther."

I watched Bee at the sink. She didn't look up as she rhythmically lathered her hands with the bar of lavender soap she kept near the faucet. Minutes passed as she turned the soap over and over again as if in a trance.

"Bee?" I said again. "Did you know her?"

She set the soap down, and slowly ran her fingers under the warm water, rinsing them for what seemed like an eternity, until she turned off the faucet and held them up to the light.

"I can never seem to find a pair of gloves that don't let dirt into my nails," she said.

"Bee," I said as she walked out of the kitchen. "Did you hear what I asked you?"

She looked back at me before turning down the hallway. "Remind me to buy a new pair of gloves next time we're in town, dear."

Later that morning, I heard a knock at the door. I looked through the window and could see it was Greg.

"Hi," he said boyishly. "Sorry to drop in unannounced, but I was passing by, and . . ." he paused, pulling something out of the brown paper bag in his hands. *Billy.* I suddenly thought of Esther's childhood love, and it occurred to me then that the way I felt about Greg mirrored Esther's feelings about Billy in the pages of the diary.

"I wanted to give you this," he continued, handing me an unlabeled manila file folder.

"What is it?" I asked, confused.

"You seemed interested in the old owner of my house, and last night when I was cleaning out some files, I found this old paperwork. I made a copy of everything for you."

"Greg, that was incredibly thoughtful," I said, smiling. "Thank you."

"No worries," he replied, turning toward the door and then

looking back before letting himself out. "I hope you find what you're searching for here."

"Me too," I said.

I opened the file folder and started thumbing through the documents. Inside were sales records for Greg's house. I scanned the pages for pertinent facts: It had been built in 1901, then sold in 1941 to a woman named Elsa Hartley. *Hartley*, I thought, *that's Elliot's last name. Could it have been his wife? Did the love affair between Elliott and Esther never happen?*

I flipped to the next page and saw that the home wasn't sold again until 1998, to Greg. And the seller's name was William Miller. I was crestfallen. So what happened to Elsa Hartley? What happened to Elliot?

I ran to the door and could see Greg's car pulling out of the long driveway. "Wait!" I yelled, waving to him.

He rolled down his window and I ran up to the car. "Do you think you could give me a ride into town?

"Sure."

"Thanks," I said, climbing in. "I have some research to do."

Greg dropped me off at the municipal building, just off Main Street. At the reception desk an older woman, maybe in her seventies, maybe older, looked up from her dark-rimmed glasses. "Yes?" she said, almost mechanically.

"Yes, hi," I said. "I'm trying to find any records you might have on someone who used to live on this island."

She looked up at me curiously, as if I could be slightly crazy, and didn't I know that information about islanders wasn't remitted to crazy people? "What are you looking for, exactly?" she asked suspiciously.

I wasn't exactly sure myself. "Well," I said, "the thing is, I'm here to find out if someone who used to live on the island is still alive." As I heard the words aloud, goose bumps erupted on my arms.

"Fill out this form," she said, sighing, "and we'll send you whatever documents we can find in six to eight weeks."

I could almost feel my heart sink and then flop to the floor. "Six to eight weeks? I can't wait that long. There must be another way."

The woman shrugged. She was a brick wall. "It's our policy," she said.

I sighed, and decided that waiting was better than never knowing, so I filled out the form, writing the names "Elliot Hartley" and "Esther Littleton" on it, and left my New York address for any paperwork to be sent.

"Thank you," I said, turning toward the door. The woman just nodded.

I walked several paces, and heard a gasp behind me.

"Wait!" the woman nearly screamed. "Miss," she said again, louder, "wait!"

I turned around and could see her waving her arms at me from behind the desk.

"I think I *can* help you," she said.

My eyes widened as I set my bag down on the counter.

"I'm sorry," she said, looking apologetic now, "I just read your form here, and well, you see, I *knew* an Elliot Hartley."

I leaned in closer. "You did?"

"Yes," she said nostalgically. "Oh, he was something. All the girls on the island thought so too. We all hoped Elliot Hartley would notice us."

"And did he?" I said. "Did you date him?"

She shook her head. "I wish I had, but there was only one woman in Elliot's heart. Everyone knew that. But they had problems, so . . ."

"What kind of problems?"

"I'm not sure exactly, but they fought a lot. They were always breaking up and getting back together. But one time, it was for good. Elliot was heartbroken. He started drinking. He started going around with a lot of women—I even danced with him once. Oh, that was a night. But then he went off to war."

"Did he ever come back?"

The woman was silent, as though deep in thought. I prayed she would say yes, that he came back, as the story indicated, that he reunited with Esther—eventually, at least—and that the final half of the story was indeed true. "Yes, he did, but he wasn't the same, mostly because the woman he loved was married to someone else."

"And this woman," I said, "the one he loved, her name was Esther, right?"

The woman shook her head. "I'm sorry, dear," she said. "I just can't remember. It could have been Esther, but it's been so long. My memory isn't what it used to be."

I nodded. "Do you remember anything about her, this woman that Elliot loved? Anything at all?"

The woman leaned back in her chair and looked up at the ceiling as if she was trying very hard to recall a moment, a thought, a conversation from so long ago. "She was beautiful," she said. "I do remember that. She was the envy of every woman on the island."

"Do you know what became of her?"

The woman shook her head. "I don't, I'm afraid. I moved with my parents to the Midwest shortly after high school. I've only been back here for the last fifteen years. So much has changed since then. Did you know that they put a McDonald's on the island?"

I nervously tugged at the tassels on my bag, eager to change the subject back to Esther and Elliot. "Terrible," I said, remembering seeing the golden arches as Bee drove me home that first night. It had been a surprise.

I cleared my throat. "I'm just wondering if you have any ideas about who I can talk to. Would anyone who is still living know more about these people?"

"Well, you could check the newspaper records down at the public library," she said. "There has to be something on file about Elliot."

"Thanks," I said, a little disappointed. Sifting through county records didn't exactly sound like the quickest way to get from point A to point B.

"Oh," I said, remembering the records of Greg's house. "Do you happen to know someone by the name of Elsa Hartley?"

"Yes," she said. "She was Elliot's sister."

That makes sense, I thought. *He went to his sister's house, her garden, to get the tulip for Esther.* I would try to find her new address, I decided, and visit her.

"Wait, you said she *was* Elliot's sister?"

The woman nodded. "She passed away several years ago, as did her husband, William. My grandson used to mow their lawn."

"OK," I sighed. *Another brick wall.* "Thanks again."

"Sure," she said nostalgically. "It's been a long time since I've heard anything of Elliot Hartley," she continued, shaking her head and smiling the way one does when recalling a fine wine. "But I'll do some digging, and if I find anything, should I call you at a certain number?"

She wrote my cell phone number down on a slip of paper. "By the way," she said, "how did you say you knew Elliot?"

"It's a long story," I said, before heading to the door.

Bainbridge Island has one library—one big and beautiful library built by the Carnegie Foundation in the early twentieth century. When I opened the door, three young children barreled out, nearly knocking my bag off my arm.

"Finny, what did I tell you about waiting for Mommy?" a rather frazzled woman, about my age, called out to her headstrong four-year-old son.

I smiled, but I was really thinking, *Please, somebody shoot me if I ever name a child Finny.* Then I headed inside, where I flagged down a librarian. "Hi," I said, "I'm looking for the place where you keep newspapers on microfiche."

"You're in luck," she said. "We just recataloged the Seattle newspapers and the local *Bainbridge Island Digest* this month. They're all online now. What year are you looking for?"

"I'm not exactly sure," I said. "But I thought I'd start with 1943."

She looked impressed. "Wow, what interests you about the island in the forties?

"Oh," I said, "just piecing together a bit of a mystery I seem to have stumbled upon."

Her eyes widened. "You're a writer, aren't you?"

"Well, yes," I said, "but . . ." I was about to tell her that this had nothing to do with my writing, that it was a personal project, but she cut me off.

"Wait, what's your name? I know your face. I'm sure I've seen you on a book jacket."

"Um, Emily Wilson."

"Ahhhhhh!" she screamed, "*The* Emily Wilson, the author of *Calling Ali Larson*?"

I nodded. I hated when this kind of thing happened, even if it was pretty rare.

"Oh my God, I can't believe it. You. Here. On Bainbridge Island! *This* is an occasion. I'm going to get the head librarian down here to meet you, and maybe we can rustle up an impromptu *reading*."

I tugged at my sweater self-consciously, but she didn't seem to notice. "Look who's here," she said to a man sitting at a table to our right. "A big New York City author!" She was practically squealing with delight, and I hated to spoil her fun, but a reading wasn't what I had in mind. And frankly, I didn't feel like Emily Wilson, the author of *Calling Ali Larson*—not anymore. My time on Bainbridge Island had changed all that. Writing that book was no longer the apex of my career. There were bigger things ahead; I felt it.

"I'm sorry," I said. "I really appreciate that, but this isn't a good time for me. I really need to get a jump on this research. Perhaps another time?"

She smiled. "Of course, I totally understand. Let me show you where the computers are."

She walked me down an old staircase to the bottom floor. The walls were covered in wood paneling, and the air changed a bit from smells-like-books to smells-like-books-mixed-with-mildew. She pointed to a computer station and showed me how to navigate through the database where I could do my searching.

"Thank you," I said.

"Let me know if you need any help."

I looked over my shoulder twice, and my hands almost trembled with eagerness as I typed in Elliot's name. I wanted to cheer when six matches came back. The first, from the *Bainbridge Island Sun*, was a story about his winning touchdown at a Bainbridge Island High football game. There was even a photo accompanying the story, of Elliot in his football gear, surrounded by his teammates and one cheerleader who gazed adoringly at him. He was handsome, just as Esther had described—this was apparent even through the grainy newspaper photo.

I clicked on the next story, which was just a brief notice about his graduation from the University of Washington, and the next: his name embedded in a long list of GIs returning home from war.

There was one more story to click on. *Let this be it*, I said to myself. *Let this be the clue that I need.*

It was a clue, all right: a marriage announcement, dated June 2, 1949. "Elliot Hartley wed Lillian Appleton in a small ceremony in Seattle with friends and family. The bride, the daughter of Susan and Theodore Appleton, is a graduate of Sarah Lawrence College. The groom is the son of Adam and Suzanne Hartley, and is a graduate of the University of Washington and an employee of the investment firm Hadley, Banks, and Morgan. The couple makes their home in Seattle."

What? None of this makes sense. How could he marry someone else? This isn't supposed to be how it ended. It's all wrong. How could he have married anyone other than Esther? And what happened to Esther? Her fate was starting to look cloudy. I looked back to the wedding date, 1949, and cringed. *What happened in those six years after Esther wrote her story? Did he wait for her? And if so, where did she go?*

Hoping to find something—anything—on record for Esther, I did a search for "Esther Littleton," but nothing came back. *Did she have a different name than the one in the story? And if so, why was Elliot's name real and Esther's fictional?* I ran my fingers through my hair, the way I do when I'm nervous or stuck on a sentence, which in my recent writing life was every few minutes.

Then it hit me. I remembered the photo of Elliot at the football game. There was that cheerleader, that adoring cheerleader. *Could she be Esther? Is there a caption next to the photo?*

I searched for Elliot's name again, and clicked on the football article. The caption read, "From left to right: Members of the football team Bobby McFarland, Billy Hinson, Elliot Hartley, and cheerleader Esther Johnson."

My hair stood on end. Esther. *It has to be her.* And as I stared into that grainy photo, I knew in my heart I was looking at the author of the story in the red velvet diary.

But who was she?

I did a new search for "Esther Johnson," and at least two dozen articles came back: BAINBRIDGE WOMAN GOES MISSING. POLICE SEARCH HOUSE, CAR, FIND NOTHING. HUSBAND QUESTIONED IN MISSING WOMAN CASE. MEMORIAL SERVICE PLANNED FOR MISSING WOMAN.

I read them all. Every word. Esther had vanished, mysteriously, on the night of March 30, 1943. Her car was found wrecked in a park on the island, with a suitcase inside. There were no eyewitnesses, no clues, and her body had never been found.

But as disturbing as these details were, one fact, perhaps the most chilling of all, hit me the hardest. Esther's husband, I read in one of the articles, was Robert Hanson, which happened to be the name of . . . *my grandfather.*

I ran outside, both to get some fresh air and to keep myself from having some sort of outburst in the library. I also needed to talk to someone. I dialed Annabelle.

The phone rang several times. *Please pick up; please pick up.* It went to voice mail.

I called again. *Annabelle, answer. Please answer.* We both abided by the two-call rule: If we called back, it was important. She answered, just like I knew she would.

"Hi," she said. "What's going on?"

"I'm so sorry, but I had to talk," I said, out of breath. "Are you in the middle of something?"

She hushed her voice a bit before saying, "I'm with Evan."

"Oh, sorry, Annie. It's just that, I think I just stumbled upon my family's deep, dark secret."

"Whoa, slow down, honey. What are you talking about?"

"My grandfather," I said, "he was married to someone else before he married my grandma Jane, and I . . ." Oh God . . . could Jane be . . . *Janice?*

I had to stop and catch my breath, remembering Esther's next-door neighbor and allowing my mind to wander a bit. "And I think it might have been my mother's real mother. And, oh God, oh God, Annie, I think she may have been killed."

"Emily, are you sure? What makes you think something like that?"

It all was making sense to me now. Grandma Jane wasn't my real grandmother; Esther was. And that thing that Bee had told my mother so long ago—could she have told her that Grandma Jane wasn't her real mother? And had she gone so far as to implicate my grandfather in her murder? Was that the reason they left the island so many years ago?

"Well," I said, still gasping a little, "you know the book I found in the guest bedroom, the one I told you about?"

"Yeah."

"Well, I think I just found out who wrote it."

"Who?"

"My grandmother, the one I never knew."

"Em, this is nuts."

"I know."

"What are you going to do?"

I told her about the book, as best I could, and the clues I'd pieced together—the woman at the municipal building and the newspaper articles.

"What about this Elliot character?" she asked. "Could there have been foul play?"

"No, no," I said. "There's no way. He loved her so much. And she was carrying his child." But then I remembered an important detail: He didn't *know* Esther was carrying his child.

"This is a mess," I said, sitting down on the grass in front of the library, unaware that the lawn was wet—and even if I had been, at that moment I wouldn't have cared. "What am I supposed to do?"

She cleared her throat. "You're going to do what you came there to do," she said.

I ran my fingers through my hair. "I can't even remember why I came here again."

"To heal, Em."

I nodded. "But what about all of this? Maybe I'm prying into things that shouldn't be tampered with. Maybe I should let all this be."

Annabelle was silent for a few moments. "Is that what your heart is telling you to do?"

I shook my head and thought about the fortune-teller in the story, the woman who had warned Esther that her writing would have significance in the future. "No," I said. "And the thing is, Annie, for the first time in a long time, I know what my heart is telling me to do."

* * *

I had never been so eager to talk to Bee. Now that I had the raw facts, I craved the details to pull it all together. Evelyn had cautioned me about talking to Bee about the book until the time was right, and I decided that the time was now.

I caught a cab back to Bee's, and after paying the fare, I practically sprinted to the door, which Bee never locked.

"Bee?" My voice was loud, determined.

I looked in the kitchen but didn't find her there, or in the living room, either. I walked down the hall to her bedroom and knocked, but there was no answer, so I cracked the door open and glanced in. She wasn't in her room.

"Bee," I called out again, this time louder, hoping she was in the lanai.

When she didn't respond, I noticed a note on the breakfast table:

Dear Emily,

An old friend of mine, also one of Evelyn's dearest friends, called and invited me to stay with her in Seattle for the night. We thought we'd reminisce over photos and catch up. I tried calling your cell, but you must not be getting reception. I wanted you to join me, but it didn't work out in time. I hope you don't mind staying by yourself tonight. The fridge is stocked. I'll be home tomorrow afternoon.

Love,

Bee

I turned on the TV. I listened to music. I caught up on e-mail. But nothing silenced the thoughts that filled my mind. They were like a song on repeat. A very bad song.

It was an awful night to be alone. So when the sun set and the house started creaking, the way old houses do when it's dark and windy and you're alone, I picked up the phone and called Jack.

I didn't expect him to be there. I remembered him saying he'd be busy today. But he was—well, *she* was. The woman who picked up the phone. Before I heard her voice, I heard a man's laughter in the background—Jack's laughter. And there was music, too, something soft and romantic.

"Hello, Jack's residence," the woman said. She sounded sure of herself, as if she'd answered the phone there before. I looked at the clock: 9:47 P.M. What was she doing there at 9:47 P.M.?

"Oh, I'm sorry," I said awkwardly. "I was calling for Jack."

She giggled. "Well, he's kind of busy right now. Can I take a message?"

"No," I said. "That's OK. Everything's OK. I'm OK."

In that moment, I felt all the rage that Esther had for Elliot, and for that matter, the rage that Jane had felt for Andre in *Years of Grace*. I knew then why Esther had thrown the ring. I knew why she had married someone else. Anger churned in my heart like the stormy waves outside the window. I didn't want to end up like Esther, but I'd be damned if I stood back and watched as another man deceived me.

Chapter 16

March 16

I woke up early that morning, much earlier than I should have, given that I stayed up half the night wondering if there was a ghost in the house. When the phone rang shortly after eight a.m., it nearly induced a heart attack.

"Hello?" I said.

"Hello, who is this?" It was a man, with a deep and somewhat gravelly voice—a mature voice, one I didn't recognize.

"Who is *this*?" I said back. I have always found it unnerving when a caller asks who you are before they tell you their name. Well, not so much unnerving as just plain rude.

"I'm trying to reach a Ms. Emily Wilson," he said.

"You're speaking to her," I said. "And you are?"

He cleared his throat. "Elliot Hartley."

I nearly dropped the phone. But I clutched the receiver, clutched it for dear life, afraid that if I didn't he'd disappear back into the pages of the book, where he'd forever stay. "Yes," I said, "this is Emily."

"I hope I'm not bothering you, but—"

"No, no," I said, cutting him off. "You're not bothering me at all."

"Good," he said. "I'm calling to ask if we could meet. I'd like to talk to you in person."

How did he find me? And where is he? And is Esther still alive? And does he somehow know I was reading her book? Did Evelyn tell him?

It seemed wrong to quiz him about these things over the phone. "That would be fine," I said. "I mean, that would be great. I was hoping our paths would cross."

"Any chance you'd like to come by for a visit today?" he asked. "There are some things I'd really like to discuss with you."

"Yes," I said quickly.

He gave me his address, which was in Seattle.

"I'll catch the next ferry," I said.

"Emily, wait," he said. "You know who I am, right?"

"Yes, Elliot, I do. You're the man my grandmother loved."

A cab dropped me off at the ferry terminal, and it wasn't until I arrived at the ferry dock that I realized I hadn't let Jack know that I wouldn't be joining him today to visit his grandfather. But after what I'd heard on the phone the night before, it didn't seem to matter.

On the ferry, I thought a lot about Esther. *Did she simply run away? If so, where is she? And if not, if her death*—I gulped—*was foul play, why hasn't anyone found the body?*

I ran through the list of people in Esther's life. My grandfather certainly had a motive: anger, revenge, jealousy, maybe. But no matter how I assembled the clues, I decided there was no way he could have gone through with it. And what about the baby—presumably my mother? Did he leave her alone while he ran off to chase down Esther? It didn't seem probable, but it was possible.

Frances and Rose were out of the question, or maybe not. There was something concerning about Esther's relationship with Frances toward the end, and on that last night, when Esther saw Frances with Elliot—maybe something horrible happened there in the moonlight. *Did Frances snap?* I wondered.

The ferry pulled into Seattle, and I joined the crowd of passengers lining up to disembark. And as I stepped off the boat, I felt butterflies in my stomach, knowing I was one step closer to Elliot.

I hailed a cab and told the driver the address. Elliot had said that the Queen Anne Retirement Home wasn't far from downtown, and he was right. Less than five minutes later I paid my fare and stood in front of the building. It was in a neighborhood not far from where Greg used to take me sometimes in the summers. He bought me my first latte at a café a block away.

"I'm here to see a Mr. Elliot Hartley," I told a man seated at a reception desk in the lobby.

He leaned over a clipboard and looked at me with a confused face. "I'm sorry, ma'am, there's no one by that name here."

I felt my palms moisten and my heart start beating faster. "What do you mean? There must be some mistake. I just spoke to him, and he said he lived here, in"—I paused to look at the room number I'd written on a scrap of paper—"room 308."

The man just shrugged. "I wish I could help you," he said. "But his name is not on the list."

Is someone playing a cruel joke on me? I wondered.

"Wait," I said, not wanting to give in just yet. "Can you check it again?"

And just then a woman walked out from behind a cubicle wall. "Ed," she said, "is there a problem here?"

He shrugged again. "She's asking for a resident who doesn't live here."

She walked over to the counter and gave me a quizzical look. "Who are you looking for, honey?"

"His name is Elliot Hartley," I said.

"All right, let me check." She pulled the clipboard from Ed's hands and looked it over for a few seconds before looking up again with a frown on her face. "Oh," she said, "that's the problem—someone has been into my Excel file again. They've sorted this incorrectly. And the last page is missing. It must still be on the printer."

I sighed, feeling relief that there was still hope. "Thanks for checking," I said.

She returned a few seconds later with a paper in her hand and a grin on her face. "Yes, he's here," she said. "Room 308. Ed is new here, so he doesn't know the residents by name yet. But Mr. Hartley didn't register with me, either, probably because most everyone here just calls him Bud."

"Bud?" I said.

"One of the nurses here nicknamed him that, and it stuck," the woman said.

"I can show you to his apartment if you like," Ed said, I think because he felt bad for the mistake.

"That would be great," I said.

We walked down a long hallway, and at the end was an elevator. Ed pressed the "3" button and the old elevator barreled up to the third floor. When the door opened, he walked out, but I just stood there.

"Ma'am," he said, "this is your floor."

"I know," I said. "I guess I'm just a little nervous."

He seemed confused. "Why would you be nervous to see your grandfather?"

I shook my head, stepping out onto the third floor cautiously, as though there could be danger ahead. The hallway smelled like library books and overcooked pot roast. "He's not my grandfather, but I suppose he almost was."

Ed shrugged again, the way he had downstairs. I figured he thought I was nuts. Heck, I kind of thought I was nuts. "Three-oh-eight," he said pointing to the door. "Good luck."

I stood in front of apartment 308 for some time, unable to knock on the door. All I could think about was that I was here, on *Elliot Hartley's doorstep. What will he look like?* I closed my eyes for a moment and saw Jack's face, and it occurred to me that this whole time reading the diary, I'd imagined Jack's face when I pictured Elliot. I shuddered a little and raised my hand to knock on the door.

I could hear rustling around inside, and someone coming closer. The door opened slowly, and a man appeared. He was handsome— not just handsome for eighty, but handsome, plain and simple, even with thinning gray hair and wrinkly skin. "I'm so glad you came," he said.

He leaned against the doorway just looking at me, with warm, dark eyes, in the way he might have looked at my grandmother. "I knew when I saw you at the cemetery that you were her granddaughter," he said. "Jack didn't have to tell me who you were. I knew."

I felt my cheeks get hot. *Of course Elliot is Jack's grandfather. How did I not connect the dots in the first place? How eerie and wonderful and confusing.*

"It's remarkable, the resemblance," he said, pausing for a few seconds more. "It's like I'm looking at *her.*"

I smiled nervously, but said nothing.

"Well, look at me just standing here," he said. "Please, come in."

His apartment was small and clean. There was a little kitchen and pint-size dining area next to the living room, which was just big enough for a small sofa and two chairs. Around the corner was the bedroom and a bathroom.

"Make yourself at home," he said, pointing to the chair by the window.

Instead, I walked over to a wall filled with framed photos—mostly baby pictures and family portraits, but it was the black-and-white wedding photo that caught my eye, the one of Elliot and his bride, a bride who wasn't, as far as I could tell, Esther.

"Your wife," I said to him. "Is she still living?"

He shook his head. "She died eleven years ago."

I could detect nothing in his voice that told me he had cared for her, or that he missed her, but then again, it was a simple question, and he stated a simple fact.

"You're probably wondering if I loved her," he said, "my wife. If I loved her in the way I loved your grandmother."

It *was* what I was wondering, but I didn't dare ask.

He nodded. "I loved Lillian, I did. But it was different with her. She was my companion. Your grandmother was my soul mate."

It seemed wrong—blasphemous, even—to speak of a dead spouse in this way. I wondered if Lillian had come to accept that she came second, next to Esther's memory. If I hadn't read the diary, and seen for myself the depth of that love, I suppose I wouldn't have understood.

Before I sat down, something on the bookshelf caught my eye. Sandwiched between a Bible and a Tom Clancy novel was the dark blue spine of a book. My heart fluttered as I extended my hand to the shelf. "Do you mind?" I asked, looking back at Elliot for permission.

"Not at all," he said.

I knew it was *Years of Grace* even before seeing the gold letters of the title on the spine.

"She loved that book," Elliot said, his voice sounding distant. "After . . . well, after everything happened, I read it so many times. I thought if I could understand the characters, maybe I could understand Esther." He sighed. "But eventually it started to blur together, the way a story does when you've read it too many times in one lifetime."

"Elliot," I said, sitting down on the couch. "What happened? What really happened to my grandmother?"

"I know you want to understand," he said. "And that's why I wanted you to come here today."

He stood up and walked to the kitchen. "Tea?"

"Sure," I said.

He filled one of those electric pots with water, then plugged it into the wall. "Let me start by saying that no one could tell your grandmother otherwise. She was passionate and strong willed. Determined. If she got an idea in her head about something, that was that."

I sat up straighter in my chair. I thought about Jack, for a split second, and wondered if I had misjudged the scenario the other night. *Did I jump to conclusions like Esther did? Am I genetically wired to repeat history?*

"We were engaged," Elliot continued, "your grandmother and I. I'd scrimped and saved and financed myself to the hilt to buy her that ring. But there was a misunderstanding. She thought I'd been seeing someone else, another woman in Seattle."

"Were you?"

He looked horrified. "Absolutely not. The woman she saw me with was an old friend who owned an apartment in the city. She was engaged herself, and selling it to me for well below market value. Your grandma always wanted an apartment on Marion Street, with big windows and a dumbwaiter. It was something, this place. I wanted to surprise her on our wedding day, but she beat me to the punch."

"Why didn't you explain it to her? Why didn't you just tell her about the surprise?"

"I tried," he said. "But there was no reasoning with Esther."

I remembered that scene in the book, the anger in Esther's voice. The desperation in her eyes as she stood there on the edge of the street—or at least that's the way I had imagined it. "So she broke off your engagement and that was that?"

"Yes, that's about how it went." He looked dejected, as if the wound was still raw, as if even after sixty-five years, he still hadn't figured out what went wrong or why, or whether he could have done something differently to change the course of time.

"And she married someone else?"

"She did," he said again, looking at his hands resting in his lap, one on top of the other. "I was angry with her for a long time, and I made her pay. I dated half the women in Seattle, and I'd bring them to the island and parade them around, hoping Esther would notice. But when she didn't, I left for the war. But I couldn't even escape her there. She plagued my heart in the South Pacific. She was all I thought of and dreamed about. She was in every thread of my being."

"But you sent her letters while you were at war, right?"

"Just once," he said, his voice thick with pent-up emotion. "I was worried her husband would find them. I didn't want to meddle, but I had to tell her my feelings, in case I didn't return."

"I know what happened when you returned," I said.

"You do?"

"Yes," I said. "I read the story."

He looked confused. "What story?"

"The story she wrote about her life, in her red velvet diary. Don't you know about it?"

"No," he said. "But I'm not surprised. Esther was always writing the most beautiful stories. She wanted to be a writer. A professional writer." He paused for a moment. "This story," he continued. "May I see it?"

"I don't have it with me," I said, "but I can send you a copy."

"Would you?"

"Of course. I don't see any reason why she wouldn't want you to see it. She loved you, even after . . ." I hesitated, questioning my intention to confront him about the details of the story. "Maybe you can help me sort out the people in the story."

"I'll try, Esther."

I was startled. "Elliot, you just called me Esther. I'm Emily."

He shook his head, as if to scold himself. "I'm sorry," he said. "It's just, all these memories."

"It's OK," I replied. "In the diary, she calls her best friends Frances and Rose. Could they, by any chance, be . . . ?"

"Evelyn is Rose," Elliot said without question. "Didn't you see it on the program at her memorial service? Her middle name is Rose. Everyone called her that back then."

I nodded.

"And Frances is—"

"My aunt," I said. "She's my aunt, isn't she?"

"Yes," he said. "Back then she used to go by Frances, her given name. Nobody started calling her Bee until many years later."

"So you"—I paused to consider what I was about to say—"you and my aunt were once . . . ?"

He knew exactly what I meant, and he didn't make any attempt to refute the idea. The next few seconds of silence, as he gathered his thoughts, told me that there was something complicated about their history. I began to understand, in some small way, the emotional baggage my aunt had carried with her all these years; I saw it downloading in Elliot's eyes.

He sighed as if he'd hoped that the conversation wouldn't turn to Bee, but now that it had, he'd have to tell me the whole story.

"For me, there was never anyone else but Esther. All the other women were just scenery. But Frances . . ." He paused. "Frances was different. She was so unlike Esther, and for a time, I fell into the comfort of that. Your aunt never meant to fall in love with me, nor did I intend to fall in love with her. She told me a hundred times that she hated that she had developed feelings for her best friend's beau. She loved your grandmother so much," he continued, his face suddenly grief stricken. "We both loved her."

He paused and looked at his hands, then up at me again. "Your aunt suffered through the ups and downs, never hoping for anything but happiness for Esther and me. She put her own happiness aside. That was your aunt. But there was a time . . ."

"What time?"

"There was a time when Esther had said good-bye to me— forever, I thought—and your aunt was there, and I let things happen that shouldn't have."

The silence in the room was so pronounced I could hear his fingers rubbing the stubble of his unshaven chin. "It was the night she disappeared," he said, his eyes welling up with tears. "She'd gone to your aunt's house, and she saw us together through the window." He closed his eyes tightly. "I can still see her there. I can still make out her face. Her eyes. The sadness. The look of betrayal."

"I know," I said.

"How do you know?"

"It was all in the story." I walked over to his chair and knelt down. "Don't blame yourself," I said.

"How can I not?" he said through tears. "I betrayed her. But, believe me, if I had any hope that she was coming for me, that she wanted a life with me . . . well, I would have never been there. That night, that horrible night. Things would have been so different. But our timing was off. Our timing was always off." He buried his face in his hands.

"Elliot," I said softly. "I need to know what happened to her that night."

He shook his head. "I'm sorry," he said. "I thought I could talk about all of this. I thought I could get this all off my chest, but I don't know. I don't know if I can."

I looked into my lap and realized my fists were clenched. "Something bad happened that night, didn't it, Elliot?"

He nodded.

"You have to tell me," I said. "For Esther."

He looked down at his hands.

"Elliot," I said. "Just answer me. Did something happen to her that night? Did somebody take my grandmother's life?"

He buried his face in his hands. "Yes!" he cried. "Yes. It was me. It was me and Bee."

Chapter 17

I probably should have left then—or maybe I should have run and called the police on my cell phone just as soon as I was safe on the street. I wondered how I would have sounded on the phone with the 911 dispatcher: "Hi, I'm calling to report the murder of my grandmother—in 1943."

But it didn't make sense, what Elliot had said about his and Bee's part in Esther's death. How could he have killed the woman he loved? Or maybe I was stunned by the finality of his statement—that Esther was, in fact, dead. *Dead.* The word didn't seem to fit with the life I had dreamed Esther would go on to lead, and deep down I'd been holding out hope that maybe she was alive somewhere, somewhere far from here, and that maybe Elliot had been in contact with her and they were continuing some kind of secret rendezvous beyond the pages of the story.

If only.

"Wait, Elliot," I said. "You're saying you killed her?"

He paused for a long time. "No," he said. "But I may as well have. It is the most grievous moment of my life, dear Emily, to have to tell you all of this, to have to tell you that I am responsible for her death. We're responsible for her death, your aunt and I."

I frowned. "I don't understand."

Elliot nodded. "After she drove away from Bee's house, we were both terrified—of where she might go, or, worse, what she might do."

"So you followed her?"

"Yes," he said.

"But why?"

"Bee wanted to apologize, but I—well, I guess I wanted to take her into my arms and tell her how much I loved her, and only her, before it was too late."

"Too late?"

His eyes clouded up again as he began to speak. "Bee drove, and I rode along. We weren't sure where she was headed, so we checked the ferry terminal first, but we didn't see her car there, so we scoured Main Street. Then it hit me. I knew. I knew where she was. The park. We'd been there a dozen times together. She loved Fay Park."

"So you found her there?"

"Yes," he said, shaking his head as if to dispel the painful memories that were playing in his mind. "It all happened so fast."

"What?"

"I saw her eyes, just a flash, in her rearview mirror. I saw the look on her face. That last look. It's frozen in my mind. Every night before I close my eyes, every damn night of my life for the last sixty years, I see that face. Those eyes—they were so sad and lost."

Elliot's hands began to tremble under the strain of the past.

"Tell me what happened next, Elliot," I said softly. "I need to know."

He took a deep breath. "She was parked there in the middle of the parking lot. So we both got out. I pleaded with Bee to stay in the car. I needed time alone with Esther, but she wouldn't hear of it. She followed me toward Esther's car, but when we reached the passenger door, Esther started up the car . . . and she . . ."

"Elliot, what? What did she do?"

Tears were streaming down his face now. "It was dark. It was so very dark, and the fog. The fog."

"Elliot, stay with me," I said slowly.

"There were headlights, and the car," he sobbed, each word smothered by more layers of grief. "We blinked against the glare, and just then she drove that car straight over the cliff. Right over it. Right in front of us."

I gasped. *What about her pregnancy? What about the baby?*

"I started running after her, running toward the edge of the cliff," he continued, trying his best to compose himself. "I thought I could save her, if she had survived the fall. I was close to jumping off that cliff after her, but your aunt coaxed me back. We stood there on the hillside, staring down at the wreck. Her car was in a hundred pieces, and the engine had caught fire. All Bee could say was, 'She's gone, Elliot. She's gone. Let her go.'"

"Didn't you call the police or an ambulance?"

He shook his head. "Bee said not to. She thought they might pin us for murder, say we forced her over that cliff."

"So what did you do?"

He reached for his handkerchief. "We drove away. I was in a state of shock. All I could think of was that I deserved to be in jail. I felt responsible somehow, as if I'd caused her death."

"But what if she survived the crash? What if she was lying in agony down there on the beach? What if you could have saved her? Elliot, what if that's why she drove over that cliff? What if she *wanted to be saved*?"

He looked at me with eyes that seemed to beg forgiveness. "I will go to my grave with those same questions haunting me. But that car, seeing the way it was crushed—as horrific as that image was, it's the one thing that gives me a fragment of peace. Nobody survives a crash like that. Bee was right. Leaving that night was our only option. In those days, we would have been convicted with zero evidence. It's just the way things worked. We were there, so any jury would have determined that we drove her to it."

I sighed. "Where does this leave Bee? Do you think she has any regret?"

"Yes," he said. "A part of her died that night. She's never been the same. It's why we haven't been able to face each other, even after all these years. There's too much history between us, too much anguish. We can't look at each other without remembering that night, and without remembering Esther."

Just then, I recalled something I'd read in one of the articles about Esther's death. While the wreckage of her car was found at the bottom of the cliff, there had been no body.

"Elliot, I read that they never recovered Esther's body. How can that be?"

"Yes," he said. "I read that too."

I wondered if there was something he wasn't telling me. How could her body miraculously disappear after such a horrendous crash? Had someone actually gone down and rescued her? Had she walked away from the crash unscathed? *Impossible*, I said to myself.

"What do you think happened?"

"I wish I could tell you that I thought she survived. Since the wreck wasn't found until the next day, some speculated that she'd washed out to sea, to that beautiful water she loved so much." He paused to consider the idea and shuddered. "Others believed she did survive. And I would be lying if I said there wasn't a part of me that didn't hold on to that hope, but it's been too long. If she had survived, wouldn't she have returned to the island, her home? Wouldn't she have returned for her baby? Wouldn't she have returned for . . . me?"

At that moment, I realized that Elliot didn't know that Esther had been carrying his child that night. It seemed cruel and unfair to share the news with him now, a "you're going to have a baby!" message some sixty years too late, so I kept quiet. He'd read about it in the book soon enough, and maybe that was the way he was supposed to find out.

"But there is something," he said, looking hopeful for a moment.

"What?"

"Well, it might be nothing. But, for the record, that night as Bee and I were driving out of the park, we did see a car pulling in."

"Anyone you recognized?"

"I can't be sure," he said, "but I've always suspected it was Billy—well, Billy Henry Mattson, but he goes by Henry now."

"Wait," I said. "Henry, the man who lives on the beach near Bee?"

"Yes, you know him?"

I nodded. *So Billy is Henry.* I thought about the way he'd acted when the conversation had turned to my grandmother and the woman's photo he kept on his mantel, the one that had mysteriously vanished. Esther had considered him a friend in her diary, yet he was always appearing out of nowhere, which struck me as strange. *Was he stalking her?* I shivered. *No,* I reassured myself. Even if he had been crazy for her, Henry wouldn't have carted off her body. But then my mind started to wander. *People aren't always who they seem to be.* I remembered a time Annabelle and I had overheard a conversation between two seemingly posh women in an upscale Manhattan restaurant. They were practically dripping with jewels, and had that socialite air to them. Then one opened her mouth and said, "I've tried all different brands, but I just love Copenhagen. I like to dip after the kids are in bed, out on the terrace."

Our jaws dropped when we heard her say it. The woman actually chewed tobacco—like the construction workers who howled at us on Broadway. It was like hearing that your best friend's dad, the football coach, was a cross-dresser. It just didn't fit.

But, no, not Henry. I tried to repress the thought, but it stubbornly held on. The island of my childhood had weathered clouds and rain, but now it was dark with secrets.

"Elliot," I said, remembering my own journey on the island. "I know what it feels like when you can't quite get at the heart of a story." I paused and gazed deeply into his troubled eyes. "What is your heart telling you about Esther after all these years?"

He looked away. "I've been trying to make sense of this for the better part of my life. All I know, and perhaps all I will ever know, is that Esther took my heart with her that night. Took it for good."

I nodded, worried that I may have pushed him too far. "Don't you worry," I said. "I'm going to do everything I can to find the answers—for you and for Esther." I looked at my watch, then stood up. "It's truly been an honor meeting you. Thank you for all you shared with me."

"It was my pleasure," he said. "Oh, Jack is coming to visit this afternoon. You could stay to see him if you'd like."

"Jack?"

"Yes," he said. "He didn't tell you?"

"Um, yes," I said, caught off guard, "but I have to catch a ferry. Bee is expecting me."

"Oh," he said. "I'd hate to see you go so quickly."

I thought about staying, but quickly strengthened my resolve when I remembered the woman who'd answered the phone at Jack's house. "I'm sorry," I said. "I just can't."

Elliot look disappointed, but conceded.

"Wait," I said, pausing to think about what I was about to say. "I don't mean to pry, but do you know if there's a woman staying with Jack? A friend or family member, maybe?"

He looked puzzled.

"It's just that"—I paused and fidgeted with my sweater—"it's just that I called his house last night and a woman picked up. I thought it was strange, that's all."

He nodded. "Oh, yes, I think he did mention a woman, someone new."

"Oh," I said blankly.

He winked at me. "I don't know how that boy is ever going to settle down with so many pretty women in his life."

"Right," I said. He may have meant it as a compliment, but his words stung. Suddenly, the past couple weeks with Jack flashed before my eyes like a cheap romance novel, one in which I had been duped. *How have I been so naive? Why didn't I see this coming? How did I let myself read into things that weren't there?*

I thanked him for the visit, and let myself out—with a heavy heart and a long list of unanswered questions.

So much for true love, I thought as a cab drove me back to the ferry, *at least in my life.*

I was both happy and worried when I arrived back at Bee's later that day. However gingerly I chose to broach the subject, it would still be as startling and provoking as picking up a very old and very valuable bottle of wine and proceeding to smash it on the floor, right in front of the people who were saving it for their fiftieth wedding anniversary.

"Hi, dear," she said. "Did you go into town?"

"No," I said, sitting down on the couch, across from her chair, where she was busy working on a crossword puzzle. "I was in Seattle this morning."

"Oh," she said. "Doing some shopping?"

"No, I was visiting someone."

She looked up, surprised. "I didn't know you had any friends in Seattle, dear. You should have told me last time we were in the city. We could have invited her to join us."

I shook my head. "He probably wouldn't have come," I said.

"He?"

"Yes, he. Elliot Hartley."

Bee dropped her pen in her lap and looked at me as if I had just said something unforgivable.

"Bee," I said, "there are some things we need to talk about."

She nodded as if she had known this day would come. And when I opened my mouth, it was like a flood; everything came out.

"I know about my grandmother," I said. "My real grandmother. I found it, Bee, the diary she wrote, and I've been reading it since I got here. It's the story of the last month of her life—right up to the end. And it wasn't until this morning that I fully recognized the characters, that you and Evelyn were there, and Henry. Elliot filled me in."

I spoke in a hurried, almost panicky voice, as if I was trying to pack an entire lifetime of secrets into a single paragraph. I knew I had little time before Bee would ice over and retreat the way she always does when someone brings up an uncomfortable subject.

"And you believed him?"

"Why shouldn't I, Bee? My grandmother loved him."

I could see a storm brewing in her eyes. "So did I," she said in a distant voice. "And look how things turned out."

"Bee," I said softly, "I know about her last night on the island. I know that she saw you two together, and how you drove off after her." I paused, worrying about what I needed to say next. "I know that you left her there, Bee. How could you leave her there like that? What if she was hurt?"

Bee's face had gone white, and when she opened her mouth to speak, I almost didn't recognize her voice. "It was a terrible night," she said weakly. "When Elliot came over, I knew he shouldn't have been with me. We both knew that. But your grandmother had ended things with him, and I longed to know how it would feel for him to hold me. I'd thought about that a million times since I met him in high school, but Esther had always had his attention, until that night, when he seemed to want *me*." She shook her head as if the very thought of that was naive, silly somehow. "Do you know what that felt like?"

I was silent.

"I told myself it was OK," Bee continued. "I convinced myself she would approve."

"But then she saw you two, and . . ."

"And I knew, we both knew, that it was a mistake."

"So you drove after her."

She nodded and buried her head in her hands. "No," she said standing up. "I can't. I won't. No, we're not talking about this."

"Bee, wait," I said. "The diary—did you read it?"

"No," she said.

"But how did it get here?"

She looked at me with wild eyes. "What do you mean, *here*?"

"Here in this house," I said. "I found it in my bedroom. In the bedside table."

She shook her head. "I don't know," she said. "I hadn't been in that room in thirty years. It used to be her favorite room. I had it painted pink, for her and the baby. She was going to leave him, you know, your grandfather."

"So why did you have me stay in that room, Bee, if you weren't going to tell me about my grandmother?"

She looked depleted, as if she'd run out of answers. "I don't know," she said. "I guess I just thought you deserved to be there, to be in her presence."

I nodded. "I think you need to read Esther's diary," I pleaded. "You'll see that she loved you. You'll see that she forgave you."

"Where is it?" she said, suddenly looking frightened or spooked, or both.

"I'll get it for you." I walked to my bedroom and returned with the red velvet journal. "Here."

She took it in her hands, but there was no warmth or recognition in her eyes, just anger, and then the tears came.

"You just don't understand," she said, not making any sense to me.

"What, Bee?"

She wiped away tears. "What she did to us. What she put us through."

I walked over to her and rested my hand on her shoulder. "Tell me, Bee. It's time I knew the truth."

"The truth is buried," she said, taking a deep breath. There was rage churning in her eyes now. "I ought to destroy this thing," she said, walking to her bedroom.

"Bee, wait," I said, following after her, but she closed the door quickly, latching it behind her.

I waited outside Bee's door for a long time, hoping she'd come out and praying that she'd break through whatever pain she was holding on to, so we could talk about my grandmother openly and honestly for the first time ever.

But she didn't. She stayed in her room all afternoon. And when the seagulls began shrieking the way they always do around dinnertime, I expected her to appear and start poking around the kitchen, but she didn't. And when the sun set, I figured she'd give in and head to the lanai to mix herself a drink. But she didn't do that, either.

So I opened a can of soup, combed through the newspaper, and tried to interest myself in some made-for-TV drama, but by nine, I found myself yawning and wondering about the month of March. I had been on the island for almost three weeks, and so much had gone on, but so much had gone *wrong*.

I'd made a promise to Elliot, and to my grandmother, to find answers. Yet, I hadn't considered that maybe my grandmother had simply wanted to leave this world. Who was I to stir up the past, to stir up *her* past?

I felt too discouraged to think about it anymore. Jack had left two messages on my cell, but I didn't return his calls. I was too weary—from his secrets, from Bee's, from Esther's. So I called the airline to change my departure. It was time for me to return to New York. I knew in my heart that if I were to learn from Esther's story it would be to stay and fight—for truth and for love. But I was much too tired for that now.

Chapter 18

March 17

"I'm coming home," I said to Annabelle the next morning over the phone. My words sounded a little more defeated and deflated than I had hoped.

"Emily," she said, "you promised yourself a month."

"I know," I said, "but things have gotten pretty intense here. Bee isn't speaking to me now, and there's nothing more to say to Jack."

"What's going on with Jack?"

I told her about my visit to see his grandfather and what he'd said about the other woman.

"Did it ever occur to you that you might let him do the explaining for himself?"

I shook my head. "No, not after what I've been through with Joel. My threshold is low. I can't go there again, Annie."

"I'm just saying," she persisted, "maybe you're overreacting. Maybe it's nothing."

"Well, I wouldn't exactly call what Elliot said *nothing*."

"You're right," she said. "It doesn't sound good. But what about this whole thing with the story of your grandmother? You're just going to give up?"

"No," I said, even though I knew I was, in a way. "I can always work on it from New York."

"I think you should stay," Annabelle said. "You have more work to do."

"Work?"

"Yes, work for her and work for you." Then she paused. "I know you haven't gotten closure yet. I know you haven't cried."

"I haven't," I said honestly. "But maybe I don't have to."

"You do," she said.

"Annie, all I know now is that I came to this island seeking stories about my family, seeking truth. But all I have to show for it is heartbreak—for me, for everyone."

She sighed. "I think you're just running away from something that you need to face. Em, you're quitting on the last mile of the marathon."

"Maybe," I said, "but I just can't run anymore."

When I ventured out of my bedroom, I looked down the hall and noticed that Bee's door was still closed, so it surprised me to find her moments later sitting at the breakfast table, arranging a vase of flowers.

"Aren't daffodils just glorious?" she said cheerfully, as if we both had a case of amnesia about yesterday.

I nodded and sat down at the table, afraid to say anything just yet.

"They were your grandmother's favorite, you know, next to tulips," she said. "She loved the spring, especially March."

"Bee," I said, my voice aching with sorrow and regret. I mourned the loss of my only connection to my grandmother and her writing. "Did you destroy it?"

She looked at me with a silent intensity. "Henry is right," she said. "You look just like her, in almost every way, especially when you're mad."

She walked over to her chair in the living room and returned with the diary in her hands. "Here," she said, handing it to me. "Of course I didn't destroy it. I spent the night reading it—every word."

"You did?" I was grinning so big that Bee couldn't help but grin back.

"I did."

"And what did you think?"

"It reminded me of what a wild and impulsive and wonderful woman your grandmother was, and how much I loved her and have missed her."

I nodded, embracing the contentment I would continue to feel even if Bee never uttered another word about my grandmother.

"I wanted to tell you, dear," she said. "I wanted to tell you everything, just like I tried to with your mother. But every time I thought about telling you the story, the pain stopped me in my tracks. All these years, I haven't wanted to step back to 1943. I haven't wanted to remember any of it."

I nodded, recalling the violets at Henry's house. "Those flowers in Henry's garden," I said, pausing for a moment to read the emotion on her face, "they reminded you of Esther, didn't they?"

Bee nodded. "They did, dear. They reminded us both. It was as if"—she looked around the room and took a deep breath—"as if she was there with us, telling us she was OK."

I reached my hand out for hers and stroked her arm gently. The floodgates had opened, and the memories were gushing out now. I felt I could ask her anything, so I did. "Bee, the painting you gave me, it's of you and Elliot, isn't it?"

"Yes," she said simply. "It's why I gave it to you. I couldn't bear to see it. It was a window into a life I'd never have, and it came to represent all that went wrong so many years ago, with your grandmother."

I sighed, feeling the weight of the sorrow in the room. "It's the reason why you haven't been comfortable with my relationship with Jack, isn't it?"

She didn't answer the question, but the look on her face told me yes.

"I understand, Bee, I do."

She looked lost in thought again. "I bet you want me to explain myself—about that night."

I nodded.

"I was wrong," she said, "to believe that I could fill Esther's place in Elliot's heart. I was a fool. And I'll never forgive myself for driving away without knowing if we could have helped her, if we could have saved her. I blame myself for her death every day."

"No, no, Bee," I said. "It happened so fast. You were trying to protect Elliot. I understand that."

"But I was protecting Elliot for selfish reasons," she said, unable to look me in the eye. "I was protecting my own interests. I was so frightened the police would charge him with murder and take him away from *me*. So I sped away, as fast as I could. If Esther chose to drive over that hillside, that was her decision, I reasoned. I was angry at her, angry that she'd do something of that magnitude to hurt him. Elliot was in shock, and I wanted to protect him. It isn't an explanation worthy of forgiveness from Esther or from you. But I want you to know—if there is someone to blame for the aftermath that night, blame me."

We sat in silence for a few minutes before I spoke again. "Don't you think it's strange that they didn't find her body?"

"I used to think about that a lot," she said. "But not anymore. Her body must have been washed out to sea after the crash. The sound was her final resting place; it had to be. Even now, late at night, when I hear the waves on the shore, I think of her out there. The lady of the sea. She's where she wanted to be, Emily. She loved the sound and its delicate creatures. Her stories, her poems, they were almost always inspired by that shore." She pointed out the window to the beach. "It's the only way I've managed to find some peace after all these years."

I nodded. "But there's just one thing, Bee," I said. "Elliot said something about seeing Henry's car drive into the park that night."

She looked up at me, confused. "What do you mean?"

"You didn't see him there?"

"No," she said a little defensively. "No, he couldn't have been there."

"But what if he *was* there, Bee?" I said, searching her face. "If that *were* the case, don't you think he'd know something?"

"He doesn't," Bee said quickly. "I don't know what Elliot told you about Henry. Sure, he may have been in love with your grandmother, but Henry was just as shocked as the rest of the island when word got out about her death."

"Oh," I said. "Well, I'd like to talk to him about it myself. Maybe he knows something."

Bee shook her head. "I wouldn't intrude on his memories, dear."

"Why?"

"It's too painful for him," she said. I wondered if she was

protecting Henry, the way she'd thought to protect Elliot that dark night.

"Esther *affected* him, Emily," she said. "It would be too hard on him to dredge back the past. If you haven't noticed, every time you're around him he acts like a spooked horse. You remind him of her."

"I understand," I said. "But—this will probably sound crazy—I somehow get the feeling that my grandmother would want me to. I think he knows more than he's letting on."

"No," Bee said. "Let it rest."

I shook my head. "I'm sorry. I have to."

She shrugged. At the heart of it all, Bee was reasonable.

"Emily," she said, "you must remember that what's done is done. There's no changing the past. In all of this, I'd hate to see you lose sight of your own story." She paused for a moment. "Isn't that why you came here?"

I acknowledged her concern with a nod.

We sat there together in silence, except for the seagulls outside, flapping around above the house almost frantically, until I found the courage to tell her I was leaving. "I'm going home to New York."

Bee looked wounded. "Why? I thought you were staying until the end of the month."

"I was," I said, looking out at the sound and doubting my decision. *Have I given things enough time?* "But everything has gotten, well, so complicated."

Bee nodded in agreement. "It hasn't exactly been smooth sailing, has it?"

"It's been a beautiful few weeks, Bee, a transforming time, and I owe it to your hospitality, and your love," I said. "But I think it's time for me to go now. I think I need time to process what I've experienced."

She looked as if she felt betrayed. "And you can't do that here?"

I shook my head, and my resolve strengthened even more when I thought of Jack. "I'm sorry, Bee."

"OK," she said. "But don't forget, this is your home. Don't forget what I told you. It's yours now and will be yours officially whenever I go. . . ."

"Which will be never," I said, forcing a laugh.

"But it will happen, sooner than both of us think," she said matter-of-factly. The ache in my heart told me she spoke the truth.

March 19

A day passed in which I did nothing but think—about Esther and Elliot, Bee, and Jack. I thought of my mom, too, and the following day I curled on the sofa in the lanai and dialed her familiar number. "Mom?"

"It's so good to hear your voice, honey," she said.

I realized I may never completely understand my mother's ways, but excavating Esther's story had come with an unexpected benefit: I could now see her in a new light. After all, she was just a child who had lost her mother.

"Mom, we need to talk about something," I said.

"Is it Joel?"

"No," I said, pausing to consider how I would proceed. "About . . . your mother."

She was silent.

"I know about Esther, Mom."

"Emily, where is this coming from? Did your aunt tell you something? Because—"

"No. I found something, something that belonged to your mother—a diary that she wrote about her life. I read it, and I know what happened to her, at least up until the end."

"Then you know that she left us, that she left me," she said, her voice suddenly tinged with anger.

"No, Mom, she didn't leave you—at least, I don't think she intended to. Grandpa threw her out."

"What?"

"Yes, he made her leave, to pay for what she did. And, Mom, there was a tragedy that night, the night she disappeared. I'm trying to unearth the answers for you, for me, for Elliot, and for—"

"Emily, why? Why are you doing this? Why can't you just let it be?" Her sentiments mirrored Bee's, for the same reasons, perhaps. They were both scared.

"I can't," I said. "I have this sense that I'm supposed to find the answers for her."

There was more silence on the other end of the line.

"Mom?"

"Emily," she finally said. "A very long time ago, I tried to find those answers too. I wanted more than anything to locate my mother, to meet her, but mostly to ask her why she left—why she left *me*. I tried, believe me, I tried. But my search turned up nothing but emptiness and heartache. I had to make a decision to stop looking. I had to let her go. And when I did, I knew, deep down, that I had to let the island go too."

I wished I could look into her eyes then, because I knew I'd be able to see the part of her that had been missing for so long. "Mom, that's just it," I said. "You may have given up the search, but I can pick up where you left off."

She exhaled deeply. "I never wanted you to know about any of this, Emily," she said. "I wanted to protect you from it. And it worried me to see that you were taking after her—your creative gifts, your spirit, even your appearance. I knew Grandma Jane could see it, just as I did, that you're the spitting image of Esther. "

My mother's words were like a needle and thread, sewing disparate fabrics of my life together into a perfect seam. I remembered that ill-fated afternoon when Grandma Jane colored my hair years ago, and realized for the first time that it wasn't *me* she had despised; it was my resemblance to Esther. It frightened her and unsettled her so much that she wanted to change the way I looked. *What power Esther had over all of them.*

"The veil," I said, remembering the hurt I'd felt when Mom had been dismissive about my wearing the family heirloom on my wedding day. "Why didn't you want me to wear it?"

"Because it was wrong," she said. "On Danielle, it was different. But I just couldn't send you down that aisle in that veil, in Grandma Jane's veil, not when you embody so much of Esther's spirit. I'm so sorry, honey."

"It's OK," I said.

"I just wanted, so much, for you to be happy."

I paused for a moment, considering my words carefully. "Mom, there's something else."

"What?"

I blinked hard, feeling the weight of what I was about to say. "Esther was pregnant the night she left, the night of the accident."

I could hear her breathing through tears. "I don't believe this," she said.

"She was expecting a baby—Elliot's baby, the man she loved—on the night she disappeared. It's all in the diary. I know this has to be hard to hear, Mom. I'm sorry."

She blew her nose. "All these years I've been so angry at my mother, this woman who supposedly left me as a baby—who leaves their *baby*?—but now, somehow the only thing I want to know is: Did she love me? Did my mother love me?"

"She loved you," I said without hesitation. It was what Esther would have wanted me to say, I told myself, and it was what my mother needed to hear.

"Do you really think so, honey?"

The tone of her voice—raw, honest, devoid of any pretense—forever changed the way I thought of my mother. At her core, she was just a little girl longing for a maternal bond. How she hid a lifetime of heartache and issues of abandonment, I'll never know, but she was wearing it all on her sleeve now, and it made me admire her in a way I didn't know I could.

"Yes," I said, reaching my hand up to the nape of my neck. "And there's something I've come across that I think she'd like you to have." I unclasped the starfish necklace and held it in my hand, nodding to myself. Esther would have wanted her daughter to have it.

I had an hour before Bee planned to drop me off at the ferry terminal for the trip to Seattle to catch my flight. I packed my suitcase, tucking the treasures I'd collected on the island inside. But after I lay my mother's childhood scrapbook on top of my cosmetic case, I shook my head. It didn't belong in New York. It belonged here, on the island, for my mother to find again. She'd be back—I knew she would—and when she returned, she needed to make this discovery, on her own.

I remembered the photo Evelyn had left for me, and I could think of no better place for it than at home in the pages of the scrapbook. I leaned back against the bed and opened the book, turning to the last page, which was blank except for four black photo corners and the handwritten, flower-adorned word above: *Mother.* I carefully set the photo in place and then closed the scrapbook, gently setting it inside the drawer of the bedside table. I wanted to give it to her, but I knew in my heart that she needed to find it herself.

"I'll be back in twenty minutes," I said to Bee a few minutes later. I closed the back door quickly behind me before she could protest.

My thoughts mirrored the ominous clouds lurking over the beach, gray and swollen. *How will Henry respond to the questions I have for him? Did he see my grandmother alive that fateful night? What did she tell him before driving over the cliff?*

I walked up the creaky steps that led to his front porch. I hadn't noticed the cobwebs in the windows, or the catawampus doorframe, so jagged and splintered. I took a deep breath and knocked. And waited. And waited some more.

After a second knock, I thought I heard something or someone inside, so I moved closer to one of the windows and leaned in and listened: footsteps. They were definitely footsteps, hurried footsteps.

Through the window, I could see the living room, which was empty, and the hallway that led to the back door. I looked closer and noticed movement toward the rear of the house, followed by the sound of a door closing. Quickly, I ran around the side yard. There were the violets again, watching, waiting, in their wise way, as Henry's car barreled out of the garage and onto the gravel driveway. I waved and yelled, hoping he'd stop, but he kept on, his car cloaked in a cloud of dust. Our eyes met for a moment in his rearview mirror, but he didn't stop.

"Good-bye, dear," Bee said, tears streaming down her cheeks as she dropped me off at the terminal. "I wish you didn't have to go."

"Me too," I said. Though I was leaving two stories unfinished on the island, mine and Esther's, I had to go. The air was thick with memories and secrets, and I was finding it difficult to breathe.

"You'll be coming back soon, won't you?" Bee said with sadness in her eyes.

"Of course I will," I replied. Even if I wasn't so sure myself, Bee needed the reassurance. I squeezed her tight before joining the other passengers and making my way to the boat. My final act on the island was to place a copy of Esther's diary, which I had painstakingly photocopied in town, into an envelope addressed to Elliot and drop it into a mailbox.

I was leaving the island I loved, and like my grandmother may or may not have done so many years before me, I left without knowing if I'd ever return.

Chapter 19

March 20

I woke up in my New York bed the next day, back in my New York life, with my old New York problems. They seemed almost frivolous in contrast to the perplexing events of Bainbridge Island: an unsolved family mystery and an unfinished love affair. Scratch that; there were zero messages from Jack on my phone—a *finished* love affair.

If I'd thought I was going to get a cheerful welcome home from Annabelle, I was mistaken. "You shouldn't have left, Em," she said in a way that no other friend could. "You need to go back."

"I thought I could do some thinking here," I said. "Maybe do some writing."

"I hate to sound blunt, darling." She said "darling" with a distinct air of sarcasm. "But haven't you said that for the last, what, five years?"

I looked down at my hands, tugging at my pinkie the way I do when I'm nervous.

"Sorry," she said. "You know that I just want to see you happy, right?"

"Of course I know that."

"Good." Then she paused, and looked back at me a bit mischievously. "Because the maid of honor in my wedding has to be happy."

My mouth fell open. "Annabelle! No way! You and Evan?"

"Me and Evan and Herbie Hancock," she said, proudly holding up her hand to show off the ring. "I don't know what happened, Em. These last few weeks, we've just clicked. And then he took me to a Herbie Hancock show and proposed between sets. And I said yes!"

I was happy for her, so very much, yet my insides trembled a little. Annabelle's happiness was shining a floodlight over my solitude.

I smiled. "So how are you going to deal with the fact that Evan isn't really the marrying kind of name?"

"To hell with that," she said. "I'm going to take my chances. And he can always legally change his name to Bruce."

She grabbed her jacket. "Sorry to rush off, but I've got to head back to my place. I'm meeting Evan for dinner at Vive tonight."

I wanted to be meeting *anyone* for dinner at Vive tonight.

"Have fun," I said.

"Oh, before I forget, there's a box of mail on the kitchen table."

"Thanks," I said, shutting the door behind her.

But after she left, I didn't turn on my laptop or read the mail. One hour turned into two, and then three. I curled up on the couch without bothering to remove my coat and shoes. It was the very definition of exhaustion. I just pulled a wool throw blanket over me, the one that Joel's aunt had knitted for our wedding, the one I'd always hated but never dared give away. It was too small and made from fibers that itched bare skin, but I was cold. I pulled it up under my chin, rested my head on the cold leather pillow, and thought about Jack, and how nice it would have been if he were here with me.

March 21

The phone rang earlier than usual the next morning. The ring, I thought, sounded like the marriage of a screech and a fire alarm. I looked at the clock: 8:02 A.M.

"Hello?"

"Em, it's me."

It was a familiar voice, but whose? In my post-sleep haze, it took me a few seconds to recall just where I'd heard it. The café? A movie? Then I realized who it was, and my heart halted. Looking back on that moment, I do believe the earth stopped spinning for a brief second the moment I recognized his voice.

"Joel?"

"I heard that you're back," he said softly, cautiously.

"What do you mean you heard I was back? How did you know I left?"

"Listen," he said, avoiding the question. "I know this is going to sound crazy. I know you want to hang up on me right now. But the truth is, Emily, I made a horrible mistake. I have to see you. I *need* to see you."

He sounded sincere, and also sad. I dug my fingernails into my arm, just to make sure I was hearing this, just to make sure this was real. *Joel still wants me, so why aren't I feeling anything?*

I sat up and shook my head. "No, I can't do this," I said, remembering what's-her-name. "For starters, you're getting *married*." The word shook me to my core. "And, by the way, thanks for that beautiful wedding invitation. How kind of you to remember me."

My sarcasm, however, was met with confusion. "Wedding invitation?"

"Don't play dumb," I said. "You know you sent it."

"No," he said. "No, there must be some mistake. I didn't send it." He paused for a few seconds. "Stephanie," he finally said. "Stephanie must have sent it. It had to be her. I can't believe she would stoop that low, but I guess I should have realized. She's not the person I thought she was, Em. Since we moved in together she's been paranoid about everything, but especially about you. She thinks I still love you, and, well, I—"

"Joel, stop."

"Just give me a half hour," he pleaded. "Just one drink. Seven o'clock, tonight, at that little spot around the corner from," he gulped, "our place."

My grip on the phone tightened. "Why in the world should I?"

"Because I . . . because I still love you," he said with such vulnerability that I actually believed him.

I tugged at the yarn on the blanket. Everything in me told me to say no, to resist that gnawing temptation, but something in my heart told me to say yes. "All right," I said.

It was reason enough to shower, put on some strappy shoes, and meet him for *one cocktail* that night. Just one.

When I walked into the bar where we'd agreed to meet, I felt more beautiful than I had in a long time. Maybe it was the island's effect on me, or perhaps it was the fact that Joel wanted me back. In any case, a lot had changed since I'd seen him last, and I wondered if he'd notice.

I could see him from across the room, standing there at the bar, standing in exactly the same way I'd seen him so many years ago on the day we met: kind of slouched over, leaning on one elbow, smiling that Joel smile. He was just as handsome, just as dangerous. When his eyes caught mine, I steadied myself and walked over to meet him. I could still have this man, and for a minute, that thought frightened me.

"Hi," he said, slipping his arm around my waist and kissing my cheek. I didn't pull away. The way he kissed my cheek, the way I stood there beside him, it was as if we were on autopilot, or operating on muscle memory.

"You look amazing," he said, pointing to a table in the corner of the bar, which wasn't really a bar. It was one of those upscale night-club places Joel had always wanted me to go to with him when I wanted to just order in and spend the night in bed together watching *SNL*.

"Are you hungry?" he asked delicately, as if he might say the wrong thing and scare me away.

"No," I said, a little startled by the directness in my tone. "But I'll have that drink I promised you."

He smiled, and rattled off my martini order to the waitress, from memory: dirty martini, extra olives. When we sat down, I glanced around the room. There were women everywhere—beautiful women in perfect outfits, with perfect hair and perfect bodies. But for the first time in, well, I have no idea how long, Joel's eyes were fixed on *me*.

When the drinks arrived, I sipped mine slowly. If it was going to be our final drink together, I told myself, it would be OK to make it last.

"So, how is *Stephanie*?" I said.

He looked down at his hands in his lap, then back at my face. "It's over between us, Emily." He was careful to make sure that each word that passed his lips wasn't wounding me. "I was a fool to think that this was love. Because it wasn't. I didn't love her, and I never could have. My decision was clouded. I see that now. I made a terrible mistake."

I didn't know what to say, so I didn't say anything at first, but as the moments passed, my anger grew. I slammed my hands down on the table. "What do you expect me to say to that, Joel? You chose her over me, and you think you can just waltz back in here and tell me, 'Oops, I messed up. I had my fun and now I'm back'? It doesn't work like that."

He looked very troubled. "I'll never forgive myself for what I did, for as long as I live." He cleared his throat. "Stephanie is in the past. I want *you*. I need *you*. I have never been so sure about something in my whole life."

It wasn't just the plea of a guy who'd changed his mind on a whim; I knew it then. This was the appeal of a man who knew he'd lost his one true thing. And for that reason, I listened.

"Don't you see?" he continued. "This could be our second chance, our second act. We could come back stronger, more in love than ever before—if you'd only forgive me."

"Hey," I said, noticing that there were tears in his eyes. "It's OK." I tilted my head a little and smiled at him. "I decided to forgive you before I even arrived."

His eyes brightened. "You did?"

"Yes," I said. He reached for my hand, and I let him hold it in his.

"What do you say, Em?" he said, eyes big and wide and vulnerable. "Will you let me come home?"

I thought of Esther and Elliot on the sidewalk in front of the Landon Park Hotel so many years ago, how she'd given up on him.

Was that my lesson? That I was supposed to try again? And I knew it then by the way he looked at me: We *could* weather this storm. We could go on. We could try again. Lots of people moved forward after infidelity. We wouldn't be the first. But that's when I had the realization that gave me the greatest closure of all: *I didn't want to.* I had healed somehow over the past few weeks on Bainbridge Island, even though I didn't know it at the time. I knew it now.

"You will always have my forgiveness," I said softly, "but, Joel, our marriage is over."

He looked confused. "But . . ."

"I've moved on," I said. "I've had to." I glanced down at my martini glass. It was empty. I'd promised him one drink, that's all. "I have to go," I said softly. "I'm sorry."

"Not yet," he said. "Just one more drink." He held up his arm as if to call over the waitress.

"No," I said, standing up. "It's time for me to say good-bye."

He tossed a fifty-dollar bill on the table and followed me outside.

"I read the book," he said on the sidewalk in front of the restaurant.

I turned around to face him. "What book?"

"*Years of Grace,*" he said. "I finally read it. I wish I had years ago. If I had, I would have known why you loved it so much. I would have known . . . how to fix us."

I felt a tugging at my heart as I saw him then, his handsome face illuminated by the streetlight above. The chiseled chin, with a faint shadow of stubble—always appealing on Joel—big fawn-like eyes, and a flush to his cheeks. It was a perfect New York March night, and quiet. There was no one but us, and the elm trees, on the sidewalk where we stood.

"We were becoming Jane and Stephen, the characters in the book," he said, wisely taking advantage of my silence. "I thought you didn't love me. I thought you had changed. That's why I—"

There was *Stephanie* again. *Stephanie*. The hurdle I could not clear. But Stephanie was inconsequential to the final act of our story. I saw that now.

"I should have realized," he continued. "I should have—"

I extended my arm and grasped his shoulder tenderly. "Joel," I said softly. "Don't. Don't blame yourself."

He looked solemn. "We could have had it all—the children, the fifty-year anniversary, the house in the country. We could have made it work, like Jane and Stephen did. We still can."

I shook my head. Joel and I were not Stephen and Jane. It was true, their marriage had faltered, and they had rallied and gone the distance, anchoring their hearts so beautifully, so self-sacrificially, on the virtues of companionship, respect, and admiration. No, Joel and I were not Jane and Stephen. We were Jane and *Andre*, whose love did not stand the test of time. "Yes, Jane and Stephen did make it work," I said quietly, "but we . . . we weren't meant to, Joel. Can't you see that? It's not how our story was meant to end."

He searched my face with wide eyes filled with sorrow. "What can I say, what can I do to change your mind?"

I shook my head. "I'm so sorry, but there isn't anything."

And then he grabbed my waist, pulling me toward him. I felt the warmth of his body against mine as he kissed me. I closed my eyes, giving the moment the respect it deserved. When I did, I could see Jane and Stephen, and Esther and Elliot. They were all there with me. But then, finally, Jack's face appeared, and something moved in my heart.

"I'm sorry," I said, pulling away. He nodded with understanding, staring at me as if I was the only woman who mattered in the world. It was how I wanted to remember him.

"I'll never give you up," he said. The words sent a chill through my body. It was, of course, what Andre had said to Jane, so early in *Years of Grace*—the words he had uttered with intention, with love, with promise. But instead of speaking to my heart the way Joel had meant them to, they only made me more certain of my decision.

"Good-bye, Joel," I said. My voice was muffled by the wind that was now whistling through the elm trees. They waved their branches in a dramatic farewell. This time, we both knew that good-bye was for good.

I walked home feeling lighter than I had in years, for I had finally cleared the space in my heart that had been weighted down for so long. I checked the mailbox before heading upstairs—nothing—but then I remembered Annabelle saying something about a box in the kitchen.

Inside the apartment, I set my coat down on an armchair, then pulled out a chair at the table and culled the mail, creating piles for bills, junk mail, and envelopes addressed to Joel. In between two credit card offers, I found a yellowed envelope. Alongside a modern-day stamp was a three-cent stamp that looked like a relic from the past. There was no return address, and my own had been penned recently in fresh ballpoint.

In my haste to open the envelope, the soft paper nearly disintegrated in my hand. Inside was a single page, written in the most beautiful penmanship I'd ever seen:

March 31, 1943

My dear,

I'm writing to you not knowing who you are or where you are or how we may be connected. Yet I do know that our hearts have crossed for some unexplainable reason, and by some force, we are sharing a moment in time, even if interrupted by many years. By now you must have read the diary, which was nothing more than the ramblings of my heart. I don't know what it will mean to you, or to anyone, but a wise person told me that someone would one day need to read it, and I trust that person is you. Do with it what you please, for I may not be here when you come across its pages.

I leave you with a thought, a thought about love that has taken me many failures to come by: Great love endures time, heartache, and distance. And even when all seems lost, true love lives on. I know that now, and I hope you do, too.

With love from many years ago,

Esther Johnson

I held my hand to my heart. *True love lives on.* It was true for Jane in *Years of Grace*, and so it was true for Esther, my grandmother. I felt a draft from the window on my cheek and a chill come over my body. Time was a funny thing, I thought. An entire lifetime had spanned since she'd written that letter—to me. She had believed I'd be here, years later, to read her words, which she'd arranged for me to discover. My heart swelled with appreciation, with love, for the grandmother I never knew. *But who sent this letter to me? And what about her daughter, my mother? Was she simply a casualty? A casualty of love?*

I thought about what Esther had said, about great love enduring, her words echoing Elliot's. *But how could they still love each other after all these years apart? After all the misunderstandings? After everything?*

I turned back to the mail, and noticed that resting at the bottom of the box was a thick manila envelope addressed to me. The postmark read "Bainbridge Island." I pulled out the contents and opened the folded page on top.

Dear Emily,

By now you are home in New York, and I wanted you to have these letters when you arrived. They're from your grandmother, Esther. I had hoped to give them to you on the island during your visit, but I wasn't sure if you'd finished the diary. Evelyn told me you were reading it. I'm glad you found it. I knew you would. Ever since I saw you that night at the ferry terminal when you arrived, I knew you were the one, the one who was meant to read Esther's words. And after all these years of watching and waiting for some sign, there you were. So, the next morning, while you were still sleeping on the sofa, I walked over to your aunt's house. While she was out in the garden, I slipped away to the room you were staying in and left the book for you. Had she known my intentions, Bee would have forbidden it. So I didn't tell her.

I should have discussed all of this with you in person, and I hope you'll forgive my weakness. You look so much like her, Emily, and being with you reminded me of her—the way I loved her, but mostly the way she never quite returned that love.

You're probably wondering what happened the night she disappeared, and if you learned that I was there with her that night, you might be wondering if I have blood on my hands. It's time I cleared the air. I've never told anyone, not your aunt, not Evelyn, certainly not Elliot, but you need to know. I'm growing old—we all are—and this is a secret I've decided shouldn't die with me, even if your grandmother wanted it to. But it's time the truth is set free. Esther would have wanted her story to live on.

That night, in 1943, I had been visiting a friend near Esther and Bobby's house. I heard shouting as I walked to my car, and then I watched as Bobby slammed the door, leaving her there on the porch. It hurt me to see her like that. She looked forlorn, and my heart broke for her. When she drove away, she had a frantic look on her face, and the car was swerving all over the street. I worried about what she might do, so I followed her to Elliot's, and then to Bee's and then to the park. She told me she was leaving the island, but she wanted to leave in a way that no one would ever find her again.

She had some grand idea about staging her death, so that no one, especially the happy couple, Elliot and Bee, would come looking for her once she was gone. Esther wanted to make a clean break. Her inspiration was "chicken," a daredevil game some high school kids on the island had played, swerving old cars to near-head-on collisions. In her version, she was going to drive the car over and jump out just before it cleared the edge of the cliff. I begged her not to do it. If she'd wanted me to, I would have run away with her that night. I loved her so.

But she had other plans: a dramatic exit from the island—one that would hurt those she loved—and a new life to start, alone.

I waited nervously in my car in the shadows, at the entrance to the park, as she revved up her engine. That's when Elliot and Bee drove in. I worried what Esther might do when faced with those two.

What happened next is still a blur, just as it was that night. Bee stopped the car. Elliot got out and just stood there, mouth wide open. What Esther did next still chills me to my bones. She drove the car over the cliff. Just like that. She was gone.

Elliot just stood there screaming. I'll never forget it. But whatever sadness Bee had for Esther, she set it aside for the sake of

Elliot. Your aunt is a good woman, Emily. You must know that by now. And on that night, saving Elliot from criminal charges seemed, to her, the most important goal. So she pulled him into the car and they sped off. I will never shake from my memory that grief-stricken look on Elliot's face. I long struggled to come to terms with what happened, and I have decided that I pity him. To watch your beloved take her life, right in front of your eyes, before you can save her? I know that scene plays in his head every night, and it's his punishment, for everything.

Because she survived.

When I got out of my car to run to the scene, to peer over the cliff to see the wreckage, I heard something in the brush on my left, and there, in the bushes, with a few bruises and scrapes, was your grandmother. She had somehow managed to roll out of the car, just before it went over. She did it, just as she'd planned. You can imagine the joy and the relief I felt when I saw her there.

She asked me to drive her to the ferry. She was going to start a new life "from scratch," she said. She handed me her red velvet journal and explained its importance. She made me promise to keep it until the time was right, so I took it home and kept it all these years.

I begged her to stay, your grandmother, but she said she'd made up her mind, and if you knew Esther, there was no changing it.

Many months passed before I heard from her, and I have to admit, I thought the worst. But the letters started trickling in, from Florida at first, and then from more exotic places like Spain, Brazil, Tahiti. She had changed her name, she told me, dyed her hair, and perhaps most shocking, to me, was the letter when she told me about Lana, the baby she gave birth to.

I looked up from the letter, my heart beating faster with every second. *Lana.* I remembered her name instantly. She was the woman, of course, Jack had mentioned. The client. *That* explained her inter-est in Jack and his art. *She must have been contacting Jack to find Elliot.* The puzzle was fitting together now, all of it. I continued reading:

> She asked about her daughter, your mother, of course, and because I stayed in touch with your grandfather, at least before he left the island with his new wife, Jane, I was able to give her updates, and this brought her great comfort, I know.
>
> She didn't want anyone to know she was alive, but toward the end, she asked me to relay her love and well wishes to Bee and Evelyn, and to Elliot, to tell them she loved them and had thought about them often over the years. I'm ashamed to say I never relayed those messages. I couldn't bring myself to do it. I didn't think they could handle the truth, after all these years, and I worried what they would think of me, keeping a secret like this from them. They had already buried her in their hearts. But if you want an honest answer, I will tell you that Esther's letters were my only connection to her, and I didn't want to share that. Not with Bee or Evelyn, and certainly not with Elliot. I didn't want to share her.
>
> The letters stopped coming several years ago, and I've missed them, deeply. I wonder about where she is, if she's all right, if she's still living. Toward the end, she stopped including her return address on the envelopes, and my attempts to find her have all failed. I'm afraid to say, dear, I believe she has passed on.
>
> Now I turn the letters over to you. I hope you'll enjoy them as I have for so many years, and I hope they will help you know Esther and love her, as I have always loved her. They are full of life and hope and expectation, but deep between the lines you can see the regret and sorrow, too. As you will see, she was quite something, as are you.
>
> Sincerely,
>
> Henry

I leaned back in my chair and sighed, clutching the letter to my chest. *So she didn't die that night. She staged it all, and Henry helped her.* I couldn't wait to tell Elliot, but then I wondered if he'd really want to know that she wrote Henry for all those years and not him. *Would he understand? Could he forgive her?*

I took a final look inside the envelope and saw that I'd missed something wrapped in stiff cardboard. When I pulled it out, I could see there was a photograph inside, the one that had been on Henry's mantel, with a sticky note attached:

I thought you'd like this picture of your grandmother. It's exactly how I remember her in my heart.

I set the photo down on the table, and reached for the stack of letters. I wanted to read every single one.

March 25

"You've been away for a while," my therapist, Bonnie, said in our session a few days later. She insisted I call her Bonnie, not Dr. Archer, and I did so, reluctantly.

"I have," I said, digging my knuckles into the blue twill armchair, feeling as I always do when I'm with Bonnie: guilty. "I'm sorry I didn't keep our meetings. I left pretty suddenly." I proceeded to tell her about everything: Bainbridge Island, Bee, Evelyn, the book, Greg, Jack, Henry, meeting Elliot, and Joel, too. And how I'd spent the last few days thinking it all through.

"You realize," she said after I'd gotten it all out, "that you don't need me anymore."

"What do you mean?"

"You have your answers," she said.

"I do?"

"You do."

"But I still can't write," I said. "I'm not cured."

"Yes, you are," she said. "Go home. You'll see."

She was right. When I got home later that morning, I pulled out my laptop and began writing. I wrote through lunch, through the noise of rush hour traffic, through dinner, and late into the night. I didn't stop until I had transcribed every word of Esther's story.

Before I closed my laptop that night, I stared at the last sentence. It was the end of the diary, yet it wasn't the end of the story. I knew that in my heart. I took a deep breath and spaced my cursor down to a fresh page. I may not have known how the story would end just yet, but when I did, I was determined to write it. For Esther. For Elliot. For Bee, Evelyn, Henry, Grandpa, Grandma, Mom, and for me.

March 30

Since I'd returned to New York, I'd tried not to think about Jack, but everywhere I turned, there he was. It was his presence I couldn't shake, and I wondered if this was what Elliot and my grandmother had meant when they talked about enduring love.

And yet Esther's story hadn't ended the way she'd planned. Maybe that was my lesson: I could accept the failure of this love and move on from it, keeping it tucked away in my heart for a lifetime.

I called Annabelle at noon to coax her away from her office for lunch. "We haven't properly celebrated your engagement," I said.

We planned to meet at one, at a restaurant near my apartment. The hostess seated me, and I waited at the table until Annabelle arrived, ten minutes late. "Sorry," she said. "Evan's mom called. She's chatty."

I grinned. "It's so good to see you, Annie."

She smiled. "Was it a good visit? I mean, I know so much happened there, but are you glad you went?"

I nodded. "Yes."

"So what are you going to do?"

I grinned. "I know exactly what I need to do," I said.

"What?"

"The book," I answered. "I'm going to finish it."

"What do you mean?"

"I'm going to finish Esther's story for her. I'm going to write the final chapter."

Annabelle grinned.

"This story has been bottled up so long," I said. "I somehow feel responsible for giving it closure."

She reached across the table for my hand. "And with it, you're finding your own closure."

I nodded. "I owe this to you."

"Nah," she said. "I just got you on the plane. You did the rest."

"Annie, I was on the verge of becoming a cat lady. Can't you just picture me there, in my apartment, surrounded by nineteen cats?"

"I can," she said, grinning. "Somebody had to save you from the felines."

We laughed, and then Annabelle looked down at her lap. "When are you leaving?"

"Leaving?"

"For Bainbridge Island."

I knew in my heart that I was going, and Annabelle did too. But when, and under what circumstances, was still to be worked out. "I don't know," I said.

But the time and date had already been decided. I just didn't know it yet.

It was after three when I got home. The message light on my phone was blinking, so I pressed the Play button.

"Emily, it's Jack."

My hair stood on end.

"It took me a while to track down this number, and to realize that you'd left the island. I was so confused about why you'd leave without saying good-bye, and then I spoke to my grandfather. He told me about your visit, and I realized what had happened. His memory has been fading recently, so if he said anything funny about me, don't take it to the bank."

The message cut off, and another started. *"Sorry. Me again. I also wanted to say, about the other night. It was you who called, right? I hope that didn't give you the wrong impression. I was working on a painting for a client. I had yellow acrylic on my hands when she picked up. Please believe me. There is nothing romantic happening there. Emily, she's in her sixties. Does this put your mind at ease?"* He paused for a moment. *"But there is something I've been keeping from you. Something we need to talk about."* He paused again. *"Emily, I miss you. I need you. I . . . love you. There, I said it. Please call me."*

I looked up his number on the caller ID and dialed him back, as quickly as my fingers could punch in the numbers. *He loves me.* But the phone just rang and rang. So I hung up and did the next best thing: I called the airline and booked a flight to Seattle, departing the next day.

"Will you be needing a return ticket?" the agent asked.

"One way," I said, without pausing to think.

I packed quickly, but after I'd zipped up my suitcase, I was overcome with the feeling that I'd forgotten something. After a walk through the apartment, checking off items on my mental list, I realized what it was: *Years of Grace*. I'd been thinking about the book ever since returning to New York, and I was desperate to read it again in light of Esther's own story.

The book waited patiently on the shelf in the living room. I pulled it out, sank into the couch, and read a few pages. I studied the title page with fresh eyes, which is when I noticed something I hadn't seen all the times I'd read the book: someone's handwriting, in black ink, very light and worn, but still there. I held the page closer to my eyes, and there, plain as day, were the words "This book belongs to Esther Johnson."

Chapter 20

March 31

I remember hearing a story in high school about a girl who had gone to Seattle with her friends but missed the ferry that would get her to the island in time for her ten p.m. curfew. Knowing that the next ferry wouldn't come for another hour, and that her father was strict and would ground her, or worse, she panicked, and when she saw the ferry pulling out of the Seattle terminal, she threw her bag down and leaped across the gangway. But instead of landing on the ferry's balcony, she landed in the water. She'd been taken to the emergency room and sent home with a broken wrist and a bruised chin. Krystalina. That was her name—it came to me just then, just as the ferry's horn sounded, just as I reached the terminal and saw the boat backing away from the dock, just as my heart sank.

I had been either camped out in airports or flying for the better part of thirteen hours (the price you pay for last-minute travel), and when I reached the ferry terminal, I contemplated making a run for it and jumping à la Krystalina when I saw that I'd missed the seven p.m. boat by a mere hair. I looked down at the churning waters below, and I decided that the island could wait a little longer. Jack could wait. Or could he?

The boat docked at 8:25 P.M. No one was waiting for me but one lonely taxi.

"Can you take me to Hidden Cove Road?" I asked the driver.

He nodded and reached for my bag. "You're traveling light," he said. "Just staying for a short visit?"

"I'm not sure yet," I said.

He nodded again, as if he knew exactly what I meant.

I directed him to Jack's house, and when we arrived, it looked dark, too dark.

"It doesn't look like anyone's home," the driver said, stating the obvious. I was annoyed when he suggested that we leave.

"Wait," I said. "Give me a minute."

This was the point in movies when the woman and the man reunite—when they run into each other's arms and lock lips.

I knocked once, and waited a minute or so. Then I knocked again.

"Anybody home?" the driver called out from the car.

I ignored him and knocked yet again, listening to the sound of my heart beating in my chest. *C'mon, Jack, answer.*

After a minute, I knew he wasn't coming. Or he wasn't home. But suddenly it was all too much for me. I sat down on the porch and buried my head in my knees.

What am I doing here? How did I come to love this man? I pondered a passage from *Years of Grace* that I had always admired: "Love was not a hothouse flower, forced to reluctant bud. Love was a weed that flashed unexpectedly into bloom on the roadside."

Yes, this love, it was not of my doing. It was natural. It was unstoppable. The realization gave me great comfort on Jack's cold and lonely doorstep.

"Miss," said the driver, "are you OK? If you need somewhere to go, I'll call my wife. She can make a bed up for you. It's not much, but you have somewhere to stay for the night." It hit me then: Everyone on Bainbridge Island has a streak of goodness in them.

I looked up and collected myself. "Thank you; that's very kind. But my aunt lives just up the beach. I'll go there tonight."

He dropped me off in front of Bee's. After I paid the fare, I just stood there for a moment, staring up at the house with my bag in my hand, wondering if I'd made the right decision to come back. I walked closer to the house, to the front door, and noticed that the lights were on. I let myself in.

"Bee?" I could see her there, sitting in her chair, just like I'd never left. After all that had happened, it was a comforting sight.

"Emily?" She got up to hug me. "What a surprise!"

"I had to come back," I said.

"I knew you would," she said. "And Jack, is he one of those reasons?"

I nodded. "I just went to his house. But he's not there."

Bee wore a solemn look on her face. "It's Elliot," she said. The way she said his name, it sent shivers down my arms. "He's sick. Jack called earlier and told me. He wanted me to know that"—she paused as her voice cracked, revealing her pent-up emotions—"to know that Elliot is . . . well, he isn't well, dear. He's dying."

I gulped.

"He's on his way to the hospital now. He just left for the ferry, in fact. If you leave now, you might catch him."

I looked at my feet. "I don't know," I said. "Do you think he'll want to see me?"

Bee nodded. "I know he'll want to see you," she said. "Go to him. She'd want you to."

Of course, she was talking about Esther, and it was Bee's words that got me to the ferry terminal that night. It was her words that changed my path forever. And with those words, I believe, she redeemed herself, for everything. She knew it. I knew it. And somehow I had a feeling that if Esther were here, she'd be nodding in approval.

"Can I borrow your keys?" I said, grinning.

She tossed them to me. "You better drive fast."

I felt my pulse race. "What about you?" I said, remembering her history with Elliot. "Don't you want to see him?"

She looked as though the answer might have been yes, but she shook her head. "It's not my place," she said.

I could see tears welling in her eyes. "You still love him, Bee, don't you?"

"Nonsense," she said, wiping away a tear.

"That package," I said, "the one Elliot gave you. What was it?"

She smiled. "It was the photo album, the one he'd given me after he came home from the war. I sent it back to him after everything happened with your grandmother. But he saved it all these years."

I squeezed her hand and grabbed my bag.

"Now, you go," she said. "Go after your Jack."

I drove Bee's Volkswagen so fast, so furiously, it was as if my life depended on it. I didn't think about police officers or accidents or anything else—just Jack. Every minute, every second counted.

I whipped the Volkswagen around the island until I made it to the ferry terminal, and as I pulled into the parking lot, my heart sank when I heard the ferry horn signaling its departure. I ran to the terminal and down the gangway, again considering taking that leap. But the ferry was too far now. I'd missed it. I'd missed Jack.

I clutched the railing tightly, scolding myself for my timing. Of course this was how it would go. In recent years, my life had been one missed connection after another. I shuffled along until I made it to the ledge, where people usually wait for friends and relatives to arrive from Seattle. The ferry was in full view. I squinted in vain for the sight of Jack, but the boat was already too distant to make out faces.

Then I heard footsteps behind me. Someone was running toward the terminal. I turned around, and there he was, sprinting toward the gangway with suitcase in hand, looking worried—that is, until he saw me.

"Emily?"

"Jack," I said, loving the sound of his name on my lips.

He dropped his bag and ran to me. "I had no idea you were going to be here," he said, pushing the hair out of his eyes, then running his hand along my face.

I let my heart do the talking. "I got your message," I said, "and I wanted to surprise you."

He grinned. "Well, you succeeded at that." He looked as if he was about to say something, but he got derailed by the sound of a ferry horn in the distance. Another ferry was coming into the harbor ahead of schedule.

"I went to your house," I said, searching his eyes for something, anything.

He reached for my hand, and his touch rushed warmth to every inch of my body.

"Bee said your grandfather is ill," I said. "I'm so sorry to hear that. You were going to see him, weren't you?"

He nodded. "I thought I'd go over tonight and stay with him so he isn't alone. He's having surgery in the morning."

"Is he going to be OK?"

"We're not sure," he said. "He's had two bypass surgeries in the last five years, and the doctors say that if this one doesn't do the trick, it might be their last attempt."

I wondered if Esther knew that the love of her life's heart was breaking, quite literally.

"You should go to him," I said. "We can see each other tomorrow, after he comes through surgery." I motioned to the ferry, now offloading passengers and nearly ready to board. "You go, catch that ferry. I'll be here waiting for you."

He shook his head. "And leave you here all beautiful and lovely? No, my grandfather would never approve. Why don't you come with me?"

I rested my head on his chest, the way I had done at Bee's house that afternoon in the lanai. "OK."

"I just keep thinking of that morning," he said, turning to face me again, "when I saw you at Henry's house."

"What do you mean?" I asked, looking up at him, hoping he was going to say what I thought he was going to say.

"I hoped we'd end up like this."

I was overcome with a feeling I'd never had before. I felt loved, but there was more. I felt adored.

Jack reached into his pocket, then for my hand.

"Emily," he said, clearing his throat. "I want you to have something. He held a small black box in his hand, and I couldn't help but remember the box Elliot had given him at Evelyn's funeral. *What's inside?* I lifted the lid with trembling fingers and could see something sparkle under the streetlights.

Jack cleared his throat. "My grandfather gave me a ring he gave to a woman he loved many years ago. I'd like you to have it."

I gasped. There was an enormous pear-shaped diamond set between two rubies, and I knew it in an instant. It was Esther's engagement ring. It had to be. Instinctively, I slipped it on my finger.

Jack saw the recognition in my eyes. "You know the story, don't you?"

I nodded. "Yes."

"How?"

"I've been doing some research this month," I said cryptically.

"So have I," he said. "I wanted to see if I could locate Esther, for my grandfather's sake. I wanted them to see each other again." He kicked a pebble on the walkway. "But it's too late now."

"What makes you think it's too late?"

Jack looked worried. "I'm afraid she passed away."

My heart sank. "How do you know?"

He rubbed his eyes, either because of exhaustion or because of sadness. "Her nurse told me. She was the woman who took care of her these past fifteen years while her health declined—she was also the one you saw me with that night in town, and the woman who answered the phone that night at my house."

"I'm confused," I said. "How did you find her?"

"She contacted me," he said. "She told me she was fulfilling Esther's dying wish to learn my grandfather's whereabouts."

I sighed. "So she died."

Jack nodded. "Yes."

I shook my head. "No," I said. "That can't be true." My heart refused to believe that the story ended this way.

"What did you say her name was?"

"Lana," he said.

I smiled knowingly. "That explains everything."

Jack looked confused. "What?"

"Jack, Lana is not her nurse. Lana is her *daughter*. *Elliot's* daughter."

Jack rubbed his forehead. "This makes no sense," he said.

"I know it doesn't. But it's true. And if Lana reached out to you and didn't tell you the true story of her relation to Esther, maybe she's not telling the full truth about her whereabouts, or the fact that she may be still *living*. I think she's trying to protect her mother.

"Wait," I continued, before Jack could respond. "You mentioned that this woman, Lana, had commissioned a painting. Was it the portrait in your studio, the one of the woman on the beach?"

"Yes," he said. "She said it was for her mother. I painted it from an old photograph."

"Jack," I said, "did it ever occur to you that the woman in the photo could have been *Esther*, that she wanted to give her mom a painting by Elliot's *flesh and blood*?"

Jack considered the idea for a moment and then shook his head. "It's just that she said her mother and her *father* were in a retirement home in Arizona. If what you're saying is true, why would she tell such an elaborate story to hide the truth?"

"It has to be because she doesn't want her mother to get hurt again," I said.

Jack shrugged. "I wish it were the case, Emily," he said. "But I just don't see it that way. I saw the way she spoke of Esther's life, and her passing. It was all very real."

The wind picked up, and Jack instinctively wrapped his arms around me like a blanket. "I wish it could have ended differently for them," he said, holding me tight. "But we can write our own story. Ours doesn't have to be tragic."

He kissed my forehead softly as the ferry's horn sounded again.

"And to think I almost ran away, from you, from all of this," I said.

He squeezed my hand. "I'm so glad you didn't."

We walked, hand in hand, onto the boat and nestled into a booth facing the Seattle side. The closer we approached the city's skyline, the more I could sense Jack's concern for his grandfather. What state would Elliot be in when we arrived? Would he be coherent? Would my presence bring him greater sadness, especially after reading the pages of the diary I'd mailed to him?

We arrived at the hospital and made our way to the fourth-floor reception desk, where we inquired about Elliot. "I'm afraid he's not doing well," said a nurse in almost a whisper. "He's been combative and disoriented since this afternoon. We're doing everything we can to make him comfortable, but the doctors say there isn't much time left. You may want to say your good-byes while you have a chance."

Jack's face was almost white as we approached the door to his grandfather's room. "I can't do this alone," he said to me.

I put my hand on his arm. "You don't have to."

Together we walked into the room, and there he was, hooked up to an arsenal of wires and machines. His skin was pale and his breathing barely registered.

"It's me, Grandpa," Jack said quietly, kneeling beside Elliot's bed. "It's Jack."

Elliot opened his eyes slowly, but just halfway. "She came," he said softly, in almost a whisper. "She was here. I saw her."

"Who, Grandpa?"

He closed his eyes, and they fluttered a little as though he was dreaming. "Those blue eyes," he said. "Just as blue as they were."

"Grandpa," Jack said softly, his eyes sparkling with hope, "who was here?"

"She told me she was getting married," Elliot said, opening his eyes again, but it was clear he was lost in his memories, and I could see the disappointment on Jack's face. "She told me she was marrying that schmuck, Bobby. Why would she marry him? She doesn't love him. She never loved him. She loves me. We belong together." He sat up and suddenly began tugging at an IV line attached to his arm. "I have to talk her out of it. I have to tell her. We'll run away together. That's what we'll do."

Jack looked worried. "He's hallucinating," he said. "The nurse warned me about this. It's the medication."

Elliot appeared wild and desperate, knocking a heart rate monitor to the floor with one weak swoop of his arm before Jack could jump up to calm him. "Hold on, Grandpa, you're not going anywhere." He turned to me. "Emily, get the nurse."

I pressed the red button near Elliot's bed, and moments later, two nurses rushed in. One helped us settle Elliot back into his bed, while the other injected something into his left arm. "This will help you rest more comfortably, Mr. Hartley," she said.

When Elliot was sleeping, I turned to Jack. "I'm going to go get something to drink. Do you want anything?"

"Coffee," he whispered, without taking his eyes off of Elliot.

I nodded.

I walked down to the cafeteria, thankful to find it still open, and poured two cups of French roast, tucking a packet of sugar and two miniature containers of half-and-half in my pocket. *How does Jack take his coffee?* I remembered Annabelle's research, but quickly pushed the thought aside and searched my wallet for $2.25 to pay for the coffee.

On the elevator, my mind turned to Elliot, and how he'd been so convinced, or rather, confused, about seeing Esther. It broke my heart the way he loved her so, even now, even at the end of his life. When I had almost made my way back to Elliot's room, I heard someone approaching behind me.

"Excuse me, ma'am," a woman said.

I turned to see one of the nurses holding a slip of paper in her hand. "You didn't happen to find a woman's scarf in the room with Mr. Hartley, did you?"

I shook my head. "No, I'm sorry, I didn't see anything."

The nurse shrugged. "All right," she said, looking at the paper in her hand. "A woman called earlier saying that her mother had left a"—she looked down at the paper—"a blue silk scarf in the room when visiting Mr. Hartley earlier today."

My eyes widened. "Did she give you her name? Did she leave a number?"

The nurse looked at me. "Do you know her?"

"I might," I said, swallowing hard.

She looked at the paper again. "Well that's odd," she said. "The nurse who worked the earlier shift took the message." She shook her head. "Looks like she didn't get a name."

I sighed.

"Well, if you find it, bring it to the nurse's station," she said. "Maybe she'll call back again. Sorry to bother you."

"How's he doing?" I whispered to Jack once inside the room. I handed him his coffee, extending my hand with the sugar packet and creamers.

"He's sleeping," he said, bypassing the sugar and selecting a single half-and-half container, which he emptied into his cup. I did exactly the same.

I kissed his cheek.

"What was that for?" he asked.

"Just because," I whispered.

I tiptoed over to Elliot's bedside and pulled the blanket up around his shoulders, and when I did, something in the covers caught my eye. Underneath the blanket, he was clutching something, a scarf. A blue scarf. He was holding it close to his chest.

I blinked back a tear, because in that moment, *I knew.*

"You're crying," Jack whispered.

"I'm crying," I said, smiling through the tears spilling out of my eyes. *I'm finally crying.* There was so much I wanted to tell him, so much I wanted to say, but it could wait. All I knew was that there were tears in my eyes just then, big fat tears, and they rolled down my cheeks with such ferocity, I hadn't thought my eyes had it in them. With each drop, I felt lighter, happier, more whole.

Jack pulled me close to him. "Thank you for being here with me."

I gave him a quick squeeze, just as the nurse opened the door to the room and whispered to me, "Ma'am, I have the name of that caller. She signed in at the front desk." Jack walked back to Elliot's bedside when he stirred, and I followed the nurse into the hallway.

"Lana," she said, showing me a clipboard on which her name was written. "Her name was Lana."

"Lana," I said, tears rolling down my face. "Of course." The hair on my arms was standing on end.

I'd never know what words passed their lips when they saw each other again after a lifetime apart. Did they embrace? Did they weep for the years they had lost? But I suppose that didn't matter, not really. *He got to see his daughter. And he got to see his Esther, once more.*

"Are you OK, honey?" the nurse asked, putting her hand on my shoulder.

I nodded. "Yes," I said, smiling. "*Yes.*"

I sat down in a metal folding chair in the hallway outside Elliot's room. The fluorescent lights hissed overhead, and the air smelled of stale coffee and Lysol. I opened my bag and pulled out my laptop with a sense of purpose and clarity that I hadn't felt in years. I stared at the flashing cursor on the blank screen, but this time it was different. I knew how to finish Esther's story now. I knew how it began, and I knew how it ended. Every word of it.

But as the digital clock in the hallway flashed from 11:59 to midnight, I realized that there was another story to write first. It was the first day of April—a new day, a new month, and the beginning of a new story, my story, and I could hardly wait to start writing it.

Acknowledgments

This book would not be a book without the wise eye of Elisabeth Weed, my literary agent, who saw a glimmer of something special in this story and waded with me through the muck of a thousand revisions until the manuscript sparkled. Elisabeth, thank you for believing in this project and for placing me in the enormously capable hands of my editor at Plume, Denise Roy.

Denise, Elisabeth told me you would be the perfect editor for me, and she was so right. You dazzled me with your brilliant editorial eye and creative ideas. I couldn't have hoped for a more talented and kind person to work with—you made even the revision rounds enjoyable. Can we do this again?

I am also incredibly grateful to my family, for their love and support—my sister, Jessica Campbell, a true best friend; and my two brothers, Josh and Josiah Mitchell—but most of all, to my parents, Terry and Karen Mitchell, who always encouraged my writing (even that embarrassing handwritten "newspaper" I distributed to the neighbors in the sixth grade—gulp). Thank you for your devotion to me (even in those horrid teenage years). And, also a thanks to the Jio family for creating a marvelous son, Jason, and for letting me plaster your family name on the cover of this book.

Much appreciation goes out to the editors, fellow authors, and writers who have cheered me on and supported me in million different ways: Allison Winn Scotch, Claire Cook, Sarah Pekkanen, and the other lovely women of the Debutante Ball; Camille Noe Pagán, Jael McHenry, Sally Farhat Kassab, Cindi Leive, Anne Sachs, Lindsey Unterberger, Margarita Bertsos, and all the other wonderful women (and men) at *Glamour*, as well as Heidi Cho and Meghan Ahearn at *Woman's Day*.

To Nadia Kashper and all the terrific folks behind the scenes at Plume, thank you for working so hard on my behalf. Also, a heartfelt thanks to Stephanie Sun at Weed Literary for being an early reader of this book, and to Jenny Meyer, my literary agent who handles foreign rights—so grateful to you that my first book will debut in bookstores in Germany and elsewhere. (Still pinching myself!)

And, to the lovely people of Bainbridge Island who have unknowingly opened up their world to readers around the world. While there is much fiction in theses pages, the essence of the island is, I hope, intact. In my opinion, it is impossible to find a more perfect place in the world than this ten-mile stretch of island.

To my boys, who I love with all my heart, I wrote this book mostly while you napped or snoozed in your beds at night, but someday you will grow up and learn that your mama is a writer—I hope this won't embarrass you too much.

Turn the page for a sneak peek of

THE
LAST
CAMELLIA

Publishing in paperback and ebook
August 2020

Prologue

The old woman's hand trembled as she clutched her teacup. Out of breath, she hadn't stopped to wash the dirt from under her nails. She hovered over the stove, waiting for the teakettle to whistle as she eyed the wound on her finger, still raw. She'd clumsily cut it on the edge of the garden shears, and it throbbed beneath the bloodstained bandage. She'd tend to it later. Now she needed to come to her senses.

She poured water in the little white ceramic pot with the hairline crack along the edge and waited for the tea leaves to steep. *Could it be?* She'd seen a bloom, as clear as day. White with pink tips. The Middlebury Pink, she was certain of it. Her husband, rest his soul, had tended to the camellia for twenty years—sang to it in the spring, even covered its dark emerald leaves with a quilt when the frost came. Special, he'd called it. The woman hadn't understood all the fuss over a scrawny tree, especially when the fields needed plowing and there were potatoes to be harvested.

If he could only see it now. In bloom. *What if someone from the village finds it?* No, she couldn't let that happen. It was her responsibility to make sure of that.

Years ago, her husband spent sixpence on the tree, which was

then just a sprout peeking out of a ceramic pot. The traveling sales-
man told him it had been propagated from a shoot at the base of the
Middlebury Pink, the most beautiful camellia in all of England,
and perhaps even the world. The only known cultivar, which produced the largest, most stunning blooms—white with pink tips—
presided over the Queen's rose garden inside the gates of the palace.
Of course, the woman hadn't believed the tale, not then, and she
had scolded her husband for his foolishness in spending such a high
price on what might be a weed, but in her heart, she did love to see
him happy. And when he looked at the tree, he was happy. "I suppose it's better than squandering money on drink," she had said.
"Besides, if it blooms, maybe we can sell the buds at the market."

But the tree didn't bloom. Not the first year or the second, or
the third or fourth. And by the tenth year, the old woman had given
up hope entirely. She grew bitter when her husband whispered to
the tree in the mornings. He said he had read about the technique in
a garden manual, but when she found him spritzing the tree with a
mixture of water and her best vegetable soap, she didn't care that he
said it would ward off pests; her patience had worn thin. Sometimes she wished for a bolt of lightning to strike the tree, split it in
two, so her husband could stop fawning over it the way he did. She
thought, more than once, about taking an ax to its slim trunk and
letting the blade slice through the green wood. It would feel good to
take out her anger on the tree. But she refrained. And after the man
died, the tree remained in the garden. Years passed, and the grass
grew high around its trunk. The ivy wrapped its tendrils around
the branches. The old woman paid no attention to the camellia until that morning, when a fleck of pink caught her eye. The single
saucer-size blossom was more magnificent than she could ever
have imagined. More beautiful than any rose she'd ever seen, it

swayed in the morning breeze with such an air of royalty, the old woman had felt the urge to curtsey in its presence.

She took another sip of tea. The timing was uncanny. Just days ago, a royal decree had been issued notifying the kingdom that a rare camellia in the Queen's garden had been decimated in a windstorm. Greatly saddened, the Queen had learned that a former palace gardener had propagated a seedling from the tree and sold it to a farmer in the countryside. She had ordered her footmen to search the country for her beloved tree's descendant and to arrest the person who had harbored it all those years.

The woman stared ahead. She turned to the window when she heard horses' hooves in the distance. Moments later, a knock sounded at the door, sending ripples through her tea. She smoothed the wisps of gray hair that had fallen loose from her bun, took a deep breath, and opened the door.

"Good day," said a smartly dressed man. His tone was polite but urgent. "Upon orders from Her Majesty, we are searching the country for a certain valuable variety of camellia." The woman eyed the man's clothing—plain, common. He was an impostor; even she could tell. Her husband had warned her of the lot—flower thieves. Of course, it all fit. If they could get to the camellia before the Queen's footmen, they could command a fortune for it. The man held a page in his hand, rolled up into a tight scroll. Unfurling it with great care, he pointed to the blossom painted on the page, white with pink tips.

The woman's heart beat so loudly, she could hear nothing else.

"Do you know of its whereabouts?" the man asked. Without waiting for her reply, he turned to search the garden for himself.

The man walked along the garden path, past the rows of vegetables and herbs, trampling the carrot greens that had just pushed through the recently thawed soil. He stood looking ahead where the tulips had reared their heads through the black earth. He knelt down to pluck a bud, still green and immature, examining it carefully. "If you see the tree," he said, twirling the tulip in his hand, before tossing it behind him, "send word to me in town. The name's Harrington."

The old woman nodded compliantly. The man gestured toward the north. Just over the hill was Livingston Manor. The lady of the house had been kind to them, offering to let them stay in the old cottage by the carriage house so long as they tended the kitchen garden. "Better not mention my visit to anyone at the manor," the man said.

"Yes, sir," the woman said hastily. She stood still, watching as he returned to his horse. When she could no longer hear the *click-clack* on the road, she followed the garden path past the pear tree near the fence until she came to the camellia bearing its one, glorious bloom.

No, she thought to herself, touching the delicate blossom. The Queen could search every garden in the land, and the flower thieves could examine every petal, but she would make sure they never found this one.

CHAPTER 1

Addison

New York City
June 1, 2000

The phone rang from the kitchen, insistent, taunting. It might as well have been a stick of dynamite on the granite counter-top. If I didn't pick it up after three rings, the answering machine would turn on. *I cannot let the answering machine turn on.*

"Are you getting that?" my husband, Rex, said from the couch, looking up from his notebook. He had an adorable fascination with old-school appliances. Typewriters, record players, and an answering machine circa 1987. But at that moment, I longed for voice mail. If only we had voice mail.

"I'll get it!" I said, jumping up from the breakfast table and stubbing my toe on the leg of the chair. I winced. One ring. Two.

The hair on my arms stood on end. What if it was *him?* He had started calling two weeks ago, and every time the phone rang, I felt the familiar terror. *Calm. Deep breath.* Maybe it was one of my clients. That horrible Mrs. Atwell, the one who'd made me redo her rose garden three times. Or the IRS. Let it be the IRS. Anyone would be more welcome than the person I feared waited on the other end of the line.

If I turned off the machine, he'd call again. Like a shark sensing blood in the water, he'd keep circling until he got what he wanted. I had to answer it. "Hello?" I said airily into the receiver.

Rex looked up, smiled at me, then returned to his notebook.

"Hello again, Addison." His voice made me shiver. I couldn't see him, of course, but I knew his face—the patchy stubble that grew around his chin, that amused look in his eyes. "You know, I don't care for your new name. *Amanda* suited you much better."

I remained silent, quickly opening the French doors and stepping outside onto the patio that overlooked a tiny patch of garden—rare for the city, but all ours. A bird chirped happily from the little camellia tree Rex and I had planted last year on our first wedding anniversary. I hated that he was trespassing on my private sanctuary.

"Listen," I whispered. "I told you to stop calling me." I looked up at the apartment building behind our townhouse, wondering if he could see me from one of the windows above.

"Amanda, Amanda," he said, amused.

"Stop calling me that."

"Oh, I forgot," he continued. "You're all fancy now. I read about your wedding in the paper." He clicked his tongue scoldingly. "Quite the fairy-tale ending for a girl who—"

"Please," I said. I couldn't bear the sound of his voice, the way it made me think of the past. "Why can't you leave me alone?" I begged.

"You mean, you don't *miss* me? Think of all the good times we had together. You remember the way we used to—"

"Stop," I said, cringing.

"Oh, I see how it is," he said. "All stuck-up now that you married the *King of England*. You think you're really something. Well, let me ask you this: Does your husband know *who you really are*? Does he know what you've *done*?"

I felt sick, woozy. "Please, please leave me alone," I pleaded, feeling my throat tightening as I swallowed.

He laughed to himself. "But I can't," he said. "No. You see, I spent ten years of my life in prison. That's a long time to think about things. And I thought a lot about you, Amanda. Almost every day."

I shuddered. With him behind bars, I'd felt a false sense of security. His incarceration, for two felony counts of money laundering and a lesser charge of statutory rape, had felt like a thick, warm blanket wrapped around me. And now that he was out, the blanket had been ripped off. I felt exposed, frightened.

"Here's the thing, baby," he continued. "I'm sitting on a very valuable piece of information. I mean, you can't blame me for wanting the same cushy life you have."

"I'm going to hang up now," I said, my finger hovering over the End Call button.

"This can all end well," he said. "You know what I want."

"I already told you I don't have that kind of money."

"You may not," he said, "but your husband's family does."

"No, don't bring them into this."

"Well," he said, "then I have no other choice." I heard the chime of an ice cream truck on the other end of the line. I remembered chasing after those trucks as a little girl, wide-eyed, hopeful. I don't know why; I never had a dollar for an ice cream sandwich, and yet they lured me still.

I pulled the phone from my ear and listened as the same notes sounded, a block away, perhaps. The melody struck terror in me. The truck was close. Too close.

"Where are you?" I asked, suddenly panicked.

"Why? You want to see me?" he said, amused. I could picture the menacing grin on his face.

My chin quivered. "Please, leave me alone," I pleaded. "Can't you just leave me alone?"

"It could have been so easy," he said. "But you've tried my patience. If I don't have the money by the end of the week, I'll have no other choice but to tell your husband everything. And when I say 'everything,' I mean *everything*."

"No," I cried. "Please!"

I walked around the building and peered beyond the fence at the side yard. The ice cream truck motored past, slowly. Children cheered and squealed as the melodic chimes poured through the loudspeaker, and yet, with each note, I became increasingly paralyzed with terror. "You have five days, Amanda," he said. "And, by the way, you look stunning in that dress. Blue's your color."

The line went dead, and I looked down at my blue linen dress, before turning to the street. The walnut tree in the distance. An old Honda with tinted windows and a rusty hood parked nearby. A bus stop that cast jagged shadows on the sidewalk.

I ran back to the house and closed the French doors, locking them behind me. "Let's go to England," I said to Rex, breathless.

He pushed his dark-rimmed glasses higher on the bridge of his nose. "Really?" He looked confused. "I thought you didn't want to make the trip. Why the change of heart?"

My in-laws had recently purchased a historic manor in the English countryside, and they'd invited Rex and me to stay there for the summer while they continued their travels throughout Asia, where Rex's father, James, was working. Rex, whose novel-in-progress was set in a manor in the English countryside, thought it would be perfect for research. And we both shared a love of old homes. From what his mother, Lydia, had said on the phone, the estate brimmed with history.

But the timing was off. My landscape design business had enjoyed a surge of activity, and I was juggling four new clients, including a massive garden installation on a rooftop in Manhattan. It was a terrible time to leave. And yet now I had no choice. Sean didn't know about the manor. He wouldn't find me there. The trip would give me time to think.

My eyes darted around the living room nervously. "Well, I don't. . . . I mean, I didn't." I sighed, collecting myself. "I've just been thinking it over, and, well, maybe we do need a getaway. Our anniversary is coming up." I sat down on the couch beside him, twirling a lock of his shiny dark hair between my fingers. "I could explore the gardens, maybe even learn a thing or two; you know everyone's crazy about English gardens here." I was talking fast, the way I do when I'm worried. Rex could tell, I know, because he squeezed my hand.

"You're nervous about the airplane, aren't you, honey?" he said.

True, I did have a bit of airplane fright, and my doctor had prescribed Xanax for such moments. But, no, Rex didn't know the real reason for my anxiety, and I could never let him find out.

There was a time when I believed I'd tell him the truth about me. But the longer I waited, the more it seemed impossible to open my mouth and utter the painful words. So I didn't. Instead, I hid behind my carefully crafted story. A girl from a wealthy family in New Hampshire whose parents had died in a car accident years ago. The money that had all been lost in a fraudulent investment scheme. Rex had believed it all, believed in *me*. He didn't wonder why I didn't get Christmas cards or birthday calls. He didn't ask if I wanted to visit my childhood home. He admired my strength, he said, that I could live in the present and not mourn the past. *If only you knew.*

I tucked my hand in his. "I'll be fine," I said. "And you said that the house would be the perfect place to really dig into your research—let's do it, Rex. Let's go."

He smiled, touching my cheek lightly. "You know I'd love to make the trip, but only if you're certain."

"I am," I said, shifting my gaze to the window and eyeing the rusty car parked on the street. I stood up and pulled the drapes closed. "The sun's so bright today." I continued, reaching for my phone, "I bet I can call the travel agency and get tickets for tomorrow."

"Really?" he said. "That quick?"

I forced a smile. "Why not? We might as well make the most of the summer."

"Well," he said, setting his notebook aside, "I'll phone my parents and see about arrangements. Wait, what about your clients?"

I winced inwardly, remembering the intricate boxwood-lined courtyard I'd planned for a client and the adjoining butterfly garden for her two little girls. I'd promised that the installation would be in place by the end of next week, for her daughter's birthday. My assistant, Cara, would have to oversee it all. She'd do a fine job, but it wouldn't be the job I'd do. The astilbes wouldn't be spaced perfectly. The hebe wouldn't be clipped into smooth spheres the way I'd envisioned. I sighed. I knew I couldn't stay, not with the dark cloud that hovered. I just had to make sure it didn't follow me to England.

"Ready?" Rex asked in the doorway the next evening. I'd managed to book us two seats on the nine p.m. direct flight to London.

"Yeah," I said from the doorstep, cinching my scarf higher on my neck. I took a few steps toward the cab waiting at the sidewalk, then froze.

Rex looked at me. "Is that the phone ringing?"

I shivered, looking back at the house. The ring was muffled but detectable.

"Should I run back and get it?"

"No," I said, hurrying to the car. "Let's not stop. We'll miss our plane."

One mother's desperate hope for survival.
One woman's search for the truth ...

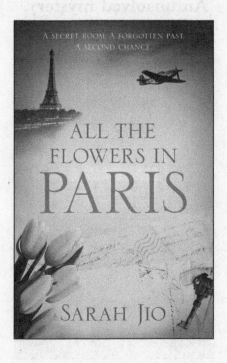

1943: In occupied Paris, Celine creates bespoke bouquets at her father's flower shop on rue Cler, whilst trying to shield her young daughter from the brutal reality of war. But when an SS officer takes an interest in Celine and her family, all their lives are put in jeopardy.

2009: Caroline wakes in Paris with no memory of her previous life. Hunting for clues to her identity in her apartment on the rue Cler, she discovers a bundle of letters written by a young widow during the Second World War. As she peels back the layers of the past, Caroline finds new purpose – but Celine's story is unfinished. Desperate to find out the truth, Caroline digs deeper, uncovering dark and dangerous secrets ...

*Can learning the truth about Celine help
Caroline unlock the mystery of her past?*

A sudden snowstorm.
A missing child.
An unsolved mystery.

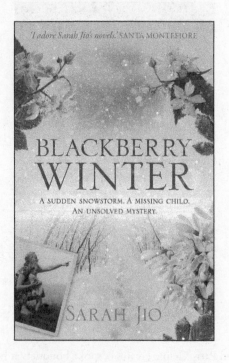

1933. Vera Ray kisses her young son goodnight and leaves to work the night-shift at a local hotel. The next morning, she discovers an sudden snowfall has blanketed the city, and her son has vanished, the snow covering up any trace of his tracks, or the perpetrator's.

2010. Journalist Claire Aldridge has been burying herself in work to avoid her own pain. When she is assigned to cover the 'blackberry winter' storm she learns of the disappearance of a three-year-old boy. He was never found. Claire vows to find the truth, but as she immerses herself in the mysteries of the past, Claire discovers that not all secrets should be revealed.

A haunting story of love, family
and the secrets that can destroy us...